MODERN HUMANITIES RESEARCH ASSOCIATION
CRITICAL TEXTS
VOLUME 72

EDITOR
STEFANO EVANGELISTA
(ENGLISH)

JEWELLED TORTOISE
VOLUME 8

EDITORS
STEFANO EVANGELISTA
CATHERINE MAXWELL

For That Moment Only, and Other Prose Works

MICHAEL FIELD

EDITED WITH AN INTRODUCTION AND NOTES BY
ALEX MURRAY AND SARAH PARKER

For That Moment Only, and Other Prose Works

by

Michael Field

Edited with an Introduction and Notes by

Alex Murray and Sarah Parker

Modern Humanities Research Association

2022

Published by

The Modern Humanities Research Association
Salisbury House
Station Road
Cambridge CB1 2LA
United Kingdom

First published 2022

ISBN 978-1-78188-974-9 (paperback)
ISBN 978-1-78188-973-2 (hardback)

Copies may be ordered from www.tortoise.mhra.org.uk

CONTENTS

ACKNOWLEDGEMENTS

We gratefully acknowledge the permission of Leonie Sturge-Moore and Charmian O'Neil to reproduce manuscript sources. We would like to thank the staff at the Bodleian Library, Western Manuscripts, and the British Library for their assistance in accessing material. Alex would particularly like to thank Bodleian Libraries for awarding him a Humfrey Wanley Fellowship to complete the project. We would like to thank Gerard Lowe and all the other staff at the MHRA for their support and patience. Alex would like to thank the School of Arts, Languages and English at Queen's University Belfast for paying for permissions for the front cover image. We have been supported and sustained by a brilliant community of scholars and would particularly like to thank Kristin Mahoney, Kate Hext, and Carolyn Dever, who read through the manuscript. Our greatest thanks go to Stefano Evangelista and Catherine Maxwell, the Jewelled Tortoise series editors, for their indefatigable support, advice, and eagle editorial eyes.

INTRODUCTION

Michael Field, the pseudonym of Katharine Bradley (1846–1914) and her niece and life partner Edith Cooper (1862–1913), are best known as lyric poets who employed Elizabethan and Romantic verse forms to explore desire, death, and beauty. Over thirty years, from their first collaborative work, the historical verse drama *Bellerophôn* (1881), to a volume dedicated to their beloved pet dog, *Whym Chow: Flame of Love* (1914), which Bradley saw through to press in between the death of Cooper (13 December 1913) and her own passing (26 September 1914), the two women published an astonishing amount, and variety, of work. Largely missing from the usual Michael Field bibliography are their experiments in prose produced in the period 1889 to 1895, which are collected in this volume. Under the influence of the young art historian Bernard Berenson and inspired by the explosion of prose poetry and short prose sketches emerging from France, the two women penned a series of delicate prose poems, or *croquis*, as Cooper preferred to label them. A number of these were intended for publication and were submitted to the leading avant-garde periodicals of the 1890s, including the *Yellow Book* (1894–1897) and *The Pageant* (1896–1897). In late 1895 Bradley and Cooper collected the majority of their prose sketches into two 'series', to which they gave the title *For That Moment Only* and set out to find a publisher. However, as their relationship with Berenson degenerated into bitter acrimony, they discarded *For That Moment Only*, and the volume, held in the Bodleian Library, Oxford, since 1942, along with a number of other manuscript prose works of the period, has remained lost to all but the most inveterate of archival scholars. In bringing these texts to publication we hope to enrich our understanding of Michael Field's works, as well as their working practices, and to place them more firmly in the currents of prose experimentation at the *fin de siècle*.

This volume then offers a slim selection of the prose of Michael Field. It might even be called a perversely slim selection. Michael Field wrote a staggering volume of prose. Their unparalleled experiment in life writing, 'Works and Days', consists of twenty-nine volumes documenting their lives and creative practice over a thirty-year period. Of the almost 10,000 pages and well over a million words the vast majority are prose (approximately 10% are given over to drafts of their lyric poetry and verse dramas). Carolyn Dever has recently argued that we should consider 'Works and Days' not as a series of diaries but as 'the great unknown novel of the nineteenth century — or better, the living record of the transition from a Victorian worldview to a modernist one'.[1] Indeed, when read as a work of autobiografiction — to use Max Saunders's term[2] — 'Works and Days' sits alongside Dorothy Richardson's *Pilgrimage* (thirteen vols, beginning in 1915 and concluding with the posthumously published final volume in 1967). While Michael Field's prose takes on radical qualities when viewed as a maximalist narrative, it is just as powerful to view them as writers of minimalist prose forms: the *croquis*, the fragment, the prose poem. These fleeting forms of modernity may seem at odds with the reputation that Bradley and Cooper have developed among scholars of late-Victorian and early twentieth-century literature. As the authors of twenty-six verse dramas — all historical in nature — and devotees of Elizabethan versification in much of their lyric poetry, Bradley and Cooper's work appears the antithesis of the fragmented and fleeting poetic forms we associate with modernism. Yet this impression — erroneous in our view — is the result of a concatenation of events, some public but largely personal, in the mid-1890s that resulted in Michael Field's most radical literary work remaining stubbornly unpublished. While there is danger in speculation, it is tantalizing to wonder how their career would have turned out had their experiments in modernity of form been otherwise: if their prose drama *A Question of Memory* (1893) had not had such a disastrous debut; if their prose poem 'Rhythm' had appeared in the second volume of the *Yellow Book* as planned; and if *For That Moment Only* had taken its place among the explosion of prose poetry in English in the mid-1890s.

This introduction sets out to locate Michael Field's prose works within their broader *œuvre*, and within the cultural currents of the *fin de siècle*. In doing so we are making the case that these works represent Michael Field's most explicit and sustained literary engagement with modernity of form. Their prose poems and *croquis* were the product of both Bradley and Cooper's reading, but also of their personal relations and experiences. Specifically, their friendship with the art historian Bernard Berenson catalysed their decision to move away from historical verse forms and to embrace the modern. Under his guidance they read a great deal of modern French literature and began to experiment with new ways of capturing their impressions. The fleeting nature of modern experience had been outlined so compellingly by Walter Pater in the 'Conclusion' to his *Studies in the History of the Renaissance* (1873), and the two women decided that it was the short prose forms that could capture what it meant to live 'for that moment only'.[3]

[1] Carolyn M. Dever, *Chains of Love and Beauty: The Diary of Michael Field* (Princeton: Princeton University Press, 2022), pp. 4–5.

[2] Max Saunders, *Self-Impression: Life-Writing, Autobiografiction and the Forms of Modern Literature* (Oxford: Oxford University Press, 2010).

[3] This phrase is taken from the Conclusion to Walter Pater's *Studies in the History of the Renaissance* (1873) and is discussed at length below.

In using intense prose to explore modernity the two women allied themselves with formal developments that would usher in literary modernism. As we show later in this introduction, moreover, their prose works explore female sensuality in ways strikingly similar to their 'New Woman' contemporaries, anticipating their modernist inheritors.

Introducing Michael Field

Katharine Bradley and Edith Cooper wrote some of the most remarkable poetry and prose of the *fin de siècle*. They also lived truly remarkable lives, finding themselves at the centre of aestheticism and Decadence in the 1890s. Bradley was born into a strongly religious family in Birmingham in 1846. Her father was a tobacco manufacturer, a background which provided her with independent means throughout her life. As a young woman, she took advantage of the opening up of higher education to women, studying at Newnham College, Cambridge, and in the Collège de France, Paris. Her niece Edith was born in 1862, the daughter of Bradley's sister Emma Harris Bradley and her husband James Robert Cooper. When Edith's mother became an invalid after giving birth to her second daughter, Amy, Bradley came to play a formative role in her development. By the time she was seventeen, Cooper shared her aunt's literary ambitions, joining Bradley in attending classes in classics and philosophy at University College, Bristol. It was also around this time that Bradley and Cooper became, in their first biographer Mary Sturgeon's words, 'dedicated to poetry and sworn in fellowship'.[4]

In 1875, Bradley published a collection, *The New Minnesinger and Other Poems*, under the pen name 'Arran Leigh'.[5] The two women then first collaborated on a verse drama entitled *Bellerophôn*, as 'Arran and Isla Leigh', which was collected with a selection of poems in 1881. But it was in 1884 that the poet 'Michael Field' was born, with the publication of a volume of verse dramas, *Callirhöe* and *Fair Rosamund*.[6] The positive critical attention that their debut received is striking, with the *Spectator* declaring 'These poems are poems of great promise. We know nothing of the author, but we have found a wealth of surprises in the strength, the simplicity, and the terseness of the imaginative feeling they display, that convinces us of his power to do much more than he has here done, — though

---

[4] Mary Sturgeon, *Michael Field* (London: Harrap, 1922), p. 21.

[5] A pseudonym possibly inspired by Elizabeth Barrett Browning's *Aurora Leigh* (1856) as well as the Brontë sisters' gender-ambiguous surnames, Currer, Ellis, and Acton Bell.

[6] The precise origins of the pseudonym are somewhat mysterious. 'Michael' was Bradley's nickname, after the Archangel Michael (perhaps due to her fiercely protective temperament). According to Ivor C. Treby, 'Field', Cooper's nickname, may relate to 'lea', an oblique reference to the original 'Leigh'; see Treby, *The Michael Field Catalogue: A Book of Lists* (London: De Blackland Press, 1998), p. 30.

even that is no trivial beginning.'[7] A somewhat less enthusiastic anonymous review in the *Athenæum* (penned by the poet Philip Bourke Marson) used the female pronoun throughout, betraying the gender of 'Michael Field'. Bradley and Cooper were convinced it was the poet Robert Browning, to whom Cooper had disclosed their authorship, who had revealed their secret. Bradley rebuked him in a letter, explaining that: 'The report of lady authorship will dwarf and enfeeble our work at every turn. [...] we have many things to say that the world will not tolerate from a woman's lips. We must be free as dramatists to work out in the open air of nature — exposed to her vicissitudes, witnessing her terrors: we cannot be stifled by drawing-room conventionalities'.[8] Despite their plea for Browning to 'set the critics on the wrong track', Michael Field was, from this point onwards, known not only as a woman poet, but a *pair* of women poets, a fact that served to combine the misogyny Bradley and Cooper feared with the enduring prejudice surrounding collaboration as opposed to singular authorship.

Bradley was unfortunately vindicated in her sense that they would never receive the recognition they deserved if 'Michael Field' was known to be a woman, or two women. A further six verse dramas in three volumes followed over the next three years, but in critical terms these brought diminishing returns, with a growing sense that the 'promise' of their debut had not been realised in a mature poetic vision. In 1889 they turned their hand to lyric poetry, publishing *Long Ago*, a collection of poems inspired by the fragments of Sappho. The reception of this volume was mixed, hailed by their friend John Miller Gray, but panned by the *Spectator* with barely concealed misogyny: 'the taste of mankind has always revolted from the unrestrained expression by a woman of the passion of love'.[9] From this point onwards the critical reception of their work was always to be tainted by sexism, and the two women began to write for a more exclusive audience, embracing the exquisite book illustrations and designs of artists such as Selwyn Image and Charles Ricketts. Nonetheless, the two women never gave up the hope of popular success, and in 1905 they jettisoned the name Michael Field altogether, publishing *Borgia: A Period Play* anonymously. Their strategy proved a success; *Borgia* attracted the only good reviews they had enjoyed in years, despite being one of their weaker plays. Bradley and Cooper henceforward adopted the moniker 'The Author of Borgia' for the dramatic works published before their deaths.

---

[7] 'A New Poet', *The Spectator*, 24 May 1884, pp. 16–18.

[8] KB to Robert Browning, 23 November 1884 in *Michael Field, The Poet*, ed. by Ana Parejo Vadillo and Marion Thain (Peterborough, Ontario: Broadview, 2009), p. 311. In keeping with the transcription practice elsewhere in our volume we have here, and in subsequent citations, silently adopted interlineal corrections from Vadillo and Thain's transcriptions and replaced '&' or '+' with 'and'.

[9] 'Michael Field's "Long Ago"', *The Spectator*, 27 July 1889, p. 119.

Despite their critical ill fortune, Bradley and Cooper certainly made their mark on the *fin-de-siècle* literary scene. While the two women had begun their publishing career living in Bristol, in 1889 the family moved to Reigate in Surrey, which allowed them to embrace literary London. Their friends and acquaintances were a veritable 'who's who' of Decadence and aestheticism, including Walter Pater, Robert Browning, Oscar Wilde, George Moore, Arthur Symons, Charles Ricketts, and John Gray. In 1899, after the death of Cooper's father, they moved to their first independent home as a couple: 1, The Paragon in Richmond, enabling them to become ever more engaged with the literary culture of the *fin de siècle*. This engagement fundamentally altered when, in 1907, first Cooper, then Bradley, converted to Roman Catholicism; a conversion partly precipitated by the death of their beloved dog Whym Chow in 1906. For the last few years of their lives, their literary output reflected their intense faith, and by the time of their deaths they were little more than a memory for the emerging writers of literary modernism.

After their deaths Bradley and Cooper's legacy was left in the able hands of the poet Thomas Sturge Moore who, following their wishes, edited, with his son, a selection of their diaries, published in 1933 as *Works and Days, From the Journal of Michael Field*. The reception of this volume was positive, in particular the review of J. C. Squire, who declared that their diaries should rank alongside those of Dorothy Wordsworth.[10] But the generation of post-war literary critics who consolidated the canons of both Victorian literature and modernism wholly neglected Michael Field, and it was not until the work of Chris White and Martha Vicinus in the 1990s that the academy finally came to appreciate the importance of Michael Field's life and work. Following this pioneering research, in the past thirty years, scholarship on Michael Field has blossomed, with their lyric poetry receiving a great deal of critical attention, and, more recently, the verse dramas beginning to garner the respect they deserve. The ongoing digitization of their diaries, 'Works and Days', will ultimately allow the most important record of *fin-de-siècle* intellectual life — as significant as Pepys's diaries have been for understanding the Restoration period — to be accessed by scholars anywhere, at any time. Yet there are still significant works by Bradley and Cooper that remain inaccessible to scholars unable to visit research libraries for an extended period, including, until now, their experimental short prose.

'A new form': Bernard Berenson's Influence on Michael Field's Prose

Bradley and Cooper's increasing interest in prose writing coincided with their burgeoning friendship with the art critic Bernard Berenson. Born Bernhard Valvrojenski, Berenson and his family emigrated from Lithuania to America in

[10] J. C. Squire, 'Strange Collaborators', *Sunday Times*, 17 December 1933, p. 10.

1875. After studying at Boston University and Harvard, Berenson moved to Italy and eventually became one of the most well-known art critics of the first half of the twentieth century. His first major publication, *The Venetian Painters of the Renaissance with an Index to their Works* (1894), was written during the time he knew Bradley and Cooper. Along with his partner and fellow critic Mary Costelloe, Berenson urged them to give up their archaic aesthetic habits and focus on cultivating a modern prose style.[11] As Bradley wrote in July 1892, following a visit to Paris with the couple: 'we are back [...] convinced of folly in dress, of poverty and affectation in English, of false method in art [...] We have heard a new god whose sole command is *Be contemporaneous.*'[12] Bradley and Cooper's relationship with Berenson was central to their ambition to forge a modern prose style. It was one of a series of important encounters with male mentor-muse figures (Robert Browning, John Ruskin, and Charles Ricketts being others) which tested and expanded the boundaries of their collaboration, providing a dynamic interaction with another perspective that proved both inspiring and challenging for their own shared creative vision.

The women first encountered Berenson in June 1890, during their tour of European art galleries, undertaken when seeking inspiration for their collection of ekphrastic poetry, *Sight and Song*. They were clearly enchanted by the handsome twenty-four-year-old; as Cooper later recounted this first meeting: 'Sim[13] found me talking to the young Russian, beautiful with the tints of Italy — an eagerness to charm in his eyes.'[14] On their return to England, they attended Berenson's lectures at the National Gallery and befriended his protégée (and, unbeknownst to them, lover) Costelloe in February 1891. The quartet became intimate; Bradley described them at one point as the 'immortal 4, Faun, Our Lady

[11] Mary Costelloe, née Mary Whitall Smith (1864–1945), was an American art historian who frequently collaborated with Berenson. Born in Philadelphia to Quaker parents Robert Pearsall Smith and Hannah Whitall Smith, Costelloe was educated at Smith College and the Harvard Annex and corresponded with Walt Whitman in her youth. In 1885, the entire family moved to England following her marriage to Benjamin 'Frank' Conn Costelloe. During this time, Costelloe became involved in the suffrage movement and began to specialize in art history. After meeting Berenson in 1888, she left her husband and two daughters (Ray and Karin Costelloe, later Ray Strachey and Karin Stephen) in order to continue her art historical studies while living with Berenson in Italy. Her first book, *Guide to the Italian Pictures at Hampton Court: with Short Studies of the Artists*, was published as by 'Mary Logan' in 1894. She co-authored *Venetian Painters of the Renaissance* (1894) with Berenson, who was listed as the sole author at her mother's request. Costelloe later married Berenson in 1900, following the death of her first husband.

[12] Michael Field [KB], 'Works and Days', London, British Library (hereafter BL) Add. MS 46780, fol. 132r (18 June 1892).

[13] 'Sim' was one of Cooper's many nicknames for Bradley. It is short for Simorg or Simurgh, a mythical bird from Persian literature.

[14] Michael Field [EC], 'Works and Days', BL Add. MS 46780, fols 111v–112r (22 June 1892). Berenson was in fact Lithuanian.

of Prose, and that Cloud that moves together.'[15] The friendship became strained, however, when the 'immortal four' visited Paris in June 1892. During this trip, Bradley and Cooper gradually realised that Berenson and Costelloe were having an affair (Costelloe was still married at the time), and that they were being used as cover for this clandestine relationship, and as a source of funds for Berenson:

> Probably knowing that as Michael and Field we are inseparable they have counted on long absences from our company and refreshing recontres at breakfast, afternoon-tea and at night. Yet such a hope on their part is unfair; for we were induced to visit Paris on the condition that we should receive guidance to an understanding of recent art and Morellian help in the Louvre.[16]

To make matters worse, Cooper began to regard her feelings as a destructive passion: 'we had no idea that he and she were inseparable companions — we had no idea that we cared so much for him — that I should sicken of very passion for him.'[17] Whilst, as Martha Vicinus observes, this infatuation had the potential to drive a wedge between Cooper and Bradley, it also functions as a shared drama that fuelled the imaginations of *both* women; in their diaries, they picture themselves as enthralled maenads, bound to follow a cruel, exacting Dionysian master: 'we cannot trust the Sapphic frenzy that forces us, in spite our ourselves, to follow him.'[18]

Their portrayal of Berenson as Dionysus and as a faun (one of their many nicknames for him) is also apparent in their prose sketches, which were frequently written after the authors had been exposed to this mentor-muse. For example, the voyeuristic admiration of male beauty found in 'A Faun' (pp. 75–77) closely echoes descriptions of Berenson in the diaries. Compare the portrait of the sleeping 'faun' with 'finely sentient' nose, eyebrows 'wonderful in ripple', and lips 'coloured as if with freshest pigment' with Cooper's 1894 diary description of Berenson:

> his eyebrows are ridges on the top of which the light is brooding and subtle as a sea-line; it flickers from the profile of his nose — as if sentience had become white fire; it blots his mouth in the same way as it splashes a

[15] KB to MC, *c.* 1894 (no date), correspondence qtd in *Michael Field, The Poet*, ed. by Vadillo and Thain, p. 329.

[16] Michael Field [EC], 'Works and Days', BL Add. MS 46780, fol. 114v (22 June 1892). Giovanni Morelli was an Italian art historian who encouraged focus on distinctive details of paintings (e.g. the rendering of hands) in order to identify the artist.

[17] Michael Field [EC], 'Works and Days', BL Add. MS 46780, fol. 114v (22 June 1892).

[18] Michael Field [EC], 'Works and Days', BL Add. MS 46780, fol. 115r (22 June 1892). On the complex sexual dynamics of Michael Field's relationship with Berenson see Martha Vicinus, 'Faun Love: Michael Field and Bernard Berenson', *Women's History Review*, 18 (2009), 753–64; Sarah Parker, *The Lesbian Muse and Poetic Identity 1889–1930* (London: Pickering and Chatto, 2013), pp. 43–70.

> laurel-leaf — just because his lips are rounded with the same energy as the leaf [...] the salient rose of the lips among the ambers of the beard![19]

Berenson's liminal beauty is portrayed as poised between human and animal, masculine and feminine, mortal and divine. Cooper described his 'terrible power of attraction' as residing in 'his likeness to Dionysus — the vine of his features'.[20] Berenson's Dionysian presence pervades the prose sketches, from the dancing vines of 'A Vision or a Waking Dream?' to the Bacchic portrait of 'An Agony'.

Despite their disconcerting Parisian discovery, Bradley and Cooper continued to be deeply influenced by Berenson. At the close of 1892, following the publication of *Sight and Song* and as they worked at their historical verse drama *Carloman* (later retitled *In the Name of Time*), Berenson wrote entreating them to 'give up their Elizabethan conceits' and to experiment with modern prose writing:

> The reasons for not writing Elizabethan verse nowadays are manifold. To begin with, Christ who had a fine palate in wine tells us not to put new wine into old bottles. I need scarcely tell you that you directly were foreseen in that command, the new wine being the new spirit, and the old bottles being the Elizabethan rhymes, vocabulary, and turns of phrase.
>
> Axiom: Wherever there is a new spirit, there will appear a new form....[21]

In direct response to this dictum, Bradley and Cooper sought to develop a 'new form' throughout 1893 in diverse yet interconnected ways: Cooper by composing prose sketches or *croquis*, and Bradley through conceiving a series of modern plays, culminating in *A Question of Memory*. This is not to say that their collaboration broke down, but rather that it took on slightly different facets, with Cooper increasingly drawn to impressionistic prose while Bradley remained largely committed to drama. Both were still engaged with, and contributed to, each other's writing projects. As the present volume attests, Bradley herself wrote *croquis*, while Cooper continued to work on their plays. Their two projects 'crossed and interlaced' (to echo Bradley's earlier description of their collaboration) rather than contradicted one another.[22] Their experiments with

---

[19] Michael Field [EC], 'Works and Days', BL Add. MS 46782, fols 95v–96r (19 July 1894).

[20] Michael Field [EC], 'Works and Days', BL Add. MS 46784, fol. 54v (The Last Night of the Old Year (31 Dec 1895)).

[21] Bernard Berenson to Michael Field, 22 December 1892, qtd in Ana Parejo Vadillo, 'Outmoded Dramas: History and Modernity in Michael Field's Aesthetic Plays', in *Michael Field and Their World*, ed. by Margaret D. Stetz and Cheryl A. Wilson (High Wycombe: Rivendale Press, 2007), pp. 237–49.

[22] In a letter to Havelock Ellis in May 1886, Bradley described their collaboration as a 'perfect mosaic: we cross and interlace like a company of dancing summer flies' (qtd in Mary Sturgeon, *Michael Field* (New York: Macmillan, 1922), p. 47). Havelock Ellis (1859–1939) was a sexologist and the author (with John Addington Symonds) of *Sexual Inversion* (1897).

prose and modern plays were interconnected in Bradley and Cooper's minds as different ways of being 'contemporaneous'.

The first burst of *croquis* were written by Cooper in the summer of 1893 after her travels in France and Italy with Bradley, Berenson, and Costelloe that spring. Several of these sketches draw on intense autobiographical moments shared with Berenson (or, rather, experienced in his presence). One of the most personal prose pieces from this period is the untitled sketch depicting a journey from Rome to the Adriatic which captures Cooper's intense feelings towards the couple, a passion mirrored by the volcanic landscape through which they travel: 'she realised her mortal passion for the man who could not be hers, her hatred for her fair-haired friend [...] the fire within her blazed up in response to the fire of this Italian day, among fire-blighted hill as naked as her own soul' (p. 135). Cooper returns to this moment at the end of 1893, in her summary of the year:

> In Italy I had a few days when there was spring-rain on my love for Bernhard, and I drank joy as the little vines drink a shower [...] Passing through the volcanic region to the Adriatic was the time of most sulphurous passion I have ever known — never shall I forget the sea-breeze and how I turned my back on Bernhard and gave my throat to the inrushing coolness that was deliverance.[23]

Cooper describes writing prose as one of the few pleasures of 1893: 'My only joy was the discovery of a power of using my own sensations in *croquis* — the direct consequence of Bernhard's influence.'[24] She follows this with reflections on modernity: 'I do not yet realise where *modernity* is taking me; I am moving with it as if down a stream, not using it enough for motive force like a water fall turning a mill.'[25] This diary entry suggests the ways in which three forces — Berenson, the *croquis*, modernity — are interconnected in Cooper's mind. The brief, flame-like *croquis* provided a means of expressing the intensity of her feelings for Berenson, capturing the excitement of travel and the pace of modern life, and epitomizing the dynamic 'motive force' that Cooper associated with modernity itself.

Meanwhile, Bradley sought to express modernity in her own way, through conceiving a series of modern plays written in prose (rather than blank verse). She and Cooper had attempted this in 1892 with *Old Wine in New Bottles*, a modern play in which Berenson appeared as the character Paul Lange (while Cooper was Rosalie). They followed this (unpublished) work with another prose

[23] Michael Field [EC], 'Works and Days', BL Add. MS 46781, fols 103r–103v (31 Dec 1893). Bradley and Cooper use varied spellings of Berenson's name, including 'Bernard' and 'Bernhard'. We have used the former as it is the spelling that Berenson himself used for his publications.

[24] Michael Field [EC], 'Works and Days', BL Add. MS 46781, fols 103v–104r (31 Dec 1893).

[25] Michael Field [EC], 'Works and Days', BL Add. MS 46781, fol. 104r (31 Dec 1893).

play, *A Question of Memory*, set during the 1848 Hungarian revolution; a more recent setting than their previous ancient or Renaissance-inspired subjects. *A Question of Memory* was performed by the Independent Theatre Society on 27 October 1893, but was poorly received and withdrawn after one night. Bradley and Cooper, undeterred, pushed ahead with their study of modern drama. As Bradley wrote to the critic (and champion of Henrik Ibsen) William Archer in December 1893:

> Of course we are learning much from frequent attendance at the theatres — we knew nothing of the contemporary stage except some few Ibsen plays; we have learnt much from rehearsal and from the untiring instruction of our stage-manager and we have learnt most of all on Oct. 27. It was like a Day of Judgement, all we had done seen from the other end — a really horrible experience.[26]

After seeing Ibsen's *The Master Builder* at the end of 1893, Bradley and Cooper became increasingly determined to achieve modernity in drama, conceiving a series of 'contemporaneous' plays, including *William Said* (1893–1894) and *Quits* (1894).[27] They were still, however, drawn to ancient subjects: throughout 1894 they developed the verse dramas *Attila, My Attila!* (1895) and *Equal Love* (1896), set respectively in late antique Rome and Byzantium. As several critics have observed, the antiquity of their plays does not necessarily contradict Michael Field's desire for modernity. As Ana Parejo Vadillo proposes, 'history is for them a screen upon which to discuss the contemporaneous'.[28] For example, the Ancient Greek *Callirrhoë* (1884) addresses debates around female education, while the following year's medieval *William Rufus* (1885) responds to the 1880s land question. In *Attila, My Attila!*, Bradley and Cooper sought to portray 'the New Woman of the fifth century', having observed parallels between *fin-de-siècle* London and imperial Rome.[29] In short, while the antiquity of Field's style and their settings cloak the contemporaneous significance of these works, their plays represent an important, if unconventional, response to modernity.

---

[26] Michael Field [EC], draft letter to William Archer, 'Works and Days', BL Add. MS 46781, fol. 98v (Dec 1893).

[27] The former, inspired by an interview with Alfred Russel Wallace on 'Woman and Natural Selection', takes eugenics and hereditary insanity as its theme; a conspicuously Ibsenite inspiration. See Michael Field [EC], 'Works and Days', BL Add. MS 46781, fol. 95r (15 Dec 1893). The latter is a dark farce of marital discord, with noticeably Wildean dialogue. The character Sergius Voronzoff represents Berenson, declaiming lines such as 'My religion says "Be contemporaneous"' and 'I feel like a Greek faun' (Oxford, Bodleian Libraries, MS Eng. misc. d. 975 *Quits* typescript, pp. 7, 16).

[28] Vadillo, 'Outmoded Dramas', p. 237. This is certainly true of *Attila*. For more on *Attila* and sexual modernity see Joseph Bristow, 'Michael Field's "Unwomanly Audacities": *Attila, My Attila!*, Sexual Modernity, and the London Stage', in *Michael Field: Decadent Moderns*, ed. by Sarah Parker and Ana Parejo Vadillo (Athens: Ohio University Press, 2019), pp. 123–50.

[29] Michael Field, *Attila, My Attila!* (London: Elkin Matthews, 1896), n.p.

Reflecting on their diverse yet concurrent experiments with 'modern' forms, Cooper meditated on the relationship between drama and *croquis* in a letter to Berenson of February 1894: 'It's quite a different thing with drama [...] a power to realise other people's actions and passions is almost incompatible with interest in the records of one's own senses. So just because *croquis* languish I am absorbed in my characters as I have scarcely ever been before.'[30] The tension, or rather dynamic interchange, between individual perception and shared, expansive vision was a consistent feature of Michael Field's collaboration. As they expressed in the Preface to *Sight and Song*, whether in composing their dramas or writing lyric poetry together, they sought to 'see things from their own centre, by suppressing the habitual centralization of the visible in ourselves'.[31] The *croquis* generated tension in their relationship not because of Cooper's passion for Berenson, but rather because this mode of writing centred on *individual* impressions. Although Bradley wrote her own prose sketches, the *croquis* were largely composed by Cooper, and she wrote them alone, focusing on crystallizing her own thoughts and sensations. In a collaborative partnership, this was a strikingly solitary, almost solipsistic project. Berenson's advice to Cooper in 1895 underscores this aspect: 'Let her then strive to express herself — all herself — her sensations are only a part of herself.'[32] This raises the implicit question: where was the space for Bradley, in this project founded on introspection and self-expression?

Berenson encouraged Cooper's venture with his own motives in mind. In a letter of 1893, he praises her ability to illuminate his own response to art: 'Before the best Bellini's and Carpaccio's [...] you would make me feel as I have never felt these days having had the luck to see mirrors throwing a light upon them which revealed in them whole tracts I had not seen before.'[33] As Bradley and Cooper observe in their diaries, Berenson was often unwilling (or unable) to express his theories in writing, preferring to articulate his ideas in conversation.[34] Berenson urged Cooper to translate his own ideas into prose — an endeavour he also encouraged in Costelloe.[35] However, Cooper became increasingly

---

30 Michael Field [EC], 'Works and Days', BL Add. MS 46782, fols 9r–9v (26 Feb 1894).

31 Michael Field, *Sight and Song* (London: Elkin Matthews and John Lane, 1892), p. v.

32 Berenson's words regarding Cooper are recounted in Michael Field [KB], 'Works and Days', BL Add. MS 46783, fol. 80r (6 May 1895).

33 Bernard Berenson to Edith Cooper (11 October 1893), qtd in Hilary Fraser, 'A Visual Field: Michael Field and the Gaze', *Victorian Literature and Culture*, 34.2 (2006), 553–71 (p. 562).

34 In one entry, Cooper laments: 'How I grieve that B. is as incapable as Socrates of writing his thoughts [...] His great effects as an artist are as fugative [*sic*] as an actor's or singer's — they pass living from his lips, and have no further life of their own — carried away in the stream of others' personalities' (Michael Field [EC], 'Works and Days', BL Add. MS 46783, fol. 79r (30 April 1895)).

35 As mentioned above, Costelloe co-authored Berenson's first book, *The Venetian Painters of the Renaissance* (1894), though, at her mother's request, her name did not appear on the title page.

disillusioned as she realized that Berenson's motivations were largely selfish. As she wrote in a diary entry of July 1894, following one of his lectures at the National Gallery:

> He then goes on to be personal and to say that Field[36] by her own confessions, by all he has been able to see of her work, has not creative faculty to compare with her critical, which she ought to use in prose and in art criticism and study! [...] He allowed all his disappointment to escape that I have not given up my life and followed him — the St. John as he used to call me beside St. Luke — Mary! He wants me to have a fine, expressive prose style to perpetuate his thoughts with the sensuous charm they need to be characteristic and that he cannot give them in writing — He would like me to be his Maenad; he has no intention of serving me.[37]

As a result of this disappointment, in late 1894 Cooper's *croquis* shift in subject-matter away from Dionysian fauns towards other themes, such as those inspired by her travels with Bradley in Yorkshire ('The Granary') and Scotland ('Gwen') in August and September 1894. During this time, Bradley produced her own prose pieces, such as 'A Face Seen in Ling' and 'Quai d'Anjou', a brief reminiscence of her death-bed vigil for Alfred Gérente, whom she loved as a young woman. With Berenson (temporarily) out of the picture, it seems the *croquis* project became more truly collaborative.

As 1894 drew to a close, Michael Field's experiments with prose were far from over. In October 1894, Bradley and Cooper gave a title to their collection, *For That Moment Only*. In her last diary entry that year, Cooper confessed her ambitions for the series in tandem with her hope of being reconciled with Berenson: '*Is it too much to hope that I can make Bernhard my friend in Florence — that seems harder to hope than that Honoria should be played and For That Moment go into a second ed. It seems harder than the hardest miracle: but who can tell what will be the end?*'[38] Cooper's entry was prescient: Berenson sent an apologetic letter in February 1895, reigniting her attachment and clearing the way for the women's visit to Italy in April 1895. Their sojourn with Berenson and Costelloe in Fiesole inspired a fresh burst of prose writings, including 'A Vision or of Waking Dream?', 'The Fate of the Crossways', and 'An Agony'. The last of these, like the earlier 'A Faun', features a Dionysian figure that bears more than a passing resemblance to Berenson. Intriguingly, the majority of these sketches were written during Berenson's *absence*, as Bradley and Cooper stayed in his rooms at Villa Kraus while he was away. As Cooper wrote in their journal:

---

[36] 'Field' was one of many pet names Bradley used for Cooper. In turn, Bradley was called 'Michael' by Cooper and a number of their friends.

[37] Michael Field [EC], 'Works and Days', BL Add. MS 46782, fols 93r–93v (15 July 1894).

[38] Michael Field [EC], 'Works and Days', BL Add. MS 46782, fol. 144v (31 Dec 1894). *Honoria* was the original title of *Attila, My Attila!*.

> it is all beginning to turn a dream that we should have lived in his house for a fortnight and slept on his wee small, down pillow, [...] — we have lived a poem we shall never live again.
>
> Imagine inhabiting Bacchus' ivy-tent while he was not there ... all the delicate poetry is in that — that he is not there.
>
> And on Monday he will come back — the strain and tragedy and the deep intoxication and the weariness at intolerable excitement will begin once more. The dew of absence! — yes, rare, inciting natures can leave behind them what they cannot give when they are present — dew, a holy spirit.[39]

This passage illuminates the complex gendered gaze at work in the *croquis*, in which Bacchic rites and beautiful male muses are frequently observed voyeuristically, usually without the (ambiguously gendered) observing subject being seen or taking an active part in events. In portraits such as 'A Faun', for instance, the *unconsciousness* of the figure is crucial to the fantasy — once he opens his eyes to gaze back at the speaker, the spell is broken.

As Cooper anticipates, Berenson's return precipitated numerous intense discussions about art and prose. Cooper found these debates increasingly oppressive, particularly as they often dissected her own prose writings. Her reaction to Berenson's lectures was passive; Bradley became frustrated: 'Last night in salon Doctrine[40] counselled Field should write articles — she lay listening as in a trance. I knew he meant criticism — but enough!'[41] The following day, Bradley and Costelloe entreated Berenson to critique Cooper's 'The Granary' (p. 86). His analysis (as recounted by Bradley in the diary) was forensic and discouraging: '"cool, sliding" — give one the creeps — and one desires to convey an impression of warmth. [...] One must not speak of an important thing having capacities. The sentence about the grain being treasure like gold is good.'[42] The terms of Berenson's critique reflect his commitment to 'tactile values' conveyed through sensory prose. In an earlier discussion, he expounded his theory that prose 'must suggest visual images, it must have a rhythm that brings enjoyment to the ear, a quality of aroma, an atmosphere that can be felt, and a relish that makes the mouth water'.[43] Cooper's 'The Granary' certainly achieves this style, appealing to touch (plunging the fingers through the grain), smell ('The whole

---

[39] 'Michael Field [EC], 'Works and Days', BL Add. MS 46783, fol. 59v (27 April 1895).

[40] 'Doctrine' was one of the names Bradley and Cooper gave Berenson.

[41] Michael Field [KB], 'Works and Days', BL Add. MS 46783, fol. 79v (6 May 1895).

[42] Michael Field [KB], 'Works and Days', BL Add. MS 46783, fol. 80r (6 May 1895). The MS version of the story reads 'chilly, sliding'.

[43] Recounted in Michael Field [EC], 'Works and Days', BL Add. MS 46783, fol. 73v (2 May 1895). For Berenson's theory of 'tactile values', see Alison Brown, 'Bernard Berenson and "Tactile Values" in Florence', in *Bernard Berenson: Formation and Heritage*, ed. by Joseph Connors and Louis A. Waldman, Villa I Tatti Series, 31 (Cambridge, MA: Harvard University Press, 2014), pp. 101–20.

granary smells of *potpourri*'), and sound ('the scratch of a rat in the walls'). Berenson, however, required more than adherence to his aesthetic laws; he also desired Cooper to cultivate an audience for her work:

> Field is not expressing herself in *croquis* — No one can express themselves until they get listeners — the condition of self-expression being the re-creation in others of one's own heart-throb. — Mere description is nothing. [...] She must give ideas — and she must find a public — this is one reason why B. does not want her to write on things that are remote.[44]

Berenson objected to Cooper's focus on describing 'sensations' rather than articulating 'ideas'. He implied that her work was inward-looking and obscure, rather than critical and outward-facing. But Cooper herself was reluctant to court an audience on these terms: 'I can't work for magazines, and my dangerous discouragement was not doctored by the suggestion.'[45]

The more Cooper was pressurized over the *croquis*, the more she withdrew from the project, discouraged. But sometimes this same pressure actually stimulated her prose writing. For example, 'Eriphion The Faun' was inspired by Cooper's being harried into reading *For That Moment Only* aloud to Berenson and Costelloe. As she recounts:

> When I fetch the M.S. I feel the sort of anguish I once had in childhood when I was sent to fetch some biscuits I knew I had eaten [...] Yes, I experienced the same deathly sickness of humiliation. I read *Nature's Bacchanals* [re-titled 'A Traveller's Tale'] with some success, and a hum of praise helps me for a bit [...] but some of the next pieces are unwisely chosen and my voice goes from bad to worse, till it is a bleeding sob, and hides the very meaning of the words it wrings out [...] B. is almost silent, doom urges me to madness; I try to read things I cannot, have to stop, and shivering from head to foot get away, and let the outrage against my nature revenge itself in a spasm of hysteria — an earthquake and geyser combined!
>
> Then in less than fifteen minutes I begin to write about the faun Eriphion who was put to the same torture I had suffered.[46]

The *croquis* mentioned here captures Cooper's wounded feelings through recounting the story of a young faun (with the 'tail and legs of a goat', p. 70) who aspires to shoot arrows like a centaur. Fashioning his own bow, at first he delights in his skill, but is eventually humiliated in front of a group of centaurs. Following this, Eriphion's innocent joy hardens into bitterness: 'he shot his darts with caution; there was a touch of fierceness and cunning in his eyes, and when he hit the mark he did not laugh out nor scarcely chuckle to himself' (p. 72). We can read the story as a parable conveying how Berenson and Costelloe's critique killed

[44] Michael Field [KB], 'Works and Days', BL Add. MS 46783, fols 79v–80r (6 May 1895).
[45] Michael Field [EC], 'Works and Days', BL Add. MS 46783, fol. 79r (5 May 1895).
[46] Michael Field [EC], 'Works and Days', BL Add. MS 46783, fols 77v–78r (4 May 1895).

off the jouissance that Cooper associated with literary creation. Like the wounded faun, she flees from her detractors, stewing in 'hysterical' resentment. This story, along with the masochistic staging and sexual undertones of the diary explanation recounting its genesis, captures the potent combination of ambition, pride, and shame that Cooper experienced when writing and 'performing' her work under the intensely critical gaze of Berenson and Costelloe, a practice that stimulated both a fear of, and a desire for, ritualistic punishment.

There was more mockery to come later in 1895, when on the publication of *Attila, My Attila!* Berenson and Costelloe greeted the play 'with jeers and uncontrollable laughter'.[47] This mockery, combined with the revelation that Berenson had plagiarized many of Nietzsche's ideas, led to the end of the friendship, and the end of the *croquis*.[48] As Cooper wrote at the close of 1895: 'The Croquis are not going to be published — Bernhard nearly slew any care I had for them. Not as *For That Moment Only* ... perchance in magazines from time to time.'[49] She follows this with a renunciation of Berenson: 'Let me set it down: I love him inexorably by fate — as I give him up by choice. In him all that fascinates me in myself parts me in another, who has the kind sort of beauty my face seeks after. It is a kind of self-joy, a kind of recognition of the dearness of one's identity — that is such a terrible power of attraction in Bernhard.'[50] This final phrase associates Cooper's desire for Berenson with a dangerous narcissism; an immersion in one's own identity. The *croquis* were the creative harvest of this self-absorption and obsession with refining and articulating one's impressions. Cooper understood herself as at a crossroads: one path that of prose, Berenson, and 'self-joy'; the other path associated with Bradley, collaboration, and the outward-looking literary form of drama, oriented towards the other, as she had earlier described it in her letter to Berenson. Ultimately, Cooper chose the latter path. She reflected on this decision a year later, at the end of 1896:

> Again, Love [i.e. Bradley] and I wandered in the afternoon and talked of Bernhard's effort to make me his comrade-in-prose and of my dread of being torn between him and Michael [again, Bradley] — my sense that I must choose life or death — and not be content with life-in-death. I chose well indeed, tho' at the cut of a staunchless wound and I can triumph now in my choice.[51]

[47] Michael Field [KB], 'Works and Days', BL Add. MS 46784, fol. 26v (29 Nov 1895).

[48] The two women began reading Nietzsche's *Götzen-Dämmerung* (*The Twilight of the Idols*) in October 1895 and soon realised that Berenson had, earlier that spring, presented Nietzsche's ideas as his own while deterring them from reading Nietzsche's work. Cooper declared that Berenson's 'dishonesty about Nietzsche has been the moral shock of this year' (Michael Field [EC], 'Works and Days', BL Add. MS 46784, fol. 55v (31 Dec 1895)).

[49] Michael Field [EC], 'Works and Days', BL Add. MS 46784, fols 54r–54v (31 Dec 1895).

[50] Michael Field [EC], 'Works and Days', BL Add. MS 46784, fols 54r–54v (31 Dec 1895).

[51] Michael Field [EC], 'Works and Days', BL Add. MS 46785, fol. 181r (15 Nov 1896).

Though she depicts it here as a tragedy, Cooper's reconfirmation of her commitment to Bradley and the drama brought her many joys in 1896. She and Bradley replaced Berenson and Costelloe with a new collaborating couple, Charles Ricketts and Charles Shannon, who proved more supportive and equally inspiring.[52] Cooper became immersed in a new project: the verse drama *The World at Auction*, which later developed into the Roman Trilogy.[53] Once again, the road to modernity was an ancient one, as Cooper felt more able to divine the contemporaneous moment through the distant past. The two women no longer experimented with the *croquis* or prose poem after 1895, though they did submit some of their existing *croquis* to the aesthetic magazine *The Pageant*, edited by Shannon and Gleeson White.[54] The pieces did not appear in the pages of the annual, but 'The Fate of the Crossways' was published in Ricketts and Shannon's *The Dial* in 1897. As the last word — at least in print — of Michael Field's prose writings, this story is appropriate, hinging as it does on a moment of crucial decision-making. As Cooper's speaker states: 'I made my choice I will not say whether to right or left' (pp. 120–21). In the narrative of Michael Field's partnership, Cooper's choice is clear.

---

[52] Charles de Sousy Ricketts (1866–1931) and Charles Haslewood Shannon (1863–1937) were artists and designers who first befriended Bradley and Cooper in January 1894. The two men met in 1882 whilst studying at the South London School of Technical Art, forming a lifelong creative and romantic partnership that in many respects resembled Michael Field's collaboration. While Shannon specialized in portraits, including etchings and lithographs, Ricketts became best known for his illustrations, book design, and, later, theatre designs, including costumes and sets. He also designed stunning pieces of jewellery for Bradley and Cooper, now held in the Fitzwilliam Museum, Cambridge. Together, Ricketts and Shannon produced the art magazine *The Dial* (which ran for five issues from 1889 to 1897) and afterwards founded the Vale Press (1896–1904), publishing several of Michael Field's verse dramas, including the Roman Trilogy (see note 53 below). Bradley had a particularly passionate, sometimes stormy, relationship with Ricketts, in which he functioned as a male muse in a comparable manner to Cooper's earlier infatuation with Berenson. Bradley composed several sonnets dedicated to Ricketts, a number of which are included in *Wild Honey from Various Thyme* (London: T. Fisher Unwin, 1908). For discussion of these poems and Bradley's complex relationship with Ricketts, see Marion Thain, *"Michael Field": Poetry, Aestheticism, and the Fin de Siècle* (Cambridge: Cambridge University Press, 2007), pp. 130–67; and Catherine Maxwell, *Scents and Sensibility: Perfume in Victorian Literary Culture* (Oxford: Oxford University Press, 2017), pp. 201–39.

[53] Michael Field's Roman Trilogy of verse dramas, consisting of *The World at Auction* (1898), *The Race of Leaves* (1901), and *Julia Domina* (1903), explores the decline of the Roman Empire in the period 182 to 212 AD. For more on the Trilogy and its role in the development of Michael Field's aesthetic see Ana Parejo Vadillo, '"This hot-house of decadent chronicle": Michael Field and the Dance of Modern Verse-Drama', *Women: A Cultural Review*, 26 (2015), 195–220.

[54] Treby, *Michael Field Catalogue*, p. 129. They submitted 'A Vision', 'An Agony', 'Eriphion the Faun', and 'The Fate of the Crossways'. None were published in *The Pageant*.

Prose Influences: Pater and French Fiction

While it may have been Berenson's insistence that they become modern that inspired Michael Field to embrace the *croquis* form, they had been writing creative and essayistic prose for a number of years before they first made his acquaintance. Their early prose model, and the writer from whom they took the title of their series of *croquis*, was Walter Pater, the Oxford don whose delicate impressionistic prose was such an influence on the aesthetes and Decadents of the *fin de siècle*. It was from Pater that the two women developed their understanding of art as having the potential to capture individual experience within the maelstrom of modernity. Bradley and Cooper had first read Pater in the early 1880s before commencing a correspondence with him (and subsequently visiting him and his sisters) in 1889. Pater had an aversion to verse drama, but when they sent him a copy of *Long Ago* (1889), their book of verse inspired by Sapphic fragments, he responded warmly, commending those poems' 'calm Attic wisdom — their sweetness of mind'.[55] Their friendship was sustained until Pater's death in 1894, when they penned a poem to him in eulogistic homage: 'a sense renewed [...] | That thou didst touch and breathe and see of old | Stole on thee with the warmth of gratitude.'[56] While they fell out with many of the other male writers who influenced their prose style — most notably John Ruskin and Berenson — their admiration for Pater remained undimmed and his aesthetic philosophy underpins their *œuvre* in manifold ways.

While they remained committed to lyric poetry and verse drama in the early 1890s, they were well aware of Pater's claim in his essay on 'Style' (1888) that 'imaginative prose' was 'the special and opportune art of the modern world'. For Pater, this status was based upon two facts: firstly, 'the chaotic variety and complexity of its interests, making the intellectual issue, the really master currents of the present time incalculable — a condition of mind little susceptible of the restraint proper to verse form', and secondly the emergence of 'an all-pervading naturalism, a curiosity about everything whatever as it really is, involving a certain humility of attitude, cognate to what must, after all, be the less ambitious form of literature'.[57] While prose may be less ambitious and require less restraint than verse, Pater suggested that the true artist would never fall prey to the excess and carelessness that marked much of the contemporary prose of the late-Victorian period, counselling writers to be on their guard against 'the otiose, the facile, surplusage'.[58] The challenge of modern prose was one of 'inspired translation',

---

[55] Walter Pater to Michael Field, 4 July 1889 in *Letters of Walter Pater*, ed. by Lawrence Evans (Oxford: Clarendon Press, 1970), pp. 157–58.
[56] Michael Field, 'Walter Pater (30 July, 1894)', *The Academy*, 11 August 1894, p. 102.
[57] Walter Pater, *Appreciations, With an Essay on Style* (London: Macmillan, 1889), p. 7.
[58] Pater, *Appreciations*, p. 16.

for 'all language involves translation from inward to outward', and that process was to be realized 'only as precise expression'.[59] The two women had read the essay and agreed with his assessments, yet were disturbed by Pater's claim that 'the scholarly conscience' was overwhelmingly male, and that the scholar would move 'warily, considerately', 'over the ground which the female conscience traverses so lightly, so amiably'.[60] Bradley recorded in 'Works and Days' a conversation with Oscar Wilde in which she declared that this was a sentence from which she 'suffered' for its prejudice was 'hard to bear'.[61]

Bradley and Cooper had been indebted to Pater's work prior to their experiments with the *croquis* form. While their verse — in particular *Sight and Song* — had regularly been in dialogue with Pater's art-historical method, Cooper had taken direct inspiration from Pater in her impressionistic essay 'Effigies' (1890), based on two trips she and Bradley had made to Westminster Abbey (one of those being for Robert Browning's funeral). As Catherine Maxwell notes, Cooper was 'almost certainly influenced' in 'Effigies' by Pater's essay on Winckelmann.[62] Yet the *croquis* they were writing between 1893 and 1895 were fundamentally different from the idealizing reveries on the statuary of dead writers. In October 1894 Cooper received from the estate of their recently deceased friend, the 'little hero' John Miller Gray, a bound volume of 'Effigies', at which she now recoiled: 'I am so much parted from it as a ghost from an old home. I laugh at my heavy prose, I am bored by it, I am terrified at it.' She gives thanks for having been exposed to Berenson: 'Today we thank the Lord that the years that produced *Effigies* were eaten — they are well-restored in *For That Moment Only*! We should never have been self-critics if we hadn't met the shock of a negative influence'.[63] Cooper might have turned her back on 'Effigies', but the influence of Paterian style was to persist. Pater's style — simultaneously evasive and precise, elegant and obscure — was itself an expression of modernity, one that Bradley and Cooper sought to emulate. Angela Leighton has argued that Pater's prose is characterized not by the primary but the secondary meanings of his words: 'Pater's is a style of pondering afterthoughts, of hesitations and pauses, which lead to something as far from assertion as it might be possible to get in the language of prose.' Yet, as Leighton notes, Pater saw the condition of modernity as 'less a thrilling novelty than a kind of after-knowledge, premised on a time

[59] Pater, *Appreciations*, p. 31.

[60] Pater, *Appreciations*, p. 8.

[61] Michael Field [KB], 'Works and Days' (22 July 1890) in Ana Parejo Vadillo, 'Walter Pater and Michael Field: The Correspondence, With Other Unpublished Manuscript Materials', *The Pater Newsletter*, 65 (2014), 27–85 (p. 52).

[62] Catherine Maxwell, 'Michael Field, Death, and the Effigy', *Word & Image*, 34 (2018), 31–39 (p. 32).

[63] Michael Field [EC], 'Works and Days', BL Add. MS 46782, fol. 131r (29 Oct 1894).

already missed or lost'.[64] The temporal structure of Michael Field's prose likewise refuses the novelty of modernity, attempting to preserve the aesthetic moment that is already fading into memory.

As they began, under the influence of Berenson, to turn away from the Elizabethan stylings of their verse dramas and *Underneath the Bough*, their relationship with Pater intensified. Where previously he had seemed to share their intense investment in the past, they now viewed him as the epitome of the modern. On receiving a copy from the author of *Plato and Platonism* (1893), Bradley wrote to Pater, addressing him as 'the contemporary of Plato' whose 'historical criticism is in deep accord with our newly awakened interest in the Present — as the point whence life flashes into meaning'. It was the dialogue between past and present that characterized his work, and that new, more modern approach to which Bradley and Cooper aspired; it was 'the pleasure' 'to write into the Present the pleasure of thinking and acting as a modern of *dead generation* of those who lived as in antiquity — and the pleasure of entering into the present of those who lived long ago [—] as only less in degree than that of thinking and acting as a true modern in one's own age'.[65] As Bradley intimates here, to 'be contemporary' was to live the past in the present and to realise the 'present-ness' of the past, to create temporal estrangement by living a bacchic life in an age of steam trains and electricity. The incongruity of the past living in the present is a feature of the 'first series' of *For That Moment Only* in particular.

The title of their prose *croquis* — *For That Moment Only* — was only chosen once the two 'series' had been completed. On returning from a holiday to Yorkshire and Scotland on which they wrote the majority of the second series, Bradley happened upon the title:

> *For That Moment Only
>
> This is the new title discovered by me for the short prose impressions. Henry [Cooper] is about to write to Ward and calls in Amy to help find a title to tie up the bundle of prose pieces. We repeat with groans of envy *La Lanterne Sourde*.
>
> But we cannot call our pieces 'The Bull's Eye'. We think of gleams, flashes, and fine flames. Lanterns, and lights, and rays, and the gamut of time. Finally I take up Pater and read:
>
> 'Every moment some form grows perfect in hand or face; some tone on the hills or the sea is choicer than the rest; some mood of passion or insight or intellectual excitement is irresistibly real and attractive to us, — for that moment only.'[66]

---

[64] Angela Leighton, 'Walter Pater's Dream Rhythms', in *Thinking Through Style: Non-Fiction Prose of the Long Nineteenth Century*, ed. by Michael D. Hurley and Marcus Waithe (Oxford: Oxford University Press, 2018), pp. 217–31 (p. 219).

[65] Edith Cooper, draft letter to Walter Pater, March 1893, in Vadillo, 'Correspondence', pp. 68–69.

[66] Michael Field [KB], 'Works and Days', BL Add. MS 46782, fol. 129v (4 Oct 1894).

It is unclear who 'Ward' here might be, but it is possibly Ward, Lock & Co., who had recently published Oscar Wilde's *The Picture of Dorian Gray* (1891). *La Lanterne sourde* (1893) is a novel by Jules Renard, the title of which translates as 'bull's eye lantern' and refers to a lantern that only emitted light in one direction from a single glass lens. As a title, it conveys the ideal of their *croquis* as prose illuminations, small, yet significant, moments in life that can be recalled in short prose fragments. Yet in settling on a quotation from the 'Conclusion' to Pater's *Studies in the History of the Renaissance* they both acknowledged the significance of the Paterian aesthetic moment to their *croquis*, but also their wider indebtedness to Pater, both as a philosophical guide and as a prose stylist.

Pater's aesthetic moment, as described in the 'Conclusion', is both the product of, and a bulwark against, the flux of modernity. The 'perpetual motion' of our 'physical life', coupled with the 'whirlpool' of the 'inward world of thought and feeling', transforms our experience of the world into a series of impressions, each one being 'the impression of the individual in his isolation, each mind keeping as a solitary prisoner its own dream of a world'. These impressions, to which 'experience dwindles down[,] are in perpetual flight', are becoming ever more elusive as we struggle to isolate and analyse the moment, 'gone while we try to apprehend it'. It is then to 'such a tremulous wisp constantly re-forming itself on the stream, to a single sharp impression, with a sense in it, a relic more or less fleeting, of such moments gone by, what is real in our life fines itself down'. This process, this movement, from the fleeting experience to the sharp impression, and then the 'dissolution of impressions, images, sensations', constitutes for Pater the 'continual vanishing away, that strange, perpetual weaving and unweaving of ourselves'. Given the chaos that characterizes our experience of modernity, we are forever seeking after those moments of ecstasy, of contemplation, of realization, moments that are given their greatest intensity and crystallization in works of art. 'For', as Pater concludes 'art comes to you proposing frankly to give nothing but the highest quality to your moments as they pass, and simply for those moments' sake'.[67] Bradley and Cooper saw their *croquis* as offering the intense concentration of experience into sharply graven impressions.

While Pater's aesthetic impressionism may have guided them, Bradley and Cooper did not turn to contemporary English prose fiction for inspiration. Of poetry, art, music, philosophy, theology, and theatre they wrote a great deal in 'Works and Days', but creative prose rarely featured. When they do engage with contemporary British prose writers — George Egerton, Vernon Lee, George Moore[68] — it is often in a gossipy and derisive manner. The writer of fiction in

[67] Walter Pater, *The Renaissance: Studies in Art and Poetry* [1893], ed. by Donald L. Hill (Berkeley: University of California Press, 1980), pp. 186–90.

[68] George Egerton was the penname of Mary Chavelita Dunne Bright (1859–1945). Egerton published some of the most remarkable New Woman fiction of the 1890s. Her short story

English whom they most admired was George Meredith, yet the work of his that they truly revered was his poetry collection *Modern Love* (1862). It was rather modern French fiction that they read enthusiastically, particularly in the early to mid-1890s. They appreciated Stendhal, whose *Le Rouge et le Noir* (1830) Cooper declared 'tremendously great in its self-restraint'.[69] Of Pierre Loti's *Pêcheur d'Islande* (1886), the realist-impressionist narrative of Breton fishermen, Cooper wrote 'few books make me cry — this one draws "tears from the depth of some divine despair"'.[70] Perhaps the European prose writer mentioned most often in 'Works and Days' in this period is Gustave Flaubert (Ibsen and Tolstoy also feature prominently). They both admired and were appalled by his writing in equal measure. Of *Salammbô* (1862) Cooper wrote:

> The more I read the more deeply I feel the shame Flaubert did to art in a few of his chapters. *Salammbô* was placarded everywhere when the English translation was issued — because it appealed to some of the vilest qualities of man in all ages, his lust of cruelty and a gorgeous animal life. The book was prostituted, because it had in it a degrading attractiveness: and yet the style, sonorous and strong as a river full to the brim, exquisite in the sensitive surface it expands to every light or reflection under the African sky, is such alone as the initiated can enjoy.[71]

Cooper's distaste for Flaubert's most overtly 'decadent' work is unsurprising given her and Bradley's often negative response to those English writers who embraced the more fleshly and morbid themes of their French heroes. Yet for all her wariness of its content, Cooper finds that Flaubert's style allows the 'initiated' to find something more vital in his prose. In her end-of-year summary for 1890 Cooper confirms the growing sense of Flaubert's importance: 'looking back on the passing year I find that Flaubert has been the master-influence on me'.[72] Of

---

collection *Keynotes* (1893) was one of the most controversial works of the decade, with its frank explorations of female sexual psychology. Bradley and Cooper despised Egerton's writing, as explored below.

Vernon Lee was the penname of Violet Paget (1856–1935). Lee was one of the most important aesthetic critics of the *fin de siècle*. A long-time resident of Florence, Lee moved in the same circles as Berenson and Costelloe, through whom she met Bradley and Cooper, who were not enamoured with her. For more on their relationship with Lee see Frankie Dytor, '"The Eyes of an Intellectual Vampire": Michael Field, Vernon Lee, and Female Masculinities in Late Victorian Aestheticism', *Journal of Victorian Culture*, 26 (2021), 582–95.

George Moore (1852–1933) was an Anglo-Irish novelist, most famous for his Künstlerroman *Confessions of a Young Man* (1888) and the Zolaesque naturalism of *Esther Waters* (1894). Moore reviewed Michael Field's verse drama *William Rufus* (1885) positively.

[69] Michael Field [EC], 'Works and Days', BL Add. MS 46779, fol. 135v (14 Nov 1891).

[70] Michael Field [EC], 'Works and Days', BL Add. MS 46777, fol. 14v (July 1888). The quotation here is from Alfred Tennyson's 'Tears, Idle Tears', included in *The Princess* (1847).

[71] Michael Field [EC], 'Works and Days', BL Add. MS 46778, fol. 125v (11 Dec 1890).

[72] Michael Field [EC], 'Works and Days', BL Add. MS 46778, fol. 127r (31 Dec 1890).

the most infamous work of French Decadence, Joris-Karl Huysmans's *À rebours* (1884), they were equally circumspect, declaring it 'the very word of decadence — the foam on the most recent decay', yet lamenting its 'meagre tragedy'. However, for all its squalid qualities, they admired the ways in which Huysmans was able to capture the anguish of Des Esseintes's forced return to Paris from exile at Fontenay, and his 'cry for faith' which possessed 'more agony in it than the last words of any Greek protagonist or of any Elizabethan hero'.[73] The influence of the French novel on Cooper and Bradley's short prose can be seen in their refusal of narrative development, their focus on small details, and their attempt to convey the nature of experience through sensory evocation. While these are all characteristics of a 'Decadent' style, Bradley and Cooper avoid the violence, the eroticism, and the excessive allusion of Flaubert and Huysmans. While their verse dramas — particularly the Roman Trilogy — would employ such Decadent tropes, Michael Field's short prose takes the formal features of French prose writing but repurposes them to capture aesthetic moments, those everyday experiences which are both profound and fleeting.

The *Fin-de-Siècle* Prose Poem and *Croquis*

Bradley and Cooper found themselves exploring new prose forms at a crucial moment in the development of experimental literature. On both sides of the Channel many writers were using shorter, more compact prose forms. From the 'prose ballad' to short stories of psychological interiority, writers were turning away from the triple-decker novel, with 'little magazines' and avant-garde annuals such as the *Yellow Book* and *The Pageant* fuelling a market for innovation. Foremost among the developments in prose at the *fin de siècle* was the prose poem. In *À rebours*, one of Des Esseintes's many enthusiasms is the prose poetry of Charles Baudelaire. Taking pride of place on the mantel that forms the centrepiece of his library at Fontenay are his favourite three works by Baudelaire, including 'Anywhere Out of the World', arguably his greatest prose poem. A little later the narrator declares that:

> Of all forms of literature, the prose poem was Des Esseintes' favourite. Handled by an alchemist of genius it should, he maintained, contain within its small compass and in concentrated form the substance of a novel, while dispensing with the latter's long-winded analyses and superfluous descriptions. Many were the times that Des Esseintes had pondered over the fascinating problem of writing a novel concentrated in a few sentences and yet comprising the cohobated[74] juice of the hundreds of pages always taken

[73] Michael Field [EC], 'Works and Days', BL Add. MS 46780, fol. 60v (7 March 1892).
[74] OED: cohobate v. 'To subject to repeated distillation, by pouring a liquid back again and again upon the matter from which it has been distilled'.

> up in describing the setting, drawing the characters, and piling up useful observations and incidental details. The words chosen for a work of this sort would be so unalterable that they would take the place of all the others; every adjective would be sited with such ingenuity and finality that it could never be legally evicted, and would open up such wide vistas that the reader could muse on its meaning, at once precise and multiple, for weeks on end, and also ascertain the present, reconstruct the past, and divine the future of the characters in the light of this one epithet.
>
> The novel, thus conceived, thus condensed in a page or two, would become an intellectual communion between a hieratic writer and an ideal reader, a spiritual collaboration between a dozen persons of superior intelligence scattered across the world, an aesthetic treat available to none but the most discerning.
>
> In short, the prose poem represented in Des Esseintes' eyes the dry juice, the osmazome[75] of literature, the essential oil of art.[76]

As a description of what the prose poem aims to achieve this passage is still largely unparalleled, outlining the central characteristics of the form: precision and concision, yet with untold depths of emotion and spiritual perspicacity. The prose poem may have been the very acme of modernity for Des Esseintes, yet any stable definition of the form is seemingly impossible. Jeremy Noel-Tod offers the following as 'the simplest common denominator' of the form: 'a prose poem is a poem without line breaks. Beyond that, both its manner and its matter resist generalizations.'[77] It is a frustratingly vague definition, but as soon as one begins to offer more precise delineations the form falls apart under a mass of contradictions. The prose poem is not to be confused with poetic prose, which could describe the formal qualities of a great many novels and works of non-fiction. Perhaps then the prose poem is characterized by its brevity. Prose poems are generally short (typically less than 500 words, often fewer) and have traces of poetic devices such as repetition, and many argue they have a certain rhythmical quality (but then again, so does a great deal of literary prose). Rod Mengham has argued that the tension between the circumscribed space of the prose poem and the infinite spaces that lie beyond it have characterized the genre since its creation, which, he compellingly notes, began with Baudelaire at the precise moment he was also translating De Quincey's prose of claustrophobia and nightmarish Piranesian depths into French. The prose poem 'quarantines itself from what lies outside it, refuses to affiliate itself to a larger context, but then does little else

75 OED: osmazome, n. 'A name formerly given to that substance or mixture of substances soluble in water and alcohol which gives meat its flavour and smell; (more generally) meat juice or extract'.

76 Joris-Karl Huysmans, *Against Nature*, trans. by Robert Baldick (London: Penguin, 1959), pp. 198–99.

77 Jeremy Noel-Tod, 'Introduction', in *The Penguin Book of the Prose Poem* (London: Penguin, 2018), pp. xix–xx.

besides refer to these extraneous things precisely as traces, shadows and echoes'.[78] These tensions between the inside world of the prose poem and the outside world are seen in many of the works by Michael Field that we have collected here, in which clouds sailing high above a moor, or waves crashing on a desolate beach, give an expansive quality to the claustral nature of the form. Yet for other prose *croquis* that have a more narrative quality — 'A Maenad', 'A Faun' — this characterization seems inappropriate.

If there is little consensus — formally — on what a prose poem may be, then there is far more agreement on the birth of the form. The origins of the prose poem can be traced back to the prominence of the prose fragment in German Romanticism — in particular in the work of Novalis and Friedrich Schlegel — and its adoption by their English counterparts, most notably Samuel Taylor Coleridge. It has been argued that the earliest English language prose poems were the works of James Macpherson (1736–1796), collected as *The Poems of Ossian*.[79] France, however, was to be the birthplace of the modern prose poem. While Aloysius Bertrand is credited with having introduced the prose poem into French with *Gaspard de la Nuit* (1842), Charles Baudelaire's posthumous volume known as both *Le Spleen de Paris* and *Petits Poèmes en prose* (1869) is routinely regarded as having brought the form to a wide readership. In the letter to Arsène Houssaye which functions as a preface to the collection, Baudelaire characterized his prose poems as follows: 'Which of us, in his moments of ambition, has not dreamed of the miracle of a poetic prose, musical, without rhythm and without rhyme, supple enough and rugged enough to adapt itself to the lyrical impulses of the soul, the undulations of reverie, the jibes of conscience?' The form that Baudelaire describes here was, however, not to be confused with mere romantic reverie; for Baudelaire, the prose poem was, fundamentally, the expression of urban modernity: 'It was, above all, out of my exploration of huge cities, out of the medley of their innumerable interrelations, that this haunting ideal was born.'[80]

While Bradley and Cooper may have attempted to realize the 'miracle of a poetic prose' described by Baudelaire, the pieces collected here are not inspired by the grand cities of modernity. Yet they did follow Baudelaire in his unsentimental descriptions of human suffering and his philosophical ruminations. Take, for example, 'The Old Woman's Despair':

> A wizened little old woman felt gladdened and gay at the sight of the pretty baby that every one was making such a fuss over, and that every one wanted

[78] Rod Mengham, 'A Genealogy of the Prose Poem', *CounterText*, 3 (2017), 176–86 (p. 180).

[79] On the Romantic inheritance of the prose poem see Cassandra Atherton and Paul Hetherington, *Prose Poetry: An Introduction* (Princeton: Princeton University Press, 2020), pp. 28–42.

[80] Charles Baudelaire, 'To Arsène Houssaye', in *Paris Spleen*, trans. by Louise Varèse (New York: New Directions, 1970), pp. ix–x.

to please; such a pretty little creature, as frail as the old woman herself, and toothless and hairless like her.

She went up to him all nods and smiles.

But the infant, terrified, struggled to get away from her caresses, filling the house with his howls.

Then the old woman went back into her eternal solitude and wept alone, saying: 'Ah, for us miserable old females the age of pleasing is past. Even innocent babes cannot endure us, and we are scarecrows to little children whom we long to love.'[81]

The misery of old age is a feature of a number of Michael Field's works collected here, including 'Rhythm', 'It Was an Old House', 'Gentle Death', and 'An Old Couple'. Bradley and Cooper use the brevity of the prose poem form to capture the poignancy of suffering without indulging in the sentiment that marred so many examinations of death in Victorian literature.

While it was the literature of France that was the great inspiration for late-Victorian prose poetry, the form was also associated with Russian literature, and Bradley and Cooper were great enthusiasts for the literature of Eastern Europe, translations of which were flooding England at the *fin de siècle* (often from the French). Among these were Ivan Turgenev, whose *Poems in Prose* were translated into English and first published in England in 1890.[82] At the time she was writing her *croquis*, Cooper informed Berenson that she was 'studying Tourguenéf' [*sic*], and it was highly likely she had read his prose poems.[83]

Baudelaire may have given birth to the form as we now know it, but by the 1890s it was ubiquitous in French letters, and writers across the Channel (and on the other side of the Atlantic) were beginning both to translate French prose poetry into English and to pen their own experiments in the genre. A signal moment in the development of the prose poem in English was the American poet Stuart Merrill's translation of the best exemplars of the form in French, collected as *Pastels in Prose* (1890). Merrill's anthology included a veritable who's who of French Decadence and Symbolism: Louis Théodore de Banville, Alphonse Daudet, J.-K. Huysmans, Villiers de L'Isle-Adam, George Auriol, Judith Gauthier, Éphraïm Mikhaël, Stéphane Mallarmé, Charles Baudelaire, Emile Hennequin, Adrien Remacle, Paul Masy, Catulle Mendès, and Henri de Régnier, amongst others. The anthology was prefaced with a brief introduction by the venerable American novelist and critic William Dean Howells, who celebrated the form's 'beautiful reticence', 'as if the very freedom which the poets had found in their emancipation from the artificial trammels of verse had put them on their honor,

---

[81] Baudelaire, *Paris Spleen*, trans. by Varèse, p. 2.

[82] Ivan Turgénieff, *Senilia: Poems in Prose*, trans. by S. J. MacMullan (Bristol: J. W. Arrowsmith, 1890).

[83] EC to Bernard Berenson (26 February 1894), reproduced in *Michael Field, The Poet*, ed. by Thain and Vadillo, p. 322.

as it were, and bound them to brevity, to simplicity'. Howells was convinced that it was 'a form which other languages must naturalize', with the hope of preserving its 'aerial delicacy' and that 'wonderful refinement, which is almost fragility'.[84] William Sharp,[85] in an appreciative review of the volume, would make it clear that this was a very different, and far more delicate, beast from English poetic prose: 'the true prose-poem is not merely a happy passage in an environment of unemotional prose: it is a consciously-conceived and definitely-executed poetic form.' It was often characterized, he noted, by 'variations and repetitions of effect, multiplications of identical lines, corresponding to the repetitive effects in the villanelle and all poems of the rondeau-kind'.[86] Sharp would himself produce some delicate prose poems under the pen name Fiona Macleod, one of which we include in this volume.

Writers in England, particularly those Francophiles we now associate with Decadence and aestheticism, were quick to take up the form, including Oscar Wilde, who published six 'Poems in Prose' in the *Fortnightly Review*, July 1894. Other significant publications include Edward Garnett's 1894 collection *An Imaged World: Poems in Prose* and Nora Hopper's *Ballads in Prose* (1894).[87] It would be misleading, however, to suggest that all progressive artists embraced the form. W. B. Yeats, in an unsigned review of Garnett's volume, would declare that while there was 'poetry in this remarkable book for many poems', 'it seldom perfectly satisfies the artistic conscience or quite lays asleep the thought that we will forget it when it is thrust into the shelf'. As beautiful as certain passages may be, 'the impression of the whole is a little vapoury'.[88] The *National Observer*'s reviewer was even less taken with this experiment, urging the young man to 'try to think without similes' and 'reduce the amount of "ego in his cosmos"'. If this could be accomplished, he might 'yet aspire to be called something more than a Joubert *manqué*. But we are not sanguine; we have seen too many such.'[89] The world-weary response of critics to Gallic novelty was predictable, yet the rise of the English prose poem was not to be sustained.

---

[84] William Dean Howells, 'Introduction', in *Pastels in Prose*, trans. and ed. by Stuart Merrill (New York: Harper & Brothers, 1890), pp. vi–vii (p. vix).

[85] William Sharp (1855–1905) was a prolific literary critic of the *fin de siècle*. Under the pseudonym Fiona Macleod he published poetry, novels, short stories, and essays, almost all set in, or inspired by, the Highlands and Western Isles of Scotland.

[86] [William Sharp], 'Pastels in Prose', *Pagan Review*, 15 August 1892, pp. 55–56.

[87] Edward Garnett (1868–1937) was a literary critic, playwright, and publisher's reader; Nora Chesson (née Hopper) (1871–1906) was a poet associated with the Celtic revival.

[88] W. B. Yeats, 'An Imaged World', in *The Collected Works of W. B. Yeats, Vol IX: Early Articles and Reviews*, ed. by John P. Frayne and Madeleine Marchaterre (New York: Scribner, 2004), pp. 249–51 (p. 251).

[89] 'A Prose-Poet', *National Observer*, 25 August 1894, p. 386. Joseph Joubert (1754–1824) was a French moralist known for his aphoristic style. The French term *manqué* implies someone who has failed to live up to their ambition.

A number of critics argue that the association with Decadence was responsible for a hostility towards the prose poem in the early years of the twentieth century in Britain. Jane Monson credits Wilde's description of one of his love letters to Lord Alfred Douglas as a 'prose poem' with inaugurating the idea that the prose poem was inherently immoral, the form coming to be seen as 'distasteful, subversive and ostentatious'.[90] It certainly seemed in the spring of 1895 that the prose poem was on trial along with Wilde in the dock. The prose poem's path to the Old Bailey began when Wilde wrote the following letter to Douglas (most likely) in January 1893:

> My Own Boy,
> Your sonnet is quite lovely, and it is a marvel that those red-roseleaf lips of yours should be made no less for the madness of music and song than for the madness of kissing. Your slim gilt soul walks between passion and poetry. I know Hyacinthus, whom Apollo loved so madly, was you in Greek days. Why are you alone in London, and when do you go to Salisbury? Do go there to cool your hands in the grey twilight of Gothic things, and come here whenever you like. It is a lovely place and lacks only you; but go to Salisbury first.
> Always, with undying love,
> Yours, Oscar[91]

The original letter found its way into the hands of blackmailers and Wilde paid to have it restored to him. It is no prose poem, but in May 1893 it was translated into French verse by the erotic French poet and dedicatee of *Salomé*, Pierre Louÿs, and published in the *Spirit Lamp*, which was edited by Douglas, prefaced with the following note: 'A letter written in prose poetry by Mr. Oscar Wilde to a friend, and translated into rhymed poetry by a poet of no importance.'[92] Both the letter and the French translation were raised by Sir Edward Clarke as part of his prosecution of Queensberry in the libel trial. Since Carson (Queensberry's lawyer) would no doubt use such letters, and Wilde's relationship with blackmailers, as part of Queensberry's defence, Clarke went on the offensive to prove that the letter was part of an elevated artistic exchange and that Wilde now viewed it as a 'prose sonnet' and, as he wanted to later republish it, was perfectly justified to pay money for its return.[93] This tactic ultimately, perhaps inevitably, failed and Wilde's impassioned letter was passed over to the Crown and became part of the evidence that would later be used to prosecute and imprison him. The prose poem was collateral damage in Wilde's fall from grace.

---

[90] Jane Monson, 'Introduction', in *British Prose Poetry: The Poems Without Lines* (Basingstoke: Palgrave Macmillan, 2018), pp. 1–18.

[91] Oscar Wilde, 'To Lord Alfred Douglas, January 1893', in *The Complete Letters of Oscar Wilde*, ed. by Merlin Holland and Rupert Hart-Davis (London: Fourth Estate, 2000), p. 544.

[92] Pierre Louÿs, 'Sonnet', *Spirit Lamp*, 4 May 1893, p. 1.

[93] Merlin Holland, *Irish Peacock & Scarlet Marquess: The Real Trial of Oscar Wilde* (London: Fourth Estate, 2003), p. 33.

The prose poem, so the narrative goes, was then forced underground, briefly re-emerging during the First World War, only to be savaged by T. S. Eliot in his 1917 essay 'The Borderline of Prose'. His target there was the prose poetry of Richard Aldington, but he would attack the young poet by intimating he was returning, misguidedly, to the aesthetic pretensions of the 1890s: 'Charlatanism, no doubt, still exists; but decadence is far decayed; [...]. Time has left us many things, but among those it has taken away we may hope to count *À rebours*, and the *Divagations*, and the writings of miscellaneous prose poets.'[94] This was part of Eliot's crusade — disingenuous and dissembling — to consign Decadence to the past when, as Vincent Sherry has demonstrated, he was deeply indebted to its forms.[95]

As convenient as this neat narrative may be, the truth is a little messier. Wilde's imprisonment did not signal the death knell for the form: a prose poem of Stéphane Mallarmé's, translated by George Moore, appeared in *The Savoy* in 1896; Alice Meynell's delicate prose sketches *London Impressions* appeared in 1898; Ernest Dowson included the prose poems 'Absinthia Taetra' and 'The Visit' in his volume *Decorations* of 1899; Arthur Machen published a number of prose poems in 1907 and 1908; and Arthur Symons's translation of Baudelaire's *Poems in Prose* would appear in 1905. Yet perhaps the demise of Oscar Wilde did have some influence on Bradley and Cooper's decision to turn their back on *For That Moment Only* and the prose poem. While their falling out with Berenson was the main catalyst for their decision, they were not immune from the chilling effect that Wilde's trials had on Decadents and aesthetes. As Bradley wrote to Berenson soon after Wilde's arrest: 'I tremble to think of how difficult in the face of this Oscar business, it will be to go on singing the praise of youth and beauty and all those things that from the beginning of the world have been priceless to every artist.'[96] Perhaps they thought the erotic undertones of 'A Maenad' or 'A Faun' might seem a little risky given the conservative backlash that shook the nation from April 1895 onwards.

The twelve months prior to Wilde's trials had seen the two women becoming more and more distant from avant-garde artistic circles, and in particular the little magazine that was to become the symbol of English literary Decadence. Bradley and Cooper were initially enthusiastic at the prospect of the *Yellow Book*. When word of this new 'quality' periodical first started doing the rounds of

---

[94] T. S. Eliot, 'The Borderline of Prose', in *The Complete Prose of T. S. Eliot: The Critical Edition: Apprentice Years, 1905–1918* (Baltimore: Johns Hopkins University Press and Faber & Faber Ltd, 2014), pp. 537–43 (p. 537).

[95] Vincent Sherry, *Modernism and the Reinvention of Decadence* (Cambridge: Cambridge University Press, 2015).

[96] Katharine Bradley, 'To Bernard Berenson, 12 April 1895', Oxford, Bodleian Libraries, MS Eng. Lett. D. 408, fols 37–38. These are transcriptions by T. Sturge Moore.

literary London at the beginning of 1894 they rubbed their hands in anticipation. 'The contributors are to be well paid', Bradley wrote, 'we feel our purses fill with guineas'.[97] Eager to get in on the act they sent the editor, Henry Harland,[98] a bundle of submissions, including 'A Garden' by Cooper (the manuscript of which we have not been able to locate) and 'Rhythm' by Bradley. It was their understanding that Harland had accepted Bradley's prose poem, but it was not to appear in the first volume, its publication apparently held over until the second volume in July. Yet their enthusiasm for Lane's new venture waned on the publication of the debut volume. Cooper began her account of their trip up to London to visit the Bodley Head and purchase the first volume with mordant histrionics: 'We have been almost blinded by the glare of hell'. The publisher had decked out their front window with the distinctive yellow-orange of the periodical's front cover, and the effect was, for Cooper, far from appealing: 'the infamous window mocked and mowed, and fizgiged, saffron and pitchy, till one's eyes were arrested like Virgil's before the wind of flame'.[99] As lurid and nauseating as they found the visual aesthetic of the *Yellow Book*, it paled beside their horror at its contents: 'it is full of cleverness such as one expects to find in those who dwell below light and hope and love and aspiration'. Yet (as discussed later) their particular ire was reserved for George Egerton, who 'does not even deserve damnation, but something weightier — crushing-out silence'. Bradley wrote to Mary Costelloe to inform her they had come down with 'the Yellow-Book Fever'. It was soon after this that Bradley sought to retract 'our little prose-poem', 'Rhythm', writing to Harland: 'I must request you to return my typed copy of *Rhythm*. I dislike the *Yellow Book* both in its first and second number, and greatly regret that in a sudden rash of sympathy I proposed to contribute to it'. Harland's response reminded them that they had to provide a self-addressed envelope as their work had in fact been rejected. It appears that they were under the impression the piece had been accepted for publication, but when it was not published in the second volume, they decided to cut all ties with the periodical and its publisher the Bodley Head.[100] With its bleak, blunt reflection on death and solitude, 'Rhythm' would have been a fitting piece for Michael Field to publish in the flagship journal of Decadence.

'Rhythm' may have been a prose poem, but *croquis*, which is simply translated as sketch, was the term preferred by Cooper to describe her prose works. The name suggests a quick, impressionistic record of a visual image, but in French prose of the period it intimated a much greater artistry. The most famous

[97] Michael Field [KB], 'Works and Days', BL Add. MS 46782, fol. 3r (Jan 1894).
[98] Henry Harland (1861–1905) was an American novelist and editor whose editorship of the *Yellow Book* made him a prominent figure in literary London of the 1890s.
[99] In the *Inferno*, Canto XXVI, Dante being led through Hell by Virgil, where they speak to the flames.
[100] Michael Field [EC], 'Works and Days', BL Add. MS 46782, fols 94r, 95v (17 July 1894).

practitioner of the *croquis* was Huysmans, whose *Croquis Parisiens* (1880) offered memorable vignettes of Parisian life, from the music hall of the Folies-Bergère, to the industrial squalor of the Bièvre river, and studies of 'Parisian characters', including the bus conductor, the washerwoman, and the chestnut seller, along with a 'prose ballad' to the tallow candle, and a 'prose poem' in honour or roast beef. Arthur Symons claimed that in these sketches Huysmans's 'faculty of description is here seen at its fullest stretch of agility; precise, suggestive, with all the outline and colour of actual brush-work'.[101] The term was taken up by other writers in France as a label for descriptive travel writing, including René Bazin's *Croquis italiens* (1890), Georges Robert's *Voyage à travers l'Algérie: Notes et croquis* (1890), and Georges Daremberg's *En Orient et en Occident: Paysages et croquis* (1893), amongst others, yet none of these later writers captured the frank realism of Huysmans's volume and the visceral, sensual quality of his sketches. Take, for instance, his panegyric to the female armpit, in which he explores the array of aromas produced by the contact of skin and sweat with various materials. An open ball gown will emit 'an aroma of valerianate of ammonia and urine', while that which escapes from an Oxford wool dress is 'less insolent, less cynical'.[102] Other contemporary French forms Michael Field attempted to emulate include the 'conte', the sardonic short story form perfected by Auguste Villiers de l'Isle-Adam, whose *Contes Cruels* (1883) they had read, and whose influence can be seen in 'Study For a Krankenhaus "Conte"'.[103]

In English the impressionistic prose sketch was mastered by Hubert Crackanthorpe,[104] whose *Vignettes: A Miniature Journal of Whim and Sentiment* (1896), published just before his mysterious death, was a landmark in the short prose form. Emanuela Ettorre characterizes the volume as follows: 'Through a modality that oscillates between the photographic and the phantasmagorical, Crackanthorpe engages in a hermeneutic process in which writing becomes a means of self-discovery, as the observation of place is transformed into a projection of his soul.'[105] His delicate yet often cynical prose poems capture the modernity of both Huysmans and Baudelaire. Take, as an exemplar, 'Paris in October':

> Paris in October all white and a-glitter under a cold, sparkling sky, and the trees of the boulevards trembling their frail, russet leaves; garish, petulant

---

[101] Arthur Symons, 'J.K. Huysmans', *Fortnightly Review*, March 1892, pp. 402–14 (p. 407).

[102] J.-K. Huysmans, *Parisian Sketches*, trans. by Brendan King (Sawtry: Dedalus, 2007), p. 127.

[103] This was one amongst a number of 'French Books' they record having read in 1889: Michael Field [EC], 'Works and Days', BL Add. MS 46777, fol. 128r (Dec 1889).

[104] Hubert Crackanthorpe (1870–1896) was a writer of bleak realism. He published two volumes of stories and a book of prose poems before his apparent suicide in Paris.

[105] Emanuela Ettorre, 'Introduction: The Stories and Prose Poems', in *Hubert Crackanthorpe: Selected Writing*, ed. by William Greenslade and Emanuela Ettorre (Cambridge: MHRA, 2020), pp. 35–65 (p. 61).

> Paris; complacently content with her sauntering crowds, her monotonous arrangements in pink and white and blue; ever busied with her own publicity, her tiresome, obvious vice, and her parochial modernity coquetting with cosmopolitanism....[106]

Crackanthorpe's 'vignette' opens with the delicate impressionism of Symons or Dowson, before degenerating into a savage attack on the self-satisfied banality of the city so beloved by Decadents. It is worth noting just how far this is from Michael Field's *croquis*. While Cooper and Bradley are self-consciously attempting to be modern, they refuse both the posture of the world-weary poet and the preoccupation with urban modernity that tended to characterize the genre. The *croquis* of Michael Field are influenced by the modernity of form that had given rise to the prose poem and the French sketch, but they appropriated and repurposed the form to their own Bacchic aestheticism.

Perhaps the most appropriate term for describing the prose works we collect here is 'impressionist'. Inspired by Pater, these short works attempt to capture the emotional states that result from significant moments of experience. Bradley and Cooper were, of course, far from alone in their commitment to literary impressionism at the *fin de siècle*. Arthur Symons was penning delicate poems of erotic encounter and urban experience; Henry James, having early in his career been dismissive of impressionism, embraced the method in his attempt to capture the dislocation and disorientation of the modern, particularly in the sketches that made up *The American Scene* (1907); Ford Madox Ford was developing a distinctive method for articulating the fragmentary experience of the city in *The Soul of London* (1905); Alice Meynell's *London Impressions* (1898) paid attention to the rhythms and patterns of the city, from fire to fog;[107] Joseph Conrad was, by the late 1890s, developing a new, impressionistic, idea of what literary art offered: 'by the power of the written word to make you hear, to make you feel — it is, before all, to make you *see*'.[108] In the majority of these examples, the impressionistic poetry and prose of the *fin de siècle* was concerned with capturing the experience of urban life. As Arthur Symons would put it, 'I think that might be the test of poetry which professes to be modern: its capacity for dealing with London, with what one sees or might see there, indoors or out'.[109] Yet the impressionistic prose of Michael Field is striking in its refusal of urban modernity

---

[106] Hubert Crackanthorpe, *Vignettes: A Miniature Journal of Whim and Sentiment* (London: John Lane, 1896), p. 28.

[107] Ford Madox Ford (1873–1939) was one of the leading figures of British modernism; Alice Meynell (1847–1922) was a leading writer of the *fin de siècle* who published a wide range of verse, criticism, and experimental essays and prose sketches.

[108] Joseph Conrad, 'Author's Note to *The Nigger of the "Narcissus"*', *New Review*, December 1897, pp. 628–31 (p. 630).

[109] Arthur Symons, 'Modernity in Verse', in *Studies in Two Literatures* (London: Leonard Smithers, 1897), pp. 186–203 (p. 188).

as a setting. It was not as if the two women avoided the city; from 1888 to 1899 they were living in Reigate, Surrey, and would often make their way up to town where they attended galleries, concerts, lectures, afternoon teas, and evening salons. Ana Parejo Vadillo argues that we should consider Michael Field to be 'suburban' poets.[110] Yet in their *croquis* and aesthetic prose we have collected here they studiously avoid describing urban streetscapes and experiences. Many of these sketches focus on rural landscapes and are inspired by their travels to the English and Scottish countryside: a glimpse of a young woman lying in the heather on a moor in 'A Face in Ling'; a young woman on a farm feeding her fowls in 'Gwen'; a desolate littoral scene in 'A Wintry Sea'; a coach journey through the Scottish Borders in 'Incongruity'. For Michael Field it was the forms in which they captured impressions, rather than the location of experience, that made their *croquis* modern.

Michael Field and Women's Short Fiction

Thus far we have traced a largely male-dominated trajectory for the prose poem in the late nineteenth century. But the *fin de siècle* is a particularly rich epoch for short fiction by women writers, and many of these works challenge and defy formal and generic categories, existing on the border between poetry and prose. Michael Field have been largely absent from scholarly discussions of New Woman short fiction due to their predominantly dismissive attitude towards other women writers. Bradley and Cooper preferred to associate with male writers rather than their female peers, usually disparaging or ignoring the latter. Their relations with women were ambivalent at best and, although they were often envious of other women writers' success, they seldom openly acknowledge their influence, as they did with their male contemporaries. But while they have not been considered among 'New Woman' writers, Michael Field's prose shares many traits with experimental short fiction produced by other women writers during the *fin de siècle* — not least their use of these elliptical forms to convey subversive sexual desires and to ponder liminal and submerged aspects of identity, in this sense anticipating the modernist prose of Virginia Woolf and Katherine Mansfield.

As observed by numerous critics, the short story form appealed to late-Victorian women writers due to its capacity to disrupt the conventions of the nineteenth-century novel. While the novel, especially the triple-decker novel, was irrevocably associated with the pressures of the circulating library and the seemingly inescapable marriage plot, the short story offered an alternative to well-trodden narrative expectations. This made it a highly attractive form for women writers who wished to candidly convey female experience in their fiction — what

---

[110] Ana Parejo Vadillo, *Women Poets and Urban Aestheticism: Passengers of Modernity* (Basingstoke: Palgrave Macmillan, 2005), pp. 154–74.

George Egerton referred to as the 'one small plot left for her to tell; the *terra incognita* of herself'.[111] With little space for full-scale plot development, the short story usually focused on a moment, or series of moments, characterized by intense emotion or epiphany. The short story writer aimed to cultivate a mood or atmosphere rather than foster causality or character development. Short stories offered fleeting snapshots (appropriate in the era of photography); a crystallized instant in keeping with Pater's 'hard, gem-like flame'. The short story, like a lyric poem, could be likened to a finely wrought work of art; it is little coincidence that *fin-de-siècle* short story collections are often titled after such bijou productions (*Monochromes* and *Cameos*, for instance).[112] Freed from fully explicating or having to resolve the plot, women writers could drop hints, and leave loose threads at the denouement of their stories. The short story form therefore afforded opportunities for subversion without being explicit; these works were founded on ambiguity and suggestion — what was left unsaid, as much as what was spelt out.

On a practical level, the short story also provided late-nineteenth-century women writers with increased opportunities to contribute to the ever-growing market of periodicals, little magazines, and newspapers. Publishing short fiction could provide a means for financial self-sufficiency, as well as an accessible route to building a reputation as an author. By the *fin de siècle*, it was possible for the woman writer to make a living by her pen through combining journalism, reviewing, and short fiction. Writers such as Alice Meynell, Katharine Tynan, and Graham R. Tomson sustained themselves (and their families) by contributing to the *Scots Observer*, the *Pall Mall Gazette*, the *Fortnightly Review*, the *Daily Chronicle*, and *The Bookman*.[113] Among the numerous periodicals of the day, the *Yellow Book* was particularly famous (if not notorious) for its inclusion of women writers, particularly those associated with the New Woman. As Margaret Stetz and Mark Samuels Lasner observe, the *Yellow Book* offered unprecedented space for experimental women's fiction: 'no other journal of the day devoted to "high" or avant-garde culture allowed women so great a voice in defining themselves and one another.'[114]

As well as short fiction in general, the prose poem held particular appeal for women writers. As Stetz has proposed, in the 1890s we can discern

[111] George Egerton, 'A Keynote to *Keynotes*', in *Ten Contemporaries: Notes Toward Their Definitive Bibliography*, ed. by John Gawsworth (London: Ernest Benn Limited, 1932), p. 58.

[112] The titles of short story collections by Ella D'Arcy (1895) and Marie Corelli (1896).

[113] Katharine Tynan (1859–1931) was a prolific Irish poet and novelist; Graham R. Tomson was the pseudonym of Rosamund Marriott Watson (1860–1911). Tomson published some of the most striking poetry of the 1890s, combining Decadent aesthetics with a passion for the natural world.

[114] Margaret D. Stetz and Mark Samuels Lasner, *The Yellow Book: A Centenary Exhibition* (Cambridge, MA: The Houghton Library, 1994), p. 38.

interconnections between genre and gender transgression: 'Surely it is no coincidence that the nineteenth-century British writers most powerfully drawn to transgress genre boundaries between prose and poetry were those whose politics — whether social, sexual, or artistic — were radical in general.'[115] Stetz points to volumes by female members of the Celtic Renaissance including Tynan, Jane Barlow, and Nora Hopper, whose works blur the boundaries between poetry and prose, employing the oral rhythms of Irish folk tales or alternating poetry and prose in a single volume.[116] In discussing Hopper's *Ballads in Prose*, Stetz observes that many of the stories feature gender-ambiguous and cross-dressing characters and carry a homoerotic charge, connecting this to the volume's formal hybridity: 'the breaking of one sort of law was often linked to the desire to break free of others.'[117]

But where do Michael Field fit into this picture? As already noted, Bradley and Cooper do not assimilate easily into the contexts above. They are rarely considered in discussions of *fin-de-siècle* women's short fiction — not least because few scholars are aware that they wrote prose at all, due to the majority of the *croquis* remaining unpublished until now. Moreover, they were suspicious, and often outright condemnatory, of the New Woman, and dismissive of women in general. As we have seen, they loathed the *Yellow Book* — partly due to its association with this divisive figure — and withdrew their work from its pages (or they 'withdrew' after their submission was rejected). Their politics cannot be described as 'radical'; their tendencies were rather conservative and reactionary. It is difficult to position them as 'New Women' without either stretching the term to breaking point, or misrepresenting Bradley and Cooper's attitudes. The term 'female aesthetes' fits them better, but even that is a stretch, as their relationship to the aesthetic movement was ambivalent, and their complex authorial persona complicates the notion of a creative identity founded on femininity.

That being said, considering Michael Field's prose fiction in the contexts of *fin-de-siècle* short fiction produced by women is a worthwhile exercise as, on closer examination, their prose writing shares affinities with a number of works produced by women during this era. Their prose experiments can be productively set alongside the work of Vernon Lee, Alice Meynell, Olive Schreiner, and George Egerton, as well as later modernist writers such as Mansfield and Woolf.[118] Their account of meeting Vernon Lee in Florence in 1895 is a characteristic case of

---

[115] Margaret D. Stetz, '"Ballads in Prose": Genre Crossing in Late-Victorian Women's Writing', *Victorian Literature and Culture*, 34 (2006), 619–29 (p. 620).

[116] Jane Barlow (1856–1917) was an Irish poet and novelist who published a number of works exploring Irish peasant life.

[117] Stetz, 'Ballads in Prose', p. 626.

[118] Olive Schreiner (1855–1922) was a South African writer and pioneering feminist and socialist intellectual best known for her novel *The Story of an African Farm* (1883).

Bradley and Cooper's disparaging attitude towards other women writers, as frequently expressed in their diaries: it is an unflattering portrait, describing her as 'very ugly [...] an intellectual vampire' and 'like a museum, rather untidily arranged'.[119] But while they were determined to distance themselves from this apparently unattractive, misguided woman, Michael Field's work exhibits several parallels to Lee's prose. Both writers are immersed in European history and sensitive to the 'spirit of place', particularly as channelled through landscape and architecture. From her earliest publication, *Studies of the Eighteenth Century in Italy* (1880), Lee displays her fascination with the enduring presence of the past, crafting impressionistic meditations on the 'spirit of place' or *genius loci*. Conventionally a Roman deity that inhabited a particular place, in Lee's work the 'genius loci' is defined as 'the substance of our heart and mind, a spiritual reality' that connects us to particular locations.[120] Michael Field also invoke this concept in a number of their prose writings; like Lee, they found themselves drawn to crossroads, hillsides, ancient churches, and streams, particularly during their travels in Italy, and these places become vibrant embodiments of certain emotional states.

Like Lee's essays, Michael Field's prose is frequently situated on the borderline between art history, travel writing, and impressionistic short fiction, finding particular inspiration in fine art and cultural artefacts. For example, Cooper's early essay 'Effigies', with its strange blending of the ghostly and macabre with elements of art criticism, resembles a number of Lee's supernatural tales, which often focus on the uncanny effects of statues, dolls, and wax effigies. Bradley and Cooper's visceral response to Renaissance paintings and their ability to 'feel into' a diverse range of subjects, whether Botticelli's Venus or the tomb of Caecilia Metella, also recall Lee's own boundary-defying experiments with psychological aesthetics, developed alongside her partner Kit Anstruther-Thomson, in which the qualities of aesthetic objects are experienced through the body.[121] While Bradley and Cooper lauded Berenson, they insistently denigrated Lee, despite the fact that she was developing aesthetic theories that closely resembled those of the 'Doctrine'.[122] Michael Field's prose reveals that they had far more in common with Lee than they were willing to acknowledge.

In contrast to their customary disparagement, Alice Meynell was one of the few women that Bradley and Cooper openly admired in their diaries. For

---

[119] Michael Field [EC], 'Works and Days', BL Add. MS 46783 fols 47r–47v (18 April 1895); fol. 56r (21 April 1895).

[120] Vernon Lee, *Genius Loci: Notes on Places* (London: John Lane, 1899), p. 5.

[121] See Vernon Lee and Clementina Anstruther-Thomson, *Beauty and Ugliness and Other Studies in Psychological Aesthetics* (London: Bodley Head, 1912).

[122] For details of the later plagiarism case between Berenson and Lee, see Mandy Gagel, '1897, A Discussion of Plagiarism: Letters Between Vernon Lee, Bernard Berenson, and Mary Costelloe', *Literary Imagination*, 12 (2010), 154–79.

example, when contemplating their nature writing in June 1894, they praise her poem 'The Love of Narcissus' as 'most beautiful and restrained art'.[123] They also admired Meynell's critical acumen. Meeting her in July 1894, Cooper writes: 'I liked her — she is refined and one discovers it by her judgements. She has been studying our work lately — I wish she would write on it.'[124] In liking Meynell, Michael Field join an already diverse circle of admirers, including Coventry Patmore, George Meredith, Francis Thompson, Katharine Tynan, and Agnes Tobin.[125] While Meynell's early poetry earned critical acclaim, it was her carefully crafted essays, many of which were originally published in the *Pall Mall Gazette* and collected in *The Rhythm of Life* (1893), that were most celebrated in the 1890s. As Talia Schaffer observes, these essays 'raise crucial questions of genre. [...] Meynell's texts are not really essays, they are not quite prose poems, and they are certainly not journalistic advice columns, though they share components of these three.'[126] While it is difficult to ascertain if Bradley and Cooper had read the volume, Bradley's prose sketch 'Rhythm' resonates with Meynell's titular essay, in which she asserts that: 'If life is not always poetical, it is at least metrical. Periodicity rules over the mental experience of man, according to the path of the orbit of his thoughts.'[127] Death and illness shadow Meynell's meditation on the rhythms of experience; both joy and pain are 'ruled by the law that commands all things — a sun's revolutions and the rhythmic pangs of maternity'.[128] In a parallel manner, Bradley's sketch emphasises the proximity of birth and death cycles; the dying woman thinks of 'her husband's body slowly rotting in the churchyard' as she 'rock[s] the baby to sleep'. The story concludes: 'Life had taught her one of its own rhythmic laws' (p. 125). It seems that Bradley, like Meynell, considered life 'metrical'.

---

[123] Cooper writes: 'I have got art expression for my senses in the *croquis*, in the flashes of nature round a human drama, but certainly not in the nature poem. Michael has done better in that *genre* than I — but even Michael must do much better still. [...] Alice Meynell's sonnet *The Love of Narcissus* is most beautiful & restrained art (she, like every other poet, is a fool when she touches the daisy)' (Michael Field [EC], 'Works and Days', BL Add. MS 46782, fols 50v–51r (1 June 1894)). 'The Love of Narcissus' is a sonnet in Meynell's *Preludes* (1875), which also contains her much-anthologized sonnet 'To a Daisy'.

[124] Michael Field [EC], 'Works and Days', BL Add. MS 46782, fols 88v–89r (12 July 1894). During this conversation, Meynell praised the shepherdess song in Field's play *The Tragic Mary* (1890).

[125] Cooper recounts an 1896 conversation about Meynell with George Meredith: 'He admires her essays, they are full of "justesse"'; 'they have a remarkable measure; they are critical in the best sense'. Michael Field, *Works and Days*, ed. by T. & D. C. Sturge Moore (London: J. Murray, 1933), p. 103. Meredith's admiration of Meynell would have endorsed Bradley and Cooper's already positive response, given that they admired his own prose style.

[126] Talia Schaffer, *The Forgotten Female Aesthetes: Literary Culture in Late-Victorian England* (Charlottesville: University of Virginia Press, 2000), p. 161.

[127] Alice Meynell, 'The Rhythm of Life', in *The Rhythm of Life and Other Essays* (London: John Lane, 1905), pp. 1–6 (p. 1).

[128] Meynell, 'Rhythm of Life', p. 6.

Akin to many of Field's prose sketches, Meynell's essays contemplate the boundaries between nature and civilization, deconstructing this binary by aestheticizing nature and naturalizing culture. For example, Meynell's essay 'The Sun' describes the sky as an artistic arrangement: 'Not a line, not a curve, but confesses its membership in a design declared from horizon to horizon.'[129] Bradley and Cooper depict nature in similarly artistic terms, writing, for example: 'No pencil is ever so delicate, so effortless in its design as the waves' (p. 177). At the height of her interest in *croquis*, Cooper discussed nature writing with Meynell during their 1894 encounter: 'I told her how the *genii loci* attended us in our work whenever we gave them a chance. [...] She had had one day's looking at uncut hayfields — I told her we had spent hours knee-to-knee with the grass.'[130] Perhaps Meynell was inspired by this conversation, as two years later she published an essay entitled 'Grass' which condemns mowing as an aesthetic crime:

> All the beauty of a blade of grass is that the organic shape has the intention of ending in a point. Surely no one at all aware of the beauty of lines ought to be ignorant of the significance and grace of manifest intention, which rules a living line from its beginning, even though the intention be towards a point while the first spring of the line is towards an opening curve. But man does not care for intention; he mows it.[131]

Meynell's interest in grass and weeds, and their ability to transgress the artificial bounds of urban spaces, is also found in 'A Pilgrim' from *London Impressions* (reproduced in this volume), which depicts the 'thistle-seed' as a '*flâneur*', narrating its journey around the London streets (p. 186).[132] Here, as in other essays, Meynell discerns lyrical 'wildness' in humdrum city scenes; a transgressing of borders echoed in her own formal blurring of the lines between poetry and prose.

Another celebrated writer that Michael Field (grudgingly) acknowledged in their diaries was Olive Schreiner, a pioneer of the English prose poem. Schreiner incorporated an experimental prose interlude ('The Hunter') into her acclaimed novel *The Story of an African Farm* (1883) and later published a volume of eleven prose allegories entitled *Dreams* (1890). The volume was a critical and popular success, going through twenty-five editions in forty years.[133] Bradley and Cooper were among its early readers, with Bradley writing in January 1891: 'This

---

[129] Meynell, 'The Sun', in *Rhythm*, pp. 17–21 (p. 18).
[130] Michael Field [EC], 'Works and Days', BL Add. MS 46782, fols 88v–89r (12 July 1894).
[131] Alice Meynell, 'Grass', in *The Colour of Life: And Other Essays on Things Seen and Heard* (London: John Lane, 1896), pp. 60–64 (pp. 63–64). Meynell certainly did not need lecturing on the 'genii loci': she later published a volume entitled *The Spirit of Place* (1898).
[132] Meynell's fascination with the fragile frontiers between nature and the urban continues in her description of the incursion of unruly weeds in city spaces in the title essay of *Ceres Runaway* (1909).
[133] Barbara Black, Carly Nations, and Anna Spydell, 'Introduction', in Olive Schreiner, *Dreams* (Peterborough, Ontario: Broadview Press, 2020), pp. 13–48 (p. 20).

afternoon I have read to Edith and Little one Olive Schreiner's *In a Ruined Chapel* and *Wild Bees*.'[134] Bradley may have been drawn to the volume due to Arthur Symons's fulsome praise published in the *Athenæum* two days prior: 'Written in exquisite prose [...] they have the essential qualities of poetry, and are, indeed, poems in prose. The book is like nothing else in English. Probably it will have no successors, as it has had no forerunners.'[135] Focusing on the longest allegory, 'The Sunlight Lay Across My Bed', Symons describes it in somewhat Paterian terms as combining elements of multifarious art-forms: 'It is at-once music and a picture. [... T]he words seem to chant themselves to a music we do not hear [...] it is a daring experiment in the direction of a more vocal prose [...] in its calculated *crescendo*, with its wonderful effects of broken time'.[136]

Though Bradley and Cooper do not explicate their own opinions on the volume, it seems likely that Symons's praise piqued their ambition to develop an aesthetic prose style. While experimenting with *croquis*, they remained aware of Schreiner and jealous of her success. For example, in 1893, they discussed Schreiner's visit to England with their mutual friend Louie Ellis:[137]

> In the evening Louie Ellis comes. We have a Sunday in the garden. She tells us of Olive Schreiner, Olive Schreiner home from the Cape, after years of brute, wild life in Africa. The ambassador pays his respects to her, Watts asks to paint her (he is refused), she goes the round of the great. Lovers from Africa come after her [...] Meditating on all this I am filled with jealousy; this woman has been worshipped — she has known solitude — she has walked naked in the open air, she has handled politics, she has set up one, and put down another.
>
> I have lived at Durdans, neither breathing nor breathed upon.[138]

Bradley envies Schreiner's celebrity, her romantic life, and her political commitments, but she sidesteps Schreiner's actual writings, which were of course the catalyst for such adulation. Three months after this conversation, Schreiner published another volume of prose sketches, *Dream and Real Life* — a volume that Michael Field were surely aware of, as they toiled over their own prose writings.

Though Michael Field's prose is markedly different from Schreiner's — their stories largely eschew the Biblical rhythms and parable structure of Schreiner's

---

[134] Michael Field [KB], 'Works and Days', BL Add. MS 46779 fol. 3r (12 Jan 1891). 'Little one' is Amy Cooper, Edith's sister.

[135] Arthur Symons, Review of *Dreams*, *Athenæum*, 10 January 1891, reprinted in Black et al. (ed.), Schreiner, *Dreams*, pp. 165–68 (p. 167).

[136] Symons, Review of *Dreams*, p. 167.

[137] Louisa 'Louie' Ellis (1864–1928) initially befriended Olive Schreiner through her brother, Havelock Ellis. She was a dressmaker who created several of Bradley and Cooper's aesthetic gowns (see Sarah Parker, 'Fashioning Michael Field: Michael Field and Late-Victorian Dress Culture', *Journal of Victorian Culture*, 18.3 (2013), 313–34 (pp. 320–21)).

[138] Michael Field [KB], 'Works and Days', BL Add. MS 46781 fol. 45v (25 June 1893).

fables — they do employ elements of allegory, and exhibit a similar emphasis on dream-like, liminal states. In stories such as 'An Agony' and 'The Fate of the Crossways' for example, Michael Field develop a brand of pagan allegory that hinges on symbolic encounters with mythic figures. As in Schreiner's allegories, these figures present an unspoken challenge to the protagonists; Hecate, for example, appears to the speaker at a decisive moment: 'I was at crossways in my journey. Should I turn to right or left?' (p. 120), while the Dionysian figure in 'An Agony' symbolizes universal suffering and the destruction of the natural world, from which the speaker turns guiltily away. Field and Schreiner's enigmatic encounters often take place in liminal spaces between dream and reality. While Schreiner's 'Three Dreams in a Desert' is structured through intervals of waking and sleeping, Field's 'Sunset' describes a lucid dream in which the speaker encounters an uncanny 'traveller in a grey suit', who may well be a ghost (p. 84). Meanwhile, 'It Was an Old House' blurs the boundary between reality and dream; after being woken by an old clock 'from a sleep in which it seemed to be I had been vainly seeking to entertain myself by dreams' (p. 164), the speaker encounters the allegorical figure of Time — who might simply turn out to be a clock repairman.

The ambiguity between dreams and reality is signalled by the title of the very first piece in *For That Moment Only*, 'A Vision or a Waking Dream?'. Michael Field's diaries also contain a number of dream-narratives, such as 'A Renaissance Dream' and Cooper's strikingly surreal hallucinations, resulting from scarlet fever, in which literary and mythic references feverishly merge with her hospital surroundings. In her delirium, Cooper plunges into an ecstatic fantasy of multiplied identity: 'I am Greek, Roman, Barbarian, Catholic; and this multiform life sweeps me toward unconsciousness — only the shine through the blinds tortures me so that I cannot lose myself' (p. 158). This aspect of Field's writing recalls Schaffer's observation that female aesthetes often use 'fantasias' to express sexual desire and unconventional identities:

> When women writers adopted phantasmatic diction, they found it permitted new sorts of gender politics. Writers situated a woman's desires in the unreal space of 'dream' and 'fantasy', thereby preventing the reader from criticizing the character according to everyday nineteenth-century sexual norms. By placing characters outside realism, authors found themselves free to depict a wide range of behaviors.[139]

Examples of such transgressive dream narratives include Kate Chopin's 'An Egyptian Cigarette'[140] and the daydream interlude in George Egerton's 'A Cross Line', in which the protagonist imagines herself as a Salomé-esque dancer. Field's 'A Maenad' resembles Egerton's vision: both stories focus on the ecstatic

[139] Schaffer, *The Forgotten Female Aesthetes*, p. 51.

[140] Kate Chopin, 'An Egyptian Cigarette', *Vogue*, 19 April 1900, pp. 252–54.

jouissance of a female dancer who represents 'the eternal wildness' that lurks beneath the skin of the contemporary Victorian woman.[141]

However, despite these parallels, Bradley and Cooper were far from admirers of Egerton's daring prose. As we have seen, on reading the first volume of the *Yellow Book*, they reserved their strongest condemnation for Egerton. Given their shared use of masculine pennames, they even jokingly contemplated changing their name to 'Messalina Garden' to escape being tainted by association.[142] Bradley continued her critique of Egerton's contribution, 'A Lost Masterpiece', in a letter to Mary Costelloe:

> Oh, I must speak out concerning George Egerton — that shameless creature — whose pages are really 'the sweepings of a Pentonville omnibus.[' ...] do glance through A Lost Masterpiece — and note the expression 'a chunk of genius.' There ought to be in letters an outcast class to whom we can relegate such offenders.[143]

Why did Michael Field find Egerton's story objectionable? Bradley's allusion to John Ruskin's critique of George Eliot implies that Egerton's realism may have been part of the problem.[144] But while Egerton's story is set in London and does feature an omnibus (something that cannot be said of Eliot's *The Mill on the Floss*), Egerton's style is aestheticized and impressionistic, rather than relying on gritty realist description. In 'A Lost Masterpiece', an ambiguously gendered narrator (usually identified as male, but never fully ascertained as such) describes fleeting impressions that arouse unexpected associations, layering past and present, poetic and mundane. For example, a glimpse of the Thames calls to mind eighteenth-century Italian paintings of Venice:

> And as this English river scene flashes by, lines of association form angles in my brain; and the point of each is a dot of light that expands into a background for forgotten canal scenes, with green-grey water, and leaning balconies, and strange crafts — Canaletti and Guadi [*sic*] seen long ago in picture galleries...[145]

In fact, the tone and style of Egerton's story resembles Michael Field's own prose. Like Bradley and Cooper in their diaries, the narrator spends his time 'recording

---

141 George Egerton, 'A Cross Line', in *Keynotes* (London: Elkin Mathews and John Lane, 1893), pp. 9–43 (p. 38).

142 Michael Field [EC], 'Works and Days', BL Add. MS 46782, fols 38v–38r (17 April 1894). 'Messalina' likely refers to the notorious third wife of the Roman emperor Claudius.

143 KB to Mary Costelloe (*c.* April 1894), reproduced in *Michael Field, The Poet*, ed. by Thain and Vadillo, p. 330.

144 Ruskin described the characters (bar Maggie and Tom) in Eliot's *The Mill on the Floss* (1860) as 'simply the sweepings out of a Pentonville omnibus' (John Ruskin, 'Fiction, Fair and Foul', *Nineteenth Century*, 10 October 1881, pp. 516–31 (p. 521)).

145 George Egerton, 'A Lost Masterpiece', *Yellow Book*, April 1894, pp. 189–96 (p. 191). 'Guadi' appears to be a misspelling of 'Guardi', as the narrator refers to the painters Giovanni Antonio Canal, known as Canaletto, and Francesco Guardi.

fleeting impressions with delicate sure brushwork for future use; touching a hundred vagrant things with the magic of imagination, making a running comment on the scenes we passed'.[146] Perhaps these echoes are the source of the problem. For in the story, Egerton performs impressionism in order to mock its pretentious, over-blown tendencies. The story is a satirical attack on masculine presumption, as Egerton's arrogant *flâneur* objectifies those around him, until an assertive woman traversing the street disrupts his train of thought: 'what business had she to thrust herself on my observation like that, and tangle the threads of a web of genius, undoubted genius?'[147] It is possible that Bradley and Cooper did not realize that Egerton is being satirical in the story; that they took her hyperbolic style seriously. This is certainly suggested by Bradley's condemnation of the phrase 'chunk of genius', which is clearly meant to be ridiculous.[148] Or perhaps they *did* recognize her stylistic mockery, and felt personally attacked due to their not-entirely-dissimilar aesthetic prose style. Either way, it seems ironic that Bradley is left as outraged by Egerton as the narrator is by the energetic woman on the street, spluttering to Costelloe: 'We must not let these women go rampant.'[149]

While one suspects that the last thing Michael Field would want is to be read alongside Egerton, their prose writings raise similar questions about female identity and desire. For example, viewing Maurice Greiffenhagen's painting *An Idyll* prompts them to contemplate women's distinct sexual experience, as they did in many of their poems: 'The diverse sexual frankness of enjoyment in giving (or rather taking) and receiving is clear as in Michael's *Tiresias* — also woman's more cloudless delight in her part than even man's in his' (p. 152). Meanwhile, Cooper's 'Between Rome and Ancona' is a strikingly frank vignette of female sexual desire and the aggressive impulses aroused in the love rival:

> She had reached that pitch of phrenzy when an emotion becomes its opposite, when love is hate and hate itself finds its object precious. She was not very far from that still higher pitch of madness when emotion bursts into some act that has nothing to do with choice. She was in hell — not the hell of what is over and done with, but the living hell of what can and may be done under temptation. (pp. 135–36)

In such writings, Michael Field play a role in unveiling the '*terra incognita*' of womanhood at the *fin de siècle*, which aligned them (even though they would be horrified by the prospect) with Egerton's own distinctive project.

Following Wilde's trials and imprisonment in 1895, Egerton was inadvertently caught up in the scandal due to her close associations with Decadence and the

---

146 Egerton, 'A Lost Masterpiece', p. 191.

147 Egerton, 'A Lost Masterpiece', p. 194.

148 Egerton, 'A Lost Masterpiece', p. 194.

149 KB to Mary Costelloe (*c.* April 1894), *Michael Field, The Poet*, ed. by Thain and Vadillo, p. 331.

Yellow Book. In the resulting backlash, she was condemned by Hugh Stutfield as one of the women 'of the new Ibsenite neuropathic school' who are obsessed with 'probing and dissecting their "primary impulses" — especially the sexual ones'.[150] The prose poem is caught up in the mêlée, as Stutfield mocks Egerton's introduction to her translation of Ola Hansson's *Young Ofeg's Ditties* (in which she describes them as 'beautiful prose-poems'); appalled, Stutfield laments: 'If this be the literature of the future, heaven help poor humanity!'[151] But while, as Stetz observes, Egerton paid a price for continuing to work 'across the boundaries of prose and poetry' in her volume of Symbolist allegories, *Fantasias* (1898), as we have already seen, it is not quite the case that possibilities for the prose poem entirely shut down in the wake of Wilde's trials.[152] In fact, in the twentieth century, the elliptical, fragmentary qualities of the prose poem continued to prove deeply enabling for women writers who wished to express transgressive desire and to ponder submerged aspects of identity. Consider, for example, Katherine Mansfield's early prose poem 'Leves Amores', written in 1907 (pp. 193–94). Titled after one of Arthur Symons's poems, Mansfield's prose poem resounds with Decadent and Symbolist echoes; as Gerri Kimber has observed, Wilde's 'influence on all her writing was considerable'.[153] But Mansfield's gender-ambiguous narrator and portrait of transformative desire also recall several of Michael Field's prose writings.

In contemplating and aestheticizing intense moments of experience, Michael Field also anticipate Virginia Woolf's focus on 'moments of being' in her short fiction and essays. Woolf describes such moments as instances in which one becomes aware of life and death, when the 'cotton wool' of mundane existence is temporarily lifted, provoking the revelation that: 'Behind the cotton wool is hidden a pattern; that we — I mean all human beings — are connected with this; that the whole world is a work of art; that we are parts of the work of art'.[154] Like Field's prose, Woolf's short fiction concentrates on epiphanic moments, contemplating how the mind processes objects and sensations by tracing associations and forging connections. We can place, for example, Woolf's 'The Mark on the Wall' (1917) alongside Field's 'A Vision or a Waking Dream?'— both stories play on the initial ambiguity of impressions, revelling in the fantastic reveries that such uncertainty affords. While Field's prose was of course largely inaccessible to Mansfield and Woolf, all four writers shared a literary inheritance,

---

150 Hugh E. M. Stutfield, 'Tommyrotics', *Blackwood's Edinburgh Magazine*, June 1895, pp. 833–45 (p. 835).

151 Stutfield, 'Tommyrotics', p. 838.

152 Stetz, 'Ballads in Prose', p. 628.

153 Gerri Kimber, '"Always Trembling on the Brink of Poetry": Katherine Mansfield, Poet', *Humanities*, 8 (2019), 1–18 (p. 5).

154 Virginia Woolf, 'A Sketch of the Past', in *Moments of Being: A Collection of Autobiographical Writing*, ed. by Jeanne Schulkind (New York: Harcourt, 1985), pp. 64–137 (p. 72).

founded in French symbolism and British aestheticism. They also share literary aspirations: the desire to create a lyrical prose capable of capturing psychological impressions and of transforming momentary experience into lasting art. For this reason, Michael Field's prose, collected in the present volume, can and should be read alongside women's short fiction of the *fin de siècle* and early twentieth century. Indeed, including Michael Field's *croquis* in this literary context illuminates and enriches our understanding of the diversity of women's prose writings across the turn of the century.

Locating the Prose

Despite the increasing critical attention being paid to the work of Michael Field, there are no extant studies of Michael Field's short prose, with the exception of Matthew Mitton's wide-ranging essay on *For That Moment Only* and the prose poem.[155] The long-form prose of the diaries has fared somewhat better, attracting early interest from Henri Locard and informing pioneering articles by Chris White and Virginia Blain.[156] More recently, Marion Thain has contemplated the 'autobiographical narrative' constructed in the diaries, while scholars increasingly draw on them at length to explore the cultural politics of Michael Field in relation to late-Victorian fashion and interior design.[157] With Carolyn Dever's recent study of the diaries, and the ongoing digitization and transcription of the volumes, critical work on the prose is set to expand rapidly. However, while the form of the prose poem and the *croquis* are largely unknown to scholars of Michael Field, the themes explored, and the imagery used, share much with the lyric poetry that the two women are most famous for.

The 1890s saw Bradley and Cooper at their most Bacchic, drawing on both Roman and Greek classics as they developed an intense, often erotic, aestheticism. Their interest in Hellenism was long established; from their first joint publication as Arran and Isla Leigh (*Bellerophôn*), through to their breakthrough verse drama *Callirhöe* and their first collection of lyric poetry, *Long Ago*, a creative response

155 Matthew Mitton, '"For That Moment Only": Michael Field and the Prose Poem', *The Michaelian*, 1 (2009), n.p. <http://www.thelatchkey.org/Field/MF1/miltonarticle.html> [accessed 23 May 2021].

156 Henri Locard, 'Works and Days: The Journals of 'Michael Field', *Journal of the Eighteen Nineties Society*, 10 (1979), 1–9; Chris White, '"Poets and Lovers Evermore": Interpreting Female Love in the Poetry and Journals of Michael Field', *Textual Practice*, 4 (1990), 197–212; Virginia Blain, 'Michael Field, the Two-Headed Nightingale: Lesbian Text as Palimpsest', *Women's History Review*, 5 (1996), 239–57.

157 See Thain's chapter 'The Diaries and Dramas: Life-writing and the Temporal Patterns of Aestheticism', in *"Michael Field": Poetry, Aestheticism, and the Fin de Siècle*, pp. 20–41; Ana Parejo Vadillo, 'Aestheticism and Decoration: At Home with Michael Field', *Cahiers victoriens et édouardiens*, 74 (2011), 17–36; Parker, 'Fashioning Michael Field'.

to Sappho's fragments. Michael Field were continually using classical frameworks to explore the paradoxes of modernity. As Stefano Evangelista notes: 'they look to Greece in order to experiment with new and productive ways in which ancient and modern culture can be brought into contact'.[158] They were also drawn to Ancient Rome and Byzantium as locales for their verse dramas, including *Equal Love* (1896), the Roman Trilogy (*The World at Auction* (1898), *The Race of Leaves* (1901), and *Julia Domna* (1903)) and *Attila, My Attila!* (1896). This investment in both Greek and Roman antiquity can be seen most clearly in the first series of *For That Moment Only*. The volume opens with the Bacchic dance of young fauns in 'A Vision or a Waking Dream', and also features an encounter with Bacchus ('An Agony'), a Dionysian vision of a young woman dancing on the Surrey wealds in 'A Maenad', the Bacchic energy of grape vines on a Tuscan hillside ('A Traveller's Tale'), and an allegorical story of a timid faun's encounters with bullying Centaurs in 'Eriphion the Faun'. Perhaps most memorable is the intense description of a young man (modelled on Berenson) in 'A Faun'. Their published work also witnesses an encounter with the ancient Greek goddess Hecate in 'The Fate of the Crossways'. In the majority of these stories the Bacchic spirit of the past exists in the vital landscapes and bodies of the present.

The religious themes that characterized Michael Field's later work after their conversion to Catholicism in 1907 are foreshadowed in several of the *croquis* which blend Hellenic paganism with religious devotion. 'The Lady Moon', for instance, opens with the proclamation 'we had done with religion' (p. 73), before unsettling this statement by portraying the pagan adoration of the moon which fixates and transfigures the speaker's companion, a young Jewish man (based on Berenson). A comparable merging of pagan and Christian spirituality is found in the personification of Bacchus as a suffering, Christ-like figure in 'An Agony'. In 1896, Cooper noted the parallels between this work and John Gray's poem 'The True Vine', written shortly after his conversion to Catholicism. Ten years later, Bradley and Cooper began their own journey towards Catholicism, though, as scholars such as Ruth Vanita and Camille Cauti have observed, their imagery continued to represent a palimpsest, layering pagan and Catholic allusions as in the earlier *croquis*.[159]

Bradley and Cooper's Dionysian spirituality finds clearest expression in their nature writing. Almost all of the *croquis* in this volume are set in rural landscapes of England, Scotland, and Italy. They are therefore representative of Michael Field's passionate appreciation of the natural world. This is hardly surprising

---

[158] Stefano Evangelista, *British Aestheticism and Ancient Greece: Hellenism, Reception, Gods in Exile* (Basingstoke: Palgrave Macmillan, 2009), p. 100.

[159] Ruth Vanita, *Sappho and the Virgin Mary: Same-Sex Love and the English Literary Imagination* (New York: Columbia University Press, 1996); Camille Cauti, 'Michael Field's Pagan Catholicism', in *Michael Field and Their World*, ed. by Stetz and Wilson, pp. 181–90.

given that their most intense period of prose writing followed the publication of *Underneath the Bough* (1893 and 1898), a collection that would feature some of their most striking attempts to reinvent pastoral forms.[160] As Kate Thomas has argued, Michael Field rejected the Decadent disdain for the rural and the natural. It was in striding over a windswept moor or wandering through a country garden in bloom that they could find the material for 'a wholly more botanical queer aestheticism'.[161] Patricia Murphy too has noted that the two women's poetry 'endows nature with erotic qualities suggesting expansive energy and impressive power to emphasize agency'.[162] Sharon Bickle links this to their feminist pagan politics, arguing that Michael Field's verse dramas position the deeply-buried powers of the Earth Mother in conflict with a hegemonic masculine world.[163] Concentrating on Michael Field's representation of figures in natural landscapes in *Sight and Song*, Dennis Denisoff connects their 'neo-paganism' to their articulations of desire: 'Field's poems rewrite myth in order to foreground an erotic release of the self to an amorous pagan ecology'.[164] The prose we have collected here demonstrates the sheer variety of the natural settings to which the two women were attracted: the bleak moors and hills of northern England and the Scottish Borders in 'Gwen', 'A Face Seen in Ling', 'Incongruity', and 'A Superstition'; the varied landscapes of central Italy in 'Between Rome and Ancona' and 'A Faun'; and the garden spaces of 'By the Sundial'. These sketches, along with a number of passages from 'Works and Days', show that Bradley and Cooper continued to 'transform their own experience into a form of Bacchic and spiritual travel'.[165]

Michael Field used their diaries to record just about every facet of their lives, from literary gossip to personal tragedy, from accounts of their travels to their impassioned love for one another. Perhaps by sheer volume alone the subject that most dominated their diaries in the years they were working on their *croquis* was art. The two women visited galleries in France, Germany, Italy, as well as in London, where they viewed a range of art, from medieval, to Renaissance,

---

[160] On the complicated publication history of *Underneath the Bough* and Michael Field as nature writers, see Alex Murray, 'Michael Field's Wordsworth', *Victorian Poetry*, 58 (2020), 427–50.

[161] Kate Thomas, 'Vegetable Love', in *Michael Field: Decadent Moderns*, ed. by Parker and Vadillo, pp. 25–46 (p. 27).

[162] Patricia Murphy, *Reconceiving Nature: Ecofeminism in Late Victorian Women's Poetry* (Columbia: University of Missouri Press, 2019), p. 97.

[163] Sharon Bickle, 'The Fierce Earth: "Michael Field's" Pagan Politics', *Hecate*, 38.1–2 (2013), 78–90.

[164] Dennis Denisoff, 'The Post-Human Spirit of the Neopagan Movement', in *Late Victorian into Modern*, ed. by Laura Marcus, Michèle Mendelssohn, and Kirsten E. Shepherd-Barr (Oxford: Oxford University Press, 2016), pp. 350–63 (pp. 359–61).

[165] Alex Murray, '"Profane Travellers" Michael Field, Cornwall, and Modern Tourism, in *Michael Field: Decadent Moderns*, ed. by Parker and Vadillo, pp. 167–87 (p. 187).

eighteenth-century, and contemporary paintings. 'Works and Days', along with a series of small notebooks when abroad, was the space in which they would record their immediate responses to an artwork. They would then sometimes translate those prose impressions into verse, in particular for their collection *Sight and Song*; thirty-one attempts, as they put it in the preface to the volume, to 'translate into verse what the lines and colours of certain chosen pictures sing in themselves'.[166] Artworks included those by Watteau, Leonardo da Vinci, Tintoretto, Correggio, Giovanni Bellini, and Giorgione, some of which had been the subject of Walter Pater's most famous ekphrastic impressionism in *Studies in the History of the Renaissance*. At the centre of that collection is desire. As Hilary Fraser argues, the volume 'articulates a dynamic stereoscopic gaze intersected by Lesbian desire' that facilitates 'the radical destabilisation of the gender binary'.[167] The visual, erotic power of the collection has led to it becoming the most examined of all Michael Field's work. The prose sketches they produced before those poems have, however, not received the same volume of attention. We have included here three of their most captivating responses to Renaissance art, all works by Botticelli. Perhaps more importantly we include their responses to two contemporary works of art: Édouard Manet's *Olympia* (1863) and Maurice Greiffenhagen's *An Idyll* (1891). These two pieces offer a tantalizing glimpse of a planned, but later abandoned, second volume of poetic 'translations' of contemporaneous paintings. However, these prose responses deserve to be analysed on their own terms as an exploration of sexuality and the power of the gaze.

The complicated sexual politics of Michael Field's poetry and pseudonymous persona have marked their reception ever since the groundbreaking work of Chris White in the 1990s.[168] The most sophisticated examinations of sexuality in their lyric verse — in particular those of Marion Thain and Kate Thomas — have offered nuanced accounts of the ways in which the temporality and polyvocality of poetic form enact and disrupt various manifestations of desire.[169] The prose poems and *croquis* we collect here encourage us to think about the relationship between literary form and desire in new ways. The gender ambiguity that characterizes so many of their speakers adds an extra dimension to established discussions of Field's polyvocal lyric voice. This liminal subject-position, aimed at a variety of objects, articulates multiple desires and identities beyond the more

[166] Michael Field, *Sight and Song* (London: Elkin Matthews and John Lane, 1892), p. v.

[167] Hilary Fraser, *Women Writing Art History in the Nineteenth Century: Looking Like a Woman* (Cambridge: Cambridge University Press, 2014), p. 84.

[168] Chris White, 'Flesh and Roses: Michael Field's Metaphors of Pleasure and Desire', *Women's Writing*, 3 (1996), 47–62.

[169] Thain, *'Michael Field': Poetry, Aestheticism, and the Fin de Siècle*; Kate Thomas, '"What Time We Kiss": Michael Field's Queer Temporalities', *GLQ: A Journal of Lesbian and Gay Studies*, 13 (2007), 327–51.

conventionally gendered lesbian subject-position hitherto associated with Bradley and Cooper, opening up further possibilities for queer, transgendered, and non-binary readings of their work. In the *croquis*, the breaking down of boundaries between masculine and feminine and human and non-human (quite literally in the case of centaurs and satyrs), and the layering of past and present, interlace with their adoption of a liminal form. The prose poem was one of the most important genres for queer modernists who wanted to explore transgressive desire both directly and obliquely — Gertrude Stein's *Tender Buttons* (1914), or Richard Bruce Nugent's 'Smoke, Lilies and Jade' (1926) are representative — and Michael Field use the form to explore the fleeting eroticism of the gaze by memorializing it in the simultaneously constrained and expansive space of the prose poem. 'A Face Seen in Ling', 'A Faun', 'A Maenad', and 'Between Rome and Ancona' all capture the arousal and frustration of the transience of desire, an impression of longing or jealousy that — so intense in the moment — must be rendered in prose so as not to be forgotten.

The need to preserve emotion in poetic form is key to a number of the published prose essays, manuscript works, and pieces from 'Works and Days' that deal with aging and death. These works were all written following the death of 'the Mother One', Cooper's mother and Bradley's sister, in August 1889. To take 'Rhythm' as an example: this *croquis* is dated by Bradley 25 September 1893. 'Works and Days' has no entry corresponding to that day, or to the week previous, but on 26 September they pasted in an article from 1886 about the death of Ferencz Renyi, the Hungarian revolutionary of 1848 on whom their play *A Question of Memory* was based. The play was in rehearsals at this point and was to be given its disastrous first and only performance a month later. Whether 'Rhythm' was inspired by the tragic stoicism of Renyi's mother is unknown, but the proximity of prose poem and play demonstrate the broader theme of death, particularly waiting for death, that is so recurrent across Michael Field's *œuvre*. In particular their prose work 'An Old Couple', published in the *Contemporary Review* in 1889, is about an aged Adam and Eve in the modern world; Bradley's 'Quai d'Anjou' is her recollection of the death in 1868 of Alfred Gérente, with whom she had been infatuated; 'Gentle Death' offers a reflection on old age and the release of death, inspired by Cicero. Perhaps most striking are the two prose sketches from 'Works and Days' that record their visits to the Paris Morgue. These moving reflections on mortality are of a piece with a number of their poems of this period, including 'Death, men say, is like a sea', 'Bring me life of fickle breath', 'Death for all thy grasping stealth', and 'Solitary death make me thine own'. Yet whereas in the lyric poems of *Underneath the Bough* death is eroticized and paganized, there is something far more mundane and muted, but also more affecting, about the intimations of mortality that pepper their prose works.

Finally, as in Michael Field's lyric poetry and verse drama, the passage of time itself is a major theme in *For That Moment Only*. As the title of the series suggests, a number of the prose pieces reflect on the ephemeral nature of existence, and how we might appreciate the fleeting moments that we are granted. In Bradley's early essay 'An Old Couple' Eve offers a potential solution: memory, which she refers to as the 'secret of hoarding the hours' (p. 101). Two years later, in 'Mid-Age', Bradley returns to this idea, emphasizing 'the conservation of those moments that may be significant or influential' as crucial to developing one's understanding and appreciation of life, as we 'cannot possess what we experience' without a certain distance in which to process, 'a little while' between (p. 104). Bradley and Cooper's multi-volume diary clearly represents their aspiration to preserve their experiences through collaborative articulation, revision, and reflection over time. Yet, couched within this imposing daily document, like set gems, we discover the *croquis*; brief, fragmentary, delicately polished attempts to crytallise the moment into art. Placed alongside Michael Field's other productions — their vast, ambitious *œuvre* of verse drama, their body of lyric poetry (published and unpublished), the prose of 'Works and Days' itself — these elusive prose pieces are easily crowded out and overlooked. And yet they represent Michael Field's most significant response to modernity, which is now finally rendered accessible for the first time.

MICHAEL FIELD CHRONOLOGY

With a particular focus on the years covered by this volume: 1889–1895

1846, 27 October	Katharine Harris Bradley born in Birmingham to Emma Harris Bradley and Charles Bradley
1860, 27 October	Emma Harris Bradley (Katharine's sister) marries James Robert Cooper
1862, 12 January	Edith Emma Cooper born to Emma and James (Katharine's niece)
1863, 5 March	Amy Katharine Cooper is born (Cooper's sister; Katharine's niece). Emma becomes an invalid as a result of difficult labour
1868, October	Bradley studies in Paris. During this time, she starts a diary and becomes infatuated with Alfred Gérente
1868, 11 November	Alfred Gérente dies unexpectedly
1874, October	Bradley begins her studies at Newnham College, Cambridge
1875, January	Bradley corresponds with John Ruskin and joins the Guild of St George
1875, 10 May	Bradley's first book, *The New Minnesinger*, is published
1879, Autumn	The Cooper family (including Bradley) move to Bristol. Bradley and Cooper attend classes at University College
1881, 21 May	*Bellerophôn*, their first collaborative work, is published ('by Arran and Isla Leigh')
1884, May	*Callirrhoë* / *Fair Rosamund* is published; their first work under the 'Michael Field' pseudonym
1884, November	Following correspondence, Robert Browning inadvertently reveals the secret of their collaboration to the wider literary world

1888, April	The family move to Blackboro' Lodge, Reigate, Surrey. Bradley and Cooper begin the first volume of their diaries, Works and Days
1889, 20 May	*Long Ago* is published
1889, 20 August	Emma Harris Cooper (Cooper's mother; Bradley's sister) dies
1889, September	'Mid-Age' published in the *Contemporary Review*
1889, 12 December	Robert Browning dies
1890, January	'A Lumber Room' published in the *Contemporary Review*
1890, 3 March	'Effigies' published in the *Art Review*
1890, June	Bradley and Cooper embark on their European travels. They encounter Bernard Berenson for the first time in Paris
1891, 27 February	They meet Mary Costelloe when lunching with Berenson
1891, 3 March	The family move to Durdans, Reigate
1891, Spring	Bradley and Cooper attend Berenson's lectures at the National Gallery
1891, August	They travel to Dresden, where Cooper falls ill with scarlet fever, and is hospitalized until late September
1892, May	*Sight and Song* published
1892, June	Bradley and Cooper visit Paris with Berenson and Costelloe, receiving art lessons. They realise that the two are having an affair
1893, March	Trips to Bramber, Littlehampton, and Pevensey
1893, April	Another visit to Paris and Italy (with Berenson and Costelloe)
1893, June	Cooper begins experimenting with *croquis*
1893, July	*Underneath the Bough* is published (a revised, reduced edition is published in November)
1893, September	*A Question of Memory* published
1893, 25 September	'Rhythm' written by Bradley

1893, 27 October	*A Question of Memory* is staged (for one night only)
1894, January	First meeting with Charles Ricketts and Charles Shannon
1894, 6 February	Henry Harland (apparently) accepts 'Rhythm' for the *Yellow Book*
1894, 17 April	They see (and loathe) the first volume of the *Yellow Book*, particularly George Egerton's contribution
1894, 7 July	Bradley reads Oscar Wilde's 'Poems in Prose' in the *Fortnightly Review*
1894, 17 July	Having seen the second number of the *Yellow Book*, Bradley requests that Harland return 'Rhythm'
1894, Aug–Sept	Trips to Haslemere, Yorkshire, Northumberland, and Scotland inspire several prose sketches, including 'A Face seen in Ling' and 'The Granary'
1894, 14 October	They decide to title their prose sketches *For That Moment Only*
1894, 11 November	Bradley reflects on Alfred Gérente's death and writes 'Quai d'Anjou'
1895, April–May	Another visit to Florence. Bradley and Cooper stay in Berenson's rooms during his absence. They spend time with Vernon Lee, Kit Anstruther-Thomson, and Maud Cruttwell
1895, 25 May	Oscar Wilde is convicted of 'gross indecency' and sentenced to two years' hard labour. His trial occupies the conversation during this Italian visit
1895, November	*Attila, My Attila!* is published, prompting bad reviews and jeers from Costelloe and Berenson, causing a break in the friendship
1897, 24 June	James Russell Cooper (Cooper's father) disappears while mountain-climbing in Switzerland. His body is not found until October
1897, December	'The Fate of the Crossways' published in *The Dial*
1898, January	The arrival of Whym Chow, Bradley and Cooper's beloved dog

1898, 24 May	*The World at Auction* published (the first of the 'Roman Trilogy')
1898, October	American edition of *Underneath the Bough* published
1899, 16 May	Bradley and Cooper move to 1, The Paragon in Richmond
1899, 25 September	Cooper's sister Amy marries John Ryan
1905, May	*Borgia* is published anonymously. Several subsequent plays are published as by 'the author of *Borgia*'
1906, 28 January	Whym Chow becomes ill and is put down
1907, April–May	Bradley and Cooper convert to Catholicism
1907, December	*Wild Honey from Various Thyme* published
1910, 22 January	Amy dies in Dublin
1911, 6 February	Cooper is diagnosed with bowel cancer
1912, April	*Poems of Adoration* published
1913, April	*Mystic Trees* published
1913, 29 May	Bradley learns she has breast cancer (but conceals this from Cooper)
1913, 13 December	Cooper dies
1914, May	*Whym Chow: Flame of Love* published
1914, 4 August	England declares war on Germany
1914, 26 September	Bradley dies

FURTHER READING

There is very little scholarship on Michael Field as writers of prose. This list of further reading is therefore designed to include scholarship that deals at length with their prose (almost always 'Works and Days' and/or their letters), as well as key works that offer an overview of the two women's lives and works.

Bickle, Sharon, ed., *The Fowl and the Pussycat: Love Letters of Michael Field 1876–1909* (Charlottesville: University of Virginia Press, 2008)

Bristow, Joseph, 'Michael Field: In Their Time and Ours', *Tulsa Studies in Women's Literature*, 29.1 (2010), 159–79

Ehnenn, Jill R., *Women's Literary Collaboration, Queerness, and Late-Victorian Culture* (Aldershot: Ashgate, 2008)

Dever, Carolyn M., *Chains of Love and Beauty: The Diary of Michael Field* (Princeton: Princeton University Press, 2022)

Donoghue, Emma, *We Are Michael Field* (Bath: Absolute Press, 1998)

Dytor, Frankie, '"The Eyes of an Intellectual Vampire": Michael Field, Vernon Lee and Female Masculinities in Late Victorian Aestheticism', *Journal of Victorian Culture*, 26 (2021), 582–95

Evangelista, Stefano, *British Aestheticism and Ancient Greece: Hellenism, Reception, Gods in Exile* (Basingstoke: Palgrave Macmillan, 2009)

Fraser, Hilary, *Women Writing Art History in the Nineteenth Century: Looking Like a Woman* (Cambridge: Cambridge University Press, 2014)

Laird, Holly, *Women Coauthors* (Urbana: University of Illinois Press, 2000)

Locard, Henri, 'Works and Days: The Journals of "Michael Field"', *Journal of the Eighteen Nineties Society*, 10 (1979), 1–9

London, Bette, *Writing Double: Women's Literary Partnerships* (Ithaca: Cornell University Press, 1999)

MacDonald, Jan, '"Disillusioned Bards and Despised Bohemians": Michael Field's *A Question of Memory* at the Independent Theatre Society', *Theatre Notebook: A Journal of the History and Technique of the British Theatre*, 31 (1975), 18–29

Mahoney, Kristin, 'Michael Field and Queer Community at the *fin-de-siècle*', *Victorian Review*, 41 (2015), 35–40

Maxwell, Catherine, 'Michael Field, Death, and the Effigy', *Word & Image*, 34 (2018), 31–39

—— *Scents and Sensibility: Perfume in Victorian Literary Culture* (Oxford: Oxford University Press, 2017)

Mitton, Matthew, '"For That Moment Only": Michael Field and the Prose Poem', *The Michaelian*, 1 (2009), n.p. <http://www.thelatchkey.org/Field/MF1/miltonarticle.html> [accessed 23 May 2021]

Moriarty, David J., '"Michael Field" (Edith Cooper and Katharine Bradley) and Their Male Critics', in *Nineteenth-Century Women Writers of the English-Speaking World*, ed. by Rhoda B. Nathan (New York: Greenwood, 1986), pp. 121–42

OLVERSON, TRACY, 'Michael Field's Dramatically Queer Family Dynamics', in *Queer Victorian Families: Curious Relations in Literature*, ed. by Duc Dau and Shale Preston (New York: Routledge, 2015), pp. 57–76

PARKER, SARAH, 'Fashioning Michael Field: Michael Field and Late-Victorian Dress Culture', *Journal of Victorian Culture*, 18 (2013), 313–34

PARKER, SARAH, and ANA PAREJO VADILLO, eds, *Michael Field: Decadent Moderns* (Athens: Ohio University Press, 2019)

PRINS, YOPIE, *Victorian Sappho* (Princeton: Princeton University Press, 1999)

RODEN, FREDERICK S., *Same-Sex Desire in Victorian Religious Culture* (Basingstoke: Palgrave Macmillan, 2002)

STETZ, MARGARET D., and CHERYL A. WILSON, eds, *Michael Field and Their World* (High Wycombe: Rivendale Press, 2007)

STURGE MOORE, THOMAS, and D. C. STURGE MOORE, eds, *Works and Days: From the Journal of Michael Field* (London: Murray, 1933)

STURGEON, MARY, *Michael Field* (London: Harrap, 1922)

TAFT, VICKIE L., '*The Tragic Mary*: A Case Study in Michael Field's Understanding of Sexual Politics', *Nineteenth-Century Contexts: An Interdisciplinary Journal*, 23 (2001), 265–95

THAIN, MARION, ed., *Michael Field and Fin-de-Siècle Culture and Society: The Journals, 1868–1914, and Correspondence of Katharine Bradley and Edith Cooper from the British Library London* (Marlborough: Adam Matthew, 2003) (thirteen reels of microfilm)

—— *Michael Field and Poetic Identity, with a Biography* (London: Eighteen Nineties Society, 2000)

—— *'Michael Field': Poetry, Aestheticism and the Fin de Siècle* (Cambridge: Cambridge University Press, 2007)

—— 'Perspective: Digitizing the Diary — Experience in Queer Encoding (A Retrospective and a Prospective)', *Journal of Victorian Culture*, 21 (2016), 226–41

—— and Ana Parejo Vadillo, *Michael Field, the Poet: Published and Manuscript Materials* (Peterborough, Ontario: Broadview Press, 2009)

THOMAS, KATE, '"What Time We Kiss": Michael Field's Queer Temporalities', *GLQ: A Journal of Lesbian and Gay Studies*, 13 (2007), 327–51

TREBY, IVOR C., *The Michael Field Catalogue* (London: De Blackland Press, 1998)

—— *Binary Star: Leaves from the Journal and Letters of Michael Field, 1846–1914* (London: De Blackland Press, 2006)

VADILLO, ANA PAREJO, *Women Poets and Urban Aestheticism: Passengers of Modernity* (Basingstoke: Palgrave Macmillan, 2005)

—— 'Aestheticism and Decoration: At Home with Michael Field', *Cahiers Victoriens et Edouardiens*, 74 (2011), 17–36

—— 'Living Art: Michael Field, Aestheticism and Dress', in *Crafting the Women Professional in the Long Nineteenth Century: Artistry and Industry in Britain*, ed. by Kyriaki Hadjiafxendi and Patricia Zakreski (Farnham: Ashgate, 2013), pp. 243–71

VANITA, RUTH, *Sappho and the Virgin Mary: Same-Sex Love and the English Literary Imagination* (New York: Columbia University Press, 1996)

VICINUS, MARTHA, *Intimate Friends: Women Who Loved Women, 1778–1928* (Chicago: Chicago University Press, 2004)

—— 'Sister Souls: Bernard Berenson and Michael Field', *Nineteenth-Century Literature*, 60 (2005), 326–54

WHITE, CHRIS, 'Flesh and Roses: Michael Field's Metaphors of Pleasure and Desire', *Women's Writing*, 3 (1996), 47–62

—— '"Poets and Lovers Evermore": Interpreting Female Love in the Poetry and Journals of Michael Field', *Textual Practice*, 4 (1990), 197–212

Further Reading on the Prose Poem and Prose Experimentation at the *Fin de Siècle*

ATHERTON, CASSANDRA, and PAUL HETHERINGTON, *Prose Poetry: An Introduction* (Princeton: Princeton University Press, 2020)

DELVILLE, MICHEL, *The American Prose Poem: Poetic Form and the Boundaries of Genre* (Gainesville: University of Florida, 1998)

DOWLING, LINDA, *Language and Decadence in the Victorian Fin de Siècle* (Princeton: Princeton University Press, 1986)

MENGHAM, ROD, 'A Genealogy of the Prose Poem', *CounterText*, 3 (2017), 176–86

MONSON, JANE, ed., *British Prose Poetry: The Poems Without Lines* (Basingstoke: Palgrave Macmillan, 2018)

MURPHY, MARGUERITTE, 'A Dangerous Hybridity: The Prose Poem at the *fin de siècle*', in *The Edinburgh Companion to the Prose Poem*, ed. by Mary Ann Caws and Michel Delville (Edinburgh: Edinburgh University Press, 2021), pp. 67–89

REED, JOHN R., *Decadent Style* (Athens: Ohio University Press, 1985)

SAINTSBURY, GEORGE, *A History of English Prose Rhythm* (London: Macmillan, 1912)

SANTILLI, NIKKI, *Such Rare Citings: The Prose Poem in English Literature* (Madison, NJ: Fairleigh Dickinson University Press, 2002)

STETZ, MARGARET D., '"Ballads in Prose": Genre Crossing in Late-Victorian Women's Writing', *Victorian Literature and Culture*, 34 (2006), 619–29

The following is a selection of prose poems or short experimental prose works of the period, including translations that may be of interest to those wishing to explore these forms further.

BAUDELAIRE, CHARLES, *Poems in Prose*, trans. by Arthur Symons (London: Elkin Mathews, 1905)

CRACKANTHORPE, HUBERT, *Vignettes: A Miniature Journal of Whim and Sentiment* (London: John Lane, 1896)

DOWSON, ERNEST, *Decorations in Prose and Verse* (London: Leonard Smithers, 1899)

GARNETT, EDWARD, *An Imaged World: Poems in Prose* (London: J. M. Dent, 1894)

HOPPER, NORA, *Ballads in Prose* (London: John Lane, 1894)

HUYSMANS, J.-K., *Parisian Sketches*, trans. by Brendan King (Sawtry: Dedalus, 2007)

LEVERSON, ADA, 'The Minx — A Poem in Prose', *Punch, Or The London Charivari*, 21 June 1894, p. 33

MACHEN, ARTHUR, *Ornaments in Jade* (New York: Alfred A. Knopf, 1924)

MALLARMÉ, STÉPHANE, 'The Future Phenomenon', trans. by George Moore, *The Savoy*, July 1896, pp. 98–99

MERRILL, STUART, trans. and ed., *Pastels in Prose* (New York: Harper & Brothers, 1890)

MEYNELL, ALICE, *London Impressions* (London: Archibald Constable: 1898)

SCHREINER, OLIVE, *Dreams*, ed. by Barbara Black, Carly Nations, and Anna Spydell (Peterborough, Ontario: Broadview Press, 2020)

TURGENEV, IVAN, *Dream Tales and Prose Poems*, trans. by Constance Garnett (London: William Heinemann, 1897)

WILDE, OSCAR, *The Complete Works of Oscar Wilde. Volume 1: Poems and Poems in Prose*, ed. by Bobby Fong and Karl Beckson, Introduction by Ian Small (Oxford: Oxford University Press, 2000)

NOTE ON THE TEXT

With the exception of the five published works, all the prose pieces we have collected here by Katharine Bradley and Edith Cooper are manuscript materials, transcribed by the editors from the Michael Field collections in the British Library and the Bodleian Library Special Collections, Oxford. Footnotes provide full citational details for each work. This is not, however, a diplomatic edition of Michael Field's prose. Our goal is to bring the prose works of Michael Field to the widest audience possible, so we have produced a standardized selection with readability our foremost concern. We have silently corrected any errors of punctuation and spelling, standardized spelling (gray/grey), replaced Bradley and Cooper's use of '&' and '+' with 'and', italicised underlined text and titles, adopted interlineal corrections, and omitted any deletions. A genetic study of Michael Field's writing practices, as well as detailed analyses of their idiosyncratic orthography, is still to be produced, and we are certain that future scholarship will explore these aspects of their work in detail. Our hope is that by bringing their prose to a new readership we will play a small role in encouraging this vital work.

All manuscript materials are fully referenced. We have used the standard format for citing 'Works and Days', indicating which of the two women had written the entry quoted using their initials, e.g. [KB], [EC]. In cases where the handwriting belongs to Bradley/Cooper, but the wording is dictated by her partner, we have indicated this in the footnotes. While we have published all extant manuscript materials of creative prose identified by Ivor C. Treby in his invaluable (and infuriating) *Michael Field Catalogue*, we have had to make a judicious selection of prose from 'Works and Days'. Our criteria for selecting works were that they were either: fictional/creative; responses to art; or that they worked as stand-alone fragments (i.e. are not embedded in larger narrative sequences). We also limited ourselves to the years 1889 to 1895 so as to coincide with the period in which Bradley and Cooper were writing prose with the intention of publication. There are, of course, a great many captivating prose passages prior and subsequent to this period, but as their interests and aesthetics changed over time, we decided a more expansive selection would not serve to illuminate the distinct project represented by *For That Moment Only* and the additional published and manuscript prose works. We have roughly clustered the selections from 'Works and Days' into four loosely thematic groupings: those responding to artworks; dream/fever writing; reflections on aging and mortality; and writing about nature and/or place.

For That Moment Only — First Series[1]

[1] 'For That Moment Only — First Series', Oxford, Bodleian Libraries, MS Eng. misc. d. 976.

A Vision or a Waking Dream?[2]

I looked down a vista of olive-trees, white and grey and blue as silver; the branches were cramped into the form of a roof, above ground half dust and half pebbles. The morning was brilliant in the world, a fresh April morning; but in the olive vista shadow still held its own.

Under this roof twenty or thirty little creatures were dancing together — their forms peculiar, rhythmic, a surprise from the rippling force of every motion, that yet was ludicrous in its freedom and self-contentment.

Their skins were brown, such brown as has in it a rich syrup-warmth; their little shanks shone demurely with fur, too young to be brown like the rest of their bodies, but visible as a sleekness with honied flush on it, lying one way from the hips to the rather rugged hoofs. I did not see faces I could describe: only in the dance I caught now and then the glimpse of a mouth with a smile running up into the cheeks, and lost there as wonderfully as a rillet in sand;[3] or eyes that slanted and spilt a bubble of laughter; or a chin with mischief round its globe, where the fur was slight as a peach's.

But one thing I saw continuously: each head as it turned between the arms had slashed ears, leaf-like, tingling with light. The little dancers moved as if to flutes; one felt the music that kept them circling was shrill and thin in its mode.

Were they a troop of Fauns[4] — this Chorus of the olive-bower?

Whatever one might call them, they belonged to Bacchus,[5] they belonged to April and to adolescence.

Could they be vines?

---

[2] Written by Cooper on Good Friday (12 April 1895) at Fiesole; see Michael Field [EC], 'Works and Days', BL Add. MS 46783, fol. 44r. Later submitted to *The Pageant* but not published. The title is taken from the final lines of Keats's 'Ode to a Nightingale': 'Was it a vision, or a waking dream? | Fled is that music: — Do I wake or sleep?'.

[3] A rillet is a small rill or stream.

[4] A faun is a half-human half-goat figure from Roman mythology. They are often referred to in works of Decadent and aestheticist literature.

[5] Bacchus (also known in Greek myth as Dionysus) is the Roman god of intoxication, religious frenzy, and the theatre.

The Hill to Loreto[6]

There was no morn: there were no stars. But far off, over the sea, lightning broke from north to south and its brilliant agitation was so continuous that the horizon, at every second, became expressive with the haste and colour of sheet after sheet. The poles of the vineyards were thrown into black darkness as the thrills of flame ran behind them. The sky trembled with life.

And suddenly round the vine-poles a tiny fire spirted, went out, spirted again:[7] then another fire and another and another flashed and dissolved with a teazing perversity,[8] till the vineyards were full of dancing sparkles that might have been struck from an anvil, if it had not been for the silence and for something strangely immanent about those cold and wanton little flashes.

Turning from the vineyards to the roadside another light arrested us — not a flash, but a steady lucidness in the herbage, blue and serene.

We had no moon nor stars on our magical route, but instead of them, lightning and fireflies and the glow-worm.

Our horse stopped and we found ourselves side by side with a black mass of farm-buildings, while the reddish glow of a lantern filled the open doorway and two blonde, reluctant shapes swayed through it. Then our driver explained that he needed the help of oxen to drag us up to Loreto.[9]

We could not see the yoke-fellows, when once they had left their stable, but while we mounted the hill a breath of divine wholesomeness floated back to us, as if we were being drawn over meadows of cut grass.

I felt that I myself could never realise the beauty of this Italian night; and like a word that had force to save me from the deadly stupor of enchantment, I murmured — *Virgil.*[10]

---

[6] 'The Hill to Loreto' was written by Cooper and likely composed in spring-summer 1893, inspired by Bradley and Cooper's visit to Italy in April–May 1893.

[7] An earlier spelling of spurted.

[8] An earlier spelling of teasing.

[9] A hill town in the Marche region of Italy that is a popular Catholic pilgrimage site.

[10] Virgil (70–19 BC) was a Roman poet who composed the *Eclogues*, the *Georgics*, and the *Aeneid*. He also appears as Dante's guide in *Inferno* and most of *Purgatorio*. He was a major influence on European literature and Bradley and Cooper often allude to his work.

An Agony[11]

The evening sky was colourless and the wheat one ardour of green in the face of it: the world was too austere to be sad — one could only feel its sadness as tranquillity, as dew about the farm.

A tremulous, visionary passion rose in me as I wandered on; and then, as if in response to it, I found suddenly I was not alone, as I had thought; for a young man, close to the path, supported himself across the branches of a maple, his arms hanging straight down from the armpits to the ends of the fingers. His naked limbs were long as a boy's, yet soft in their modelling as a woman's, dark-golden by nature, but reddened with sunburn. His hair was ruddier by several shades than his chest, and a strange crown of Oriental design covered it like a bower — the rays of the crown being vine-stems; and their leaf-buds stood out at such intervals as are usually left between jewels in a setting. Loops of vine-sprays and vine-buds fell from his neck to the waist, and at his loins a clump of boughs spread out into open leafage.

His head was bent, his mouth in shadow: under the tiara his dim brow stretched wide, with fretted eyebrows and eyelids that kept me quiet by their quietness. Then I saw that large drops, white, limpid, patient, came through the lids and hung unfallen.

---

[11] 'An Agony' was composed by Cooper in April 1895, during Bradley and Cooper's stay in Fiesole. A year later, on Good Friday (3 April) in 1896, Cooper writes: 'I read Michael The True Vine — John Gray's beautiful little masterpiece of this year's *Blue Calendar* [...] How strange that just this time last year at Fiesole I had a vision so like his, that took prose-form in *An Agony*. My young Dionysus, suffering for men, was brown, his hair bud-wreathed. Gray's rhythm and colour and solemnity impress me whenever I read the poem. I should choose to have written it.' Michael Field [EC], 'Works and Days', BL Add. MS 46785, fol. 48r. 'An Agony' was later submitted to *The Pageant* but not published. John Gray (1866–1934) was part of Wilde's circle in the early 1890s and published *Silverpoints* (1893), one of the premier poetry collections of British Decadence. In 1895 he embraced Roman Catholicism and took holy orders, becoming ordained in 1901. He became an important presence in the two women's lives, particularly after they converted to Catholicism in 1907. This sketch is about the true vine, a parable given by Jesus in John 15. 1–17.

I knew I was in the presence of Bacchus; I knew it by his garlands, his budding crown, by the ease of his limbs — and he, The Vine, was weeping.

In the top of the maple-tree, over which he hung, a pruning-knife was hitched.

Then I understood, as far as confused passion can, the God was weeping at some hurt that had wounded to the quick, that he must bear in loneliness for the sake of the vintage, and of the men who should drink it, though they had injured him.

Twilight grew over the vineyard: something was shaken down, glittering as it fell, was scattered and lost in the soil — a tear. I looked with relief at the quiet lids; another tear was oozing and was almost round.

Then I moved sharply away — forever.

~

A Maenad[12]

It was April, an April without showers, with grey, inoperative clouds floating over the sunshine from time to time, making the air cold as they passed, but never drawing all the light out of the landscape. While we shivered below them we saw far off the tips of a young larch-wood in verdant glitter, or the distance as full of colour as if it were growing blue-bells. We were sitting under a beech-tree and a tuft of box. In front of us was the chalk-down, beyond that the azure half-transparent view of Surrey wealds.[13]

We were vibrant and impetuous as the forces that splendidly and naively were coming once more into existence round us. The imperishable truth of the Bacchic legend was re-incarnated in us all, but took the most perfect form in the youngest of our party — a girl scarcely out of her teens. She lay prone on the grass, her figure nonchalant and absolutely at rest, though guarding a wonderful suggestion

---

[12] This *croquis* by Cooper first appears in 'Works and Days' where it is preceded by the following note in the hand of Cooper: 'A *croquis* taken from our experience yesterday, April 13, at Box Hill [Surrey], in company with the Fitzpatricks — "Friar" and Kathleen — or as we named her, "the Quail"'. Michael Field [EC], 'Works and Days', BL Add. MS 46782, fol. 35r (14 April 1894). Maenads were, in Greek mythology, female followers of the god Dionysus. The name means 'raving one' and they were often depicted in states of intoxication or mania. The most famous depiction of maenads was in Euripides' *The Bacchae*, which informs this *croquis*. Bradley and Cooper had previously depicted the maenads of Dionysus in *Callirrhoë* (1884). Cooper is also likely drawing on Walter Pater's essay 'The Bacchanals of Euripides' (1889). John Keats's *Endymion* (1818) is also in the background. He completed the poem while staying at the Fox and Hounds Inn at the base of Box Hill. In Book IV the Indian Maiden recalls the moment when the Bacchanal implore her to join them:

> We follow Bacchus! Bacchus on the wing,
> A conquering!
> Bacchus, young Bacchus! good or ill betide,
> We dance before him thorough kingdoms wide: —
> Come hither, lady fair, and joined be
> To our wild minstrelsy!

[13] The Downs is a chalk escarpment that crosses the counties of Surrey, Hampshire, Sussex, and Kent.

of pliancy. Her features were irregular — the nostrils somewhat flat, a sweet uncouthness about the lips. The dusky oval of her face was crossed by black brows, lovely in utter blackness and in their union over the nose like a Greek's. Below them, in a thicket of eyelashes, yellow eyes played squirrel-pranks. Her short hair looked like a rich soil heaped up by the spade — full of strength and purple-dark curves. I had made her a wreath of larch-spines, set with the larches' stammel conelets,[14] and the green shone in spikes out of her curls that supported it triumphantly.

She wore a black skirt, and little black velvet jacket, over a bodice of shamrock green; and a great black hat, with cloudy ostrich-plumes, swung behind her like a warrior's shield. I had admired her all morning: suddenly I asked her to dance.

She sprang to the summons, hitched up her skirt round her black pantaloons, pulled off her shoes, and in her black stockings began to dance a hornpipe on the grass. I watched in an ecstasy of delight her lovely feet and ankles, her black, girt[15] shape with the green sleeves and green wreath, her liberated face following in expression the liberty of her feet as they hopped and spun and kicked and scarcely touched the ground. She sprang high, then fell on her toes that carried her forward of their own motion; her arms bent themselves over her head or swung out toward the veiled horizon of Surrey-wealds: and there was nothing against her arms and head and shoulders but the sky — one instant a monotone of cloud, the next a sheet of sunlight.

What would a man have given to watch a sight so kindlingly beautiful! But it was one of those sights that are sacred to half the world of mortals; and when a couple of tourists broke on the solitude, our maenad fled into the box-grove. The men looked at the remaining trio; they saw feet only covered with stockings, shoes among the beech-roots, while scattered over cloaks and hats were branches of box and branches of sweet-briar. The tourists lowered their eyes and passed the group rigidly. How much the spirit of Pentheus lived in the breast of those two Cockneys![16] How we longed to tear them to pieces!

The moment they were out of sight — lo and behold, our maenad was with us again, carrying out of the wood a beech-bough, covered with leaves in their dazzling youth, and a bough of willow covered with catkins. She rushed into the dance, waving her boughs at the command of her feet, sliding on the grass to give us a leafy curtsy, rising again to leap and pirouette, as much abandoned to movement as sap or light or air. Black and green, she rioted once more on the

---

[14] Stammel is a shade of red. The Weald is the flat area between the North and South Downs.

[15] 'Girt' is the past particle of 'gird', meaning that the girl's waist is encircled with a belt or a band.

[16] In Euripides' *The Bacchae* Pentheus, the King of Thebes, attempts to ban the worship of Dionysus; on entering the forest to confront the god of intoxication he is attacked and torn limb from limb by the Bacchanal.

hill-side — her eyes full of the same grace as her limbs, her black brows as shapely as her black ankles, her sleeves as vivid as her wreath and branches.

Then she lay down weary on the grass;

then she put on her shoes;

then at the bottom of the hill she put her hat over her wreath of living ruby and emerald;

then she had tea at the inn and started home by train.

I grant she did all this: yet I had seen as pure a maenad as ever danced over Cithaeron.[17] The far days of Greece had been today with us, among the box-groves on a Surrey down:

Io Bacchus! Erae![18]

---

[17] A mountain range in Central Greece where, in Euripides' *The Bacchae*, the rites of the god Dionysus took place.

[18] 'Io' is a celebratory exclamation in Latin, while 'Erae' translates as 'mistresses'.

A Traveller's Tale[19]

All Bacchanals have human shape: have they? *All Bacchanals laugh and cry and dance and drink like men and women*:[20] do they? No, I answer once for all. Nature has her own Bacchanals, who break into laughter and shout, though no sound is heard; who dance though they never move from the spot where ecstasy fills them; who absorb strength and joy while drinking, though they have never lifted a wine-cup.

I myself saw these Bacchanals, one April day, in Tuscany — just as Ulysses saw wonderful things on his journeys. I had left Siena early:[21] rain fell after weeks of drought, and there was nothing in the sky but a white general glare from a general leaden cloud, while on the roof of the railway-wagon a hiss, that broke into innumerable taps, beset my ears. Weary from lack of sleep, discouraged at a bad day, I tried to rest — but all in vain. So, shaking off my sullenness, I got up and looked out of the window. Lo! — what did I see? Thousands of little vines in Bacchic elation drinking, drinking — oh a triumph of drinking! In dumb-show they clapped,[22] they made merry; and one forgot all that poets have said, or artists painted, or sculptors cut in honour of fauns and satyrs, as vineyard after vineyard tossed its wet young branches, and the gracious little shoots became tipsy, and joy kindled the new foliage till it was the only brightness under heaven, and each plant capered divinely from its very roots in the rain-wind. Ha, ha! They swept my spirit out to join them in the wantonness of their sacrament — for *that* it was. They were drinking without measure that in October men might drink the juice of their full grapes; they were drinking for the sake of Dionysus, as his truest votaries, the bearers of his holy gift. It was delicious to see how they themselves

[19] Written by Cooper in April 1895, and originally entitled 'Nature's Bacchanals'. Cooper reports that she read it aloud to Berenson and Costelloe on Saturday 4 May 1895 'with some success' (Michael Field [EC], 'Works and Days', BL Add. MS 46783, fol. 77v).

[20] A 'bacchanal' can be both an event — a Bacchic celebration — and a follower of Bacchus.

[21] A city in Tuscany famed for its medieval architecture.

[22] An echo of Isaiah 55. 12: 'For ye shall go out with joy, and be led forth with peace: the mountains and the hills shall break forth before you into singing, and all the trees of the field shall clap their hands.'

loved to drink, what passion and fun they put into their worship. They swayed, as little and delicate as Ampelus,[23] the youth Iacchus loves,[24] their tendrils twisted tremulously like the tails of satyrs or remained ringed tight like little horns. All the revellers were crowned with their own vine-leaves, drenched and fresh; while the longest shoots were tossed-up *thyrsi*,[25] swaying backward and forward. The expression of the small green tangles was wayward, hilarious as that on fauns' faces. These young vines danced so madly that the hills they covered almost appeared to dance beneath them. Here and there more venturesome Thyads[26] would twirl on the very railway banks, shaking the dew off their chaplets frenetically, with movements of laughter and movements of spite. The rain foamed round the vine-stocks; it set them free and the whole country with them, loosing all impulses of growth. And as I watched this rout of nature's Bacchanals, these crested vines so innocent in their licence, I found they were refreshing my eyes and my blood with more than the refreshment of sleep.

---

[23] Ampelus is the personification of grape vines in Greek mythology. It may be that Cooper is drawing on a statue in the Uffizi Gallery in Florence in which Dionysus leans on a satyr, often identified as Ampelus. The statue has a clear homoeroticism that accords with the intimations of same-sex desire in this sketch.

[24] Iacchus is a Greek deity associated with Dionysus.

[25] A thyrsus was a spear or staff carried by Dionysus and his followers. They are a recurring symbol in the work of Michael Field.

[26] Thyads were another name for the Bacchantes.

Eriphion the Faun[27]

Eriphion the Faun had often peeped at the Centaurs[28] from behind mountain-cypresses, or, hidden in the boughs of a wayside olive, had listened with starting heart-beats to the rattle of their hoofs down the stony tracks. He admired their bodies, twice the bulk of his own: he who had only the tail and legs of a goat, what was he by the side of these goodly creatures, half-men, half-horses! He could not carry himself as they did, over hill and dale; nor choose to rest under the shadow of a cloud that darkened the plains a mile off; nor when the rivulet was dry round its boulders, gallop away to the river swimming out of sight. Yet more than all else Eriphion envied every Centaur his bow and arrows — the curved horns set so firmly in the centre-piece, the leather bow-string; the reed-arrows, clipt by their brazen arrow-heads, and feathered with plumage of the black eagle — themselves so long and light.

'I cannot alter my shape,' thought Eriphion, 'and the gods would never trouble to change such a kid of a little fellow as I am into anything great: but should I choose to arm myself with bow and arrows that is my own affair — if I could but manage to be clever.'

So one day he broke a wand of ash and grooved it with his teeth; then at noon next day he spied in the thicket a strong vine, seasoned by the winter's rigour, that would perfectly string his bow: last of all he pulled up tufts of moss to make believe he had a centrepiece, and wound them on the ash-wood, in the midst of its curve, plaiting them with the skin of an osier.[29]

---

[27] Although the MS version in the manuscript of 'For That Moment Only' is in Bradley's handwriting, 'Eriphion the Faun' was written 'in less than fifteen minutes' by Cooper on 4 May 1895 (Michael Field [EC], 'Works and Days', BL Add. MS 46782, fols 77v–78r). The circumstances surrounding its composition are recounted in the Introduction (pp. 14–16). It was originally entitled 'Liber' — a Roman deity associated with Bacchus, whose name means 'the Free One'. Eriphion means 'little goat' in Greek. The story was submitted to *The Pageant* but not published.

[28] Centaurs are creatures from Greek myth with the upper body of a man and the lower body of a horse.

[29] An osier refers to a willow tree whose supple branches are used for basket weaving.

That evening, when the bow was finished, he took his gourd-mandolin and danced before his work under the moon, his little black goat-legs frightful in their liveliness, and his eyes glittering in the dusk, as a well in the obscurity of its shaft.

He woke next-day to live for his arrows — peeling withies of ash and biting each of them,[30] at one end, till it was really sharp. Feathers were wanting, but after long search he found the body of a jay and plucked its blue quills. These he dipped in fruit-tree gum; and by the third day at moonrise, his arrows were pointed and winged.

Then again he took his gourd-mandolin and danced on the silver ground boisterously, his eyes dancing with a keener sparkle than his bright, little hoofs.

He rose early, and sought out an open space among some oaks where he could test his archery, and aim his weapons at a scar on one of the trunks left by a woodman's axe. Again and again the dart missed, yet he shrieked with joy; and at last he bellowed as if his laughter were almost pain. In his transport he did not hear the approach of a Centaur, not till the archer-horse loomed over him, with curious eyes, and grim, gaping mouth. A second — and Eriphion, caught in the Centaur's arms, was pitched on horseback, and felt under him the swift trot of his captor. The arrow that had touched its goal was left at the foot of the oak; his other arrows and his bow were in the Centaur's grasp, while the enemy's huge bow-case almost thrust Eriphion from his seat.

Higher and higher they mounted through the cypresses, through the stone-pines, till they came to a small plateau before treeless rocks, watered by a high spring. There several Centaurs lay on their sides, kicking with languor from the heat, and lashing the insects off their haunches, while they covered their eyes with their human arms. When they heard their companion advance, one or two looked up, and at their laughter of surprise the others also paused themselves, and the whole troop was soon on foot. Then Eriphion's captor broke the silence and told the tale of the clever Faun who had made himself weapons and even winged them to their goal. So Eriphion's fear became a sense of anxious triumph, as he was put down and his bow and arrows returned to him, while the Centaurs formed round him a fence of innumerable legs.

Then a tree was marked, the only tree on the plateau, and Eriphion was set opposite and told to aim as he had done in the woods below.

Now was the time to bring fame to his cherished handiwork! — he burnt in a terrified way to excel: but the moment the Centaurs shouted he felt he was small and wretched; his goat-legs shook, his blunt goat-nose quivered, his eyes brimmed, and the arrow fell at his feet.

The Centaurs laughed neighingly. Blind, he took another arrow from the loop of his nebris[31] — the tears over-brimmed, and the arrow fell at his feet. With

[30] A withy is a flexible branch, usually of a willow, used for binding.
[31] The skin of a fawn, worn by Dionysus and his followers.

twitching fingers he secured his remaining arrow, then plunged for his life between the nethers of a near Centaur, and ran from the camp, down through the stone-pines, down through the cypresses to the olive woods, to the vineyards, to the oak under which his victorious arrow still lay: there at the root of the tree, he sobbed out his anguish, howling against his hands, while the tears flowed from his eyes to lips and from lips to bosom and then down through the moss. His nature had borne outrage — its virgin shyness had been deflowered, and his open joy in his weapon was a thing of the past.

Eriphion left the arrow and his tears on the ground: he wandered deeper in woods that entangle a centaur's gallop; he shot his darts with caution; there was a touch of fierceness and cunning in his eyes, and when he hit the mark he did not laugh out nor scarcely chuckle to himself. He no longer hid behind mountain cypresses on the outlook for heroes: indeed, he never saw another Centaur; for at the sound of hoofs he ran among the junipers and crouched deep down where the branches were lifeless.

Eriphion did not weep again in his whole life; but his little gourd-mandolin was left untuned.

His bow and arrows he strained in his grasp even when asleep; and in a few years' time he had learnt to kill jays and other birds deftly, taking a silent pleasure in his ravage and dreaming of it all night under the moon.

The Lady Moon[32]

We were a party of profane travellers: the young man opposite me was a Jew, but a Jew lost to the traditions of his people.

Indeed, more or less, we all thought we had done with religion.

We were driving up a valley that mounted from the shore to the high crest of a little city on the Adriatic Marches.[33] Over the sky, which was very large and tranquil, there was paleness that looked like a preparation for light, although the earth was completely in dusk. Fields of sainfoin[34] covered the hills each side of our old wagonette,[35] and had almost the hue of clotted blood in the obscurity that lay on them. Behind us stretched the Adriatic, wavering from grey to silver: in front we could see the towers of the little city deep as very old bronze. No trees, no vineyards — only the pastoral slopes and a sky that looked holy.

We had been silent for a long while, resting in the coolness and feeling the exhilaration shadow can give, when, almost before I was aware of it, the young man opposite raised his hat, and with an expression on his face like that in the evening sky, said rapturously:

'Ah, there is the Lady Moon!'

I followed his eyes, and undoubtedly there she was, as pale almost as the paleness that received her, as thin as a little moon can be, full of blessed, unspent light.

Then, turning my eyes away from her, I looked at him. The sympathy between the two was infinite, yet he was not her lover — this young man, with her first

---

[32] Written by Cooper *c.* November 1894. The full text appears in 'Works and Days' in Bradley's hand on 8 November 1894, accompanied by a note that reads 'Henry's croquis revised' (Michael Field [KB], 'Works and Days', BL Add. MS 46782, fols 132r–132v). The *croquis* was later praised by Berenson: 'Of the croquis the "Lady Moon" is best' (Michael Field [EC], 'Works and Days', BL Add. MS 46782, fol. 86r (10 May 1895)). The young man in this story is clearly modelled on Berenson, who was Jewish. Bradley and Cooper regularly draw attention to his Jewish background in their diary descriptions.

[33] A central Italian region of mountains and hills fronting on the Adriatic Sea.

[34] A perennial herb (Old French 'healthy hay'), grown as stockfeed for cattle.

[35] A small horse-drawn cart in which the passengers sit facing one another.

film of brightness on him, rimming his face with charm; and though no shepherd-boy of Latmos could have made a motion at once so courteous and so finely caressing as that with which he lifted his hat, she had never stooped to him as to Endymion — never![36] That was not their secret. But his people had bowed before her, month by month, for centuries, and had greeted the freshness of her crescent-line with their eyes, with offerings and the blast of trumpets.[37]

I looked again at the face adoring her as a joy:

No, we had not yet done with religion.

[36] The mythic figure of Endymion is a shepherd on Mt Latmos, in Anatolia, Turkey. Endymion is the lover of Selene, the moon goddess. Cooper most likely has John Keats's *Endymion* (1818) in mind.

[37] Since their fellow-traveller is Jewish, the speaker/narrator is most likely referring to Rosh Chodesh, the first day of the month in the Hebrew calendar, which coincides with the new moon.

~

A Faun[38]

We had reached the Piazza of Tivoli[39] by the steam-tram, and had made our way as quickly as possible to the *Vicolo della Sibilla*,[40] where we had breakfasted on salad and fish from the Anio and country wine.[41] Then we had stretched ourselves from column to column of the adjoining Temple, on the very edge of the great ravine, full of trees and water-channels and waterfalls. It was June and very hot: the sunshine seemed to have nothing to do with the sky, but to be down with us on the earth, leaving the blue over our heads intact. The bare mountains looked almost repulsive in such heat, while the nudity of the columns became all the more beautiful. In the distance we could see one fall, like a vein of marble, the spray in front of it bluish as a cloud of incense; and over the spray a rainbow flickered as if it would burst. We had talked of our various destinies as people do on whom excessive outer loveliness weighs till they are heart-sick: and finally, with one impulse of reaction had started to visit the distant fall; and, climbing down paths, edged by butcher's broom[42] or boulders in a tangle of ilex-roots — the rush of sound from hidden water-courses audible at every turn — we had come out on a broad terrace opposite our Temple. There, from one crag, we could watch the murky silence of the fall and hear its explosion as it fell, a burst so loud it stunned us and brought with it such overwhelming sense of sleep, we were soon driven back along the terrace, where we rested in groups against its upper slope. Some lent forward and chatted; some threw themselves down and slept.

---

[38] Written by Cooper *c.* 1893. The 'faun' described is clearly modelled on Berenson. See Introduction (pp. 7–8).

[39] Town in central Italy some twenty miles East of Rome. The destination is the Tempio della Sibilla, a second-century Roman temple that was a famous beauty spot and a popular destination for those on the Grand Tour. It was the object of a number of eighteenth- and nineteenth-century paintings and sketches.

[40] A small laneway just off the main Via della Sibilla which leads to the Temple.

[41] Anio is the Latin name of the river Aniene that runs through the town.

[42] *Ruscus aculeatus*, an evergreen shrub.

Among us was a young man with strange, irregular features: we had often told him he was like a faun; even his character had, on one side, the incalculable sincerity, the *aplomb*, the freshness and malice of a wood-god. Now it chanced, as I leant forward listening to the conversation of a scholar of uncertain age, that I caught sight of this young man asleep. He lay with his knees up and his hands behind his head, which was thrown back into the herbage with a fierce exhaustion that would have its fill of rest. His short locks were dark and damp on his forehead. The nose, though rather wide, had a finely sentient look about it; the jaw had the satyr's squareness. His eyebrows were wonderful in ripple, only the wave lines left on sand will give an idea of their inevitable and naive beauty — a silver light haunted them. The sunshine was a white enamel on his temples, his cheeks were ruddy-hot and his mouth thrust its lips clear out of the beard — lips coloured as if with freshest pigment and simple in their insolence.

I did not listen to my companion, but watched the sleeper with an absorption of all my other senses into sight. He belonged to the curious scene around him, to those woods and rocks, to the temple over them — he slept as though the waterfall regulated his breath; his eyebrows moved with the intense light and depressed themselves charmingly under the fret of it. He lay on the ground with the freedom of an animal.

We think of Fauns as marble;[43] we rarely imagine them in all their weird gracefulness of flesh and blood, vivid with the health of a pleasurable existence: but here was one in modern clothes, a creature the Earth had formed, not to be her enemy as man usually is, but to be her foster-child. The Great Mother claimed him, and true to the bond between them, although unconscious of it, he lay there sleeping, thrown across a bank, damp with his struggle against the heat yet overcome. Several times I thought that his lashes of a dark silver were going to lift, but he slumbered on for some twenty minutes or more and then awoke so peacefully I found that his eyes were open. How they were the eyes of a Faun! Clear as springs, they looked as if they had never mirrored what was not beautiful, they were so joyous, yet they mocked their own poetry through some perverse instinct in their depths.

His companions woke up soon after and we all agreed we must return to the town. With one last wood-glance at the men and women among whom he lay the Faun laughed jeeringly and put on his sailor-hat. He was now a young man, very much of today, who talked of the people he knew: but as we climbed back along the thickets he still seemed to me scarcely human, a creature who made me feel shy as deep woods always do.

---

[43] Cooper here is likely alluding to the opening of Nathaniel Hawthorne's novel of young Americans in Italy, *The Marble Faun* (1860). The character Donatello, a young Italian, is compared extensively to the sculpture of a faun by Praxiteles in the Musei Capitolini in Rome.

In half-an-hour we were drinking lemon-squash at a Casino,[44] to the accompaniment of an Italian band; and a little later we mounted the steam-tram and were jolted across the Campagna to Rome in the chill of sunset.

'O poor Faun, poor Faun, poor Faun!'[45]

---

[44] A casino here refers to an Italian summer house.

[45] This exclamatory final line also appears in their notebooks from that trip: 'The Doctrine is sad because his father is dying, and his family poor. Alas, poor faun, poor faun.' Oxford, Bodleian Libraries, MS Eng. misc. e. 341, fol. 9r.

For That Moment Only — Second Series[1]

[1] 'For That Moment Only — Second Series', Oxford, Bodleian Libraries, MS Eng. misc. d. 976.

Darkened Eyes[2]

Rose and wine-coloured blossoms, vague with a silver tissue of light, were opening on the stalks of the holly oaks and drawing the bees; beyond them the burnt-up discs and flapping rays of very tall sun-flowers bowed gauntly from their stems, while under the regiment of holly oaks deep clove-carnations fell over of their own weight, and a thick square of mallows showed a whiteness as sheeny and as cooling as that of satin.

The sunshine explored and thrilled the flowers, heightening their colours as the tints of a face are heightened by emotion; the grass, still profuse from weeks of summer rain, was vaporous gold, while an unsuspected lustre in the air struck dazzling on spider-webs that suddenly revealed it. Turning from the garden to the house, I was met by a young servant.

'O Ellen', I exclaimed, 'it is beautiful in the garden.'

'And, do you know … isn't it strange' she laughed — 'the Master has only just come in, and he says: things are not looking as bright as usual in the garden this morning.'

The Master was an old man.

---

[2] Written by both Bradley and Cooper on 18 August 1894. As Cooper recounts: 'We write *Darkening Eyes* without need of correction' (Michael Field [EC], 'Works and Days', BL Add. MS 46782, fol. 110r). The use of 'we' suggests this is a true collaboration. Treby speculates that the 'master' may be Ruskin, given that Bradley referred to him as such in her letters (Treby, *Michael Field Catalogue*, p.85). However, we see no evidence to substantiate this; they did glimpse the aged Ruskin in late September 1894 on a holiday to the Lake District, but the *croquis* was written in August 1894 and there is no indication in 'Works and Days' of a person or event that may have inspired the sketch. Perhaps the 'master' is James Cooper, Edith's father.

~

Gwen[3]

'Is that Gwen feeding her fowls?'

I looked from the moor toward the gaunt house and noticed between the heather and yard-gate a whirl of snow round a blue figure, with red cap, and hair gleaming as light does on rank bents.[4]

'Yes, that must be Gwen; let us go and watch her.'

But suddenly, as we approached, there was a flash of radiance, startling as a comet's tail, and Gwen rushed with the speed of light, irradiating her red cap with the gleam of her hair, and followed by the whole flock of Dorkings,[5] to the edge of a small pond, some yards from the gate.

That nimble tumult, reduced to a kind of order by velocity, obeyed the young form, running along with a box of Indian corn, like David with his sling.[6] The radiance struck a spot of earth by the pond, and became once more a whirl of snow round the child, as she scattered the little stony grains, yellow as a kind of sea-side pebble, in showers on the fowls' white plumage.

The next moment Gwen caught up a stone and swung it out at a lame sheep that had intruded audaciously on the meal of her poultry. Whish! The stone sped beyond its aim, but frightened the creature away.

Gwen laughed like a boy at the sheep and the white Dorkings: there was nothing womanly in her yet. And the undeveloped moorland, hard and free about her, was strangely in accord with the sound of her laugh.

---

[3] Written by Cooper. First appears in 'Works and Days', transcribed during a trip to Ilkley, Yorkshire. Michael Field [EC], 'Works and Days', BL Add. MS 46782, fols 109v–110r (17 Aug 1894).

[4] A bent is a name given to a reedy grass, or a pasture of such grass.

[5] A Dorking is a breed of English domestic fowl.

[6] Biblical story from the Book of Samuel about a Philistine giant who is defeated by the young David, who strikes him with a rock fired from his sling.

~

A Face Seen in Ling[7]

I am crossing a moor in declining sunlight. The vaporous western horizon breaks into a dazzling feather-light of *cirri*,[8] over a rift of sudden acute blue, between toneless stretches of rain-cloud. I look till my eyes ache, and then, turning eastward, discover a few steps off to my left, on a higher slope, a woman lying full length in the ling,[9] as rigid and uncompromising as if she were dead, her profile outlined in white against the sky. Her soft hair is blown over her grey cap; the harsh ridges of a heath-coloured mackintosh cover her form up to the chin. Her face alone is exposed and lies deep in the ling, so that one little spray, in its rebound, pushes toward the exquisite lobes of her ear.

Full of all darkness that is not black, the indigo bosses[10] of the undergrowth press up stubbornly against the wash of pale hair over the forehead, while the delicate sprinkling of silver flowers on their surface subdues and carries into infinite distance the tawny background, moulding the cheek — a cheek of pure pallor and in perfect youth.

There is nothing in the sky so beautiful as that smooth face laid clear to the light, and I remain with my back to the west till sundown.

---

[7] While the *croquis* has been copied out in the Oxford MS by Cooper, it originally appears in 'Works and Days' in Bradley's hand, written during a trip to Ilkley in Yorkshire: Michael Field, 'Works and Days', BL Add. MS 46782, fol. 108v (Aug 1894). On the next page is the following passage that, while not appearing in the Oxford MS, seems to be an attempt to rewrite the opening: 'In the west there is a stretch of purple vaporous cloud, and springing from it flocks of dazzling cirri that diminish in their radiance till at last faint as feathers they float on the acute blue of the sky above my head.
— Till at last they float as mere lucid feathers on the acute blue of the mid sky.'

[8] The plural of cirrus, a type of thin, wispy cloud.

[9] Ling is the name given to a number of varieties of heather.

[10] In this context 'bosses' refers to a rounded protuberance, most likely of grass.

By the Sundial[11]

It was the first day of autumn. There was a sparkle to the sky and water, and a freshness in the atmosphere that were not there before. The trees, the fields, the rocks were all golden: the September morning was terrible in dew, and it seemed, she thought, as if the light here hung up in glistering banners on the wet branches, as she hurried toward the sundial where her host had promised to lay some nuts to attract the squirrels, and where she hoped to find them feeding. But she had torn down through the brushwood too quickly: when she reached the dial there was nothing on its face but the strong shadow of the narthex.[12] Disappointed, she was turning along a little green side-path, when a young man came up — blonde, in grey suit, blue shirt and tie and sash, a big St Bernard of the fashionable chestnut-colour, by his side. He was at the very acme of youth, in perfectly-poised health and exhilarated with the walk. Though the air was sparkling, almost bitingly crisp, and the sky dazzling, yet in all the fierceness of that bright dew-light he was an object still brighter. He had the unused look of the sea.

After brief greeting he passed on to the house.

The shadow of the dial shifted.

[11] Written by Cooper *c.* August–September 1894, during a visit to Haslemere. Cooper describes a sundial in the garden of Logan Pearsall Smith. We have transcribed her description of the garden and the installation below in the sketch 'Haslemere' (Michael Field [EC], 'Works and Days', BL Add. MS 46782 fols 104v–105r (Aug 1894)).

[12] The vestibule of a church. Cooper may possibly have meant 'gnomon', the part of a sundial that casts a shadow.

~

A Wintry Sea[13]

The waves were nearly hidden by encroaching fog, out of which they came, all of a sudden, powerful, with wind-scattered edges, and a flow on to the shore that was singularly cold to watch, moving up it like a shudder.

The breeze, confused with fog, blew in a vicious way, yet hardly made any ground, so that the measure of the waves as they swept in was full and uncontrolled.

Winter had taken possession of the sea.

On the shore an old man was standing at my side, his grey hair caught like the edges of the waves and whirled about in mournful slashes. The vicious wind wrung the tails of his coat, his felt cap was only kept on by the working of his eyebrows, and for a long time his eyes had followed the irrepressible desolation with which the grey billows rushed forward and broke.

His eyes were grey too, or an aged grey, sweet but rather opaque.

His white face listened: it was wintry as the sea, and it looked as if prepared for a message.

He remained silent, looking out. But my heart beat warningly, and, with the instinct of an onlooker to terminate an intercourse intolerable to witness, I said sharply 'Come away: it is cold.'[14]

---

[13] Written by Cooper *c.* 1894. Treby speculates that the 'old man' may be Cooper's father, James Russell Cooper; *Michael Field Catalogue*, p. 85.

[14] This final paragraph is in the hand of Bradley and appears to be an editorial insert.

The Granary[15]

Everyone is gone to church. I am shut alone in the granary.

It is long as a banqueting-room, almost as low as a vault. Rafters hold up the pointed wooden roof, and cross-beams make a level ceiling, through which are glimpses of the rafters and a foggy cloud of spider-webs. There are tiny windows almost on the floor, latticed, not so much for shade but that sun and air may come in discreetly.

This hall of tempered light houses great mounds, almost of the same hue as the rafters, spread out in deep tranquillity. Shadow lies like a turf over them, and sunshine touches them here and there with the poignant gladsomeness of its amber. When I plunge my fingers through them they are chilly, sliding, inestimable by the sense of touch as a sea-beach; and they leave on the skin, as I draw away my hand, a dryness that stings.

The whole granary smells of *potpourri*:[16] the windows ferment with flies, and yet, beside the agitation they make or the scratch of a rat in the walls, there is no sound save the actualness of silence, that is felt as if heard.

How the grain sleeps!

An awful presence in this long hall — a power as great as gold, hoarded its capacity within it, waiting under shade and gleam, under rafters hieratic in their ranges, till its day of rest is accomplished. *Holy, holy, holy, Lord God of Sabaoth*![17]

---

[15] Written by Cooper *c.* September 1894, during a trip to Northumberland. A draft appears among the loose materials that make up the final volume of 'Works and Days' (Michael Field [EC], 'Works and Days', BL Add. MS 46804, fol. 87r), followed by an entry by Bradley: 'Tuesday. We drive away — we leave "the stocks," the Cheviots, the granary — the objects we have learnt to love, — the Borders' (fol. 87v). For Berenson's critique of this *croquis*, see Introduction (pp. 13–14).

[16] A mixture of dried herbs, flowers, and spices used to perfume rooms. Herbs were often dried on floors during the spring and summer, as seems to be the case here.

[17] This line is taken from the Sanctus, a Christian liturgical hymn. Sabaoth is a Hebrew word meaning 'host' that is left untranslated in the English New Testament.

Incongruity[18]

The brake turned from St Mary's Loch and entered the Dens of Yarrow.[19] The stream goes the same way, full of shining water from the Loch, in the midst of hills with strange, flat curves like those of a corpse under its shroud.

On this special September afternoon the sky had an uncertain greyness, almost soft with light, but darkening continually toward storm. A few sheep pastured on the higher slopes.

I sat behind the coachman, a commonplace tourist on each side of me, while a boy and dog shared the back of the brake with a fat constable. The coachman had smart eyes, jerked round every five minutes, and a warm, immense voice devoted to the duties of the guide.

'Dry 'ope Tow'r.'[20]

Ah — Tower! I iterated.

'The home o' the Flower o' Yarrow.'[21]

— I saw her near it lovely and lonely as grass of Parnassus by a boulder.[22]

But the brake dashed on.

'Douglas Burn!'[23]

---

[18] Written by Cooper in late September 1895. During this trip Bradley wrote several poems about Yarrow. Chief among their reasons for visiting was that the landscape was associated with James Hogg and Sir Walter Scott.

[19] The *croquis* narrates a coach journey that Cooper and Bradley took from St Mary's Loch along Yarrow Water to the Gordon Arms in the Scottish Borders.

[20] Dryhope Tower is a fortified keep in the valley of Yarrow Water, built in the sixteenth century. It belonged to the Scotts of Dryhope, ancestors of Sir Walter Scott.

[21] Mary (or Marion) Scott (1548–1598) was famed for her beauty and known as the 'Flower of Yarrow'. She was later immortalized in a Border song of the same name.

[22] In Greek myth Mount Parnassus is the spiritual home of poetry.

[23] Douglas Burn is the site of the mythic Douglas tragedy, in which seven sons of the House of Douglas were slain as they sought to defend the honour of their sister, Lady Margaret, after she has been seduced by Sir William. The legend is told in 'The Douglas Tragedy', collected by Scott in *Minstrelsy of the Scottish Border* (1802–1803). As Scott's prefatory note to the ballad states: 'From this ancient tower Lady Margaret is said to have been carried by her lover. Seven large stones, erected upon the neighbouring heights of Blackhouse, are shown, as marking the

'What happened there?'

'Seven sons o' the Douglas war slain in yon lone den.'

The scene of the tragedy lay open, a great frankness in the manner of its exposure, a ghastly frankness that proved characteristic of Yarrow.

— I saw the seven mailed bodies scarcely distinguishable from the stones of the Burn, their youth as valueless as the age of the surrounding braes.[24]

'Eddin 'ope, where Hogg lived.'[25]

'Ah — Hogg!'

— I saw Scott meet him close to that homestead, for they had each for each the very sympathy of the soil.

'An' there's the Gordon Arms where the Constable gets out.'

— Climax of the Present, I saw him do it!

---

spot where the seven brethren were slain; and the Douglas-burn is averred to have been the stream, at which the lovers stopped to drink: so minute is tradition in ascertaining the scene of a tragical tale, which, considering the rude state of former times, had probably foundation in some real event.' Walter Scott, *Minstrelsy of the Scottish Border*, 4 vols (Edinburgh: James Ballantyne, 1803), III, 244.

[24] A brae is the term used in Scotland for a steep bank or hillside.

[25] James Hogg (1770–1835), Scottish poet and novelist, lived in the region around Yarrow.

~

The Fairy Knight[26]

It was spring — a morning of no special loveliness, with the daily blue sky of a fine May. The air had a fragrant warmth, delicious to the skin, and lips and nostrils; birds were singing so that their voices gave a sense of glitter to the ear, as if it were listening to a tangle of sunbeams: the light was affectionate, and the young shoots bent softly with younger flowers.

A girl of eight was standing in a large farmyard; the cows were gone to pasture, the horses and men to work. She was alone with her kitten and even her kitten had escaped and hung on the branches of a plum-tree, defiant, terrified, and clinging as though it were made of putty.

All at once a peasant-boy, not quite as old as she, crossed the yard to the back-door, gave some message, and strutted away toward the gate. She called him to her with the voice of a queen —

'Please catch my kitten for me.'

Without a word he began to climb: in the midst of the tiny, blighted leaves of the plum-tree she saw his glowing red cheeks and blue eyes, as full of wonder as the kitten's, only more dignified because of their stolid courage. He got hold of Pussie with a grasp and slipped down the tree, rosy and quick, as an apple falls. Then both he and she played with the rescued kitten, she looking animated and he foolish. It was spring … and after ten minutes of eager condescension on her part and of flattered amazement on his, they walked away from their playmate, hand in hand. She took him through the garden-door; she passed the kitchen and parlour windows with the audacity of innocence; she felt the fairyland of this fine day had got its knight. She promised he should have dinner — hot, roast beef; nothing was too much to promise, everything must come to pass, and she knew the beef was roasting. She took him to the greenest bowers of the garden; her heart was lavish, and his round blue eyes maintained a calm wonder that made enchantment itself seem commonplace as the blue sky. She promised that a dinner and a visit to the Shady Walk should be his whenever he came to ask for them. Suddenly she saw the larkspurs in noble, crisp first-bloom on her mother's

[26] Written by Cooper *c.* 1895.

favourite bed — she must not keep back anything, all must be given! She broke down a spike recklessly and offered it.

Then a strange powerlessness came over her. A voice said sharply —

'What brings you here?'

Her mother was addressing the Fairy Knight.

'Go away at once!'

And she saw him slouch off toward the garden-door, with that in his face which would have been a sob if it had not been paralysed by wonder.

She was scolded and made to feel ashamed; yet, still holding the broken head of larkspur in her hand, she protested —

'I said he might stay for dinner; I promised it.'

But such promises are made for parents to break.

It did not seem at all like spring now she was left with her mother.

Grandfather's Chair[27]

'I always get my own way.'

'Do you? I wish you'd teach me how to get mine.'

'I must give you some *private* lessons.'

These words passed in an undertone between a guest and a daughter of the house at a country breakfast-table. A moment after the chairs were shoved back and Papa went away to choose the portion of scripture for morning-prayers. When he was gone his daughter exclaimed enviously —

'Miss Braithwaite always gets her own way. Don't you wish she could teach us how to get ours with father?'

'Yes, indeed!' murmured her sister.

'And I with mine!' said the pretty prattler between them.

'I always do what I want to do and then laugh. Pluck and perfect good-temper are the secrets of success.'

The rebels were sitting in a row against a folding door, their neat little morning slippers thrust beyond the tweed skirts; and a flush of unwonted fellow-feeling drew the four girls to each other.

Only one man was in the room — a young colonist, fresh from cattle-hunting in the West, with eyes like azure lakes, gold moustache and a complexion as fine and pure as his own Californian air. Alone in the presence of women a proud bashfulness frankly lighted up his face.

'We always leave the grandfather's chair for you', one of the girls had remarked, and he had slipped in, rosy, secure of his freedom, his eyes motionless as if resting on the verge of a prairie.

The rebels went on with their confidences that grew more and more into demands. Every girl, they said, had a right to her own time and to the natural play of her own being.

'I don't think you ought to hear all this' — one of the four addressed the young colonist. His smile grew more consciously radiant, but the clear eyes never moved in their outlook.

---

[27] Written by Cooper *c.* 1895.

'We may theorise about woman's freedom,' she continued, 'but Mr Hooper is thinking how different it will be when he brings a wife to that beautiful home, with the redwood floors, he is going to build out yonder. Isn't that what you are thinking?'

He grew rose to the clipped roots of his hair, but did not answer or shift his glance.

So the girls went on talking heedlessly, while he sat in the grandfather's chair, immobile and brilliant as a young sphinx at dawn.

Cupid at College[28]

How busy the light always looks when it comes through college-windows; how austerely busy as it flickers about the bare passages, or, streaming over a wall, lights the Himalayas on some geological map into a quince-coloured ridge, and gives gloss to the livid bones of a plesiosaurus![29]

But that morning the light was busy with a group of girls, waiting by a closed door on which the sun, after gilding their plaits and waves, finally struck. The damsels carried books of Euclid under their arms,[30] yet they seemed to find plenty of amusement in the serious position they occupied, and laughter that was a giggle of happiness and had no other cause kept rising wantonly and making the best terms it could with decorum. All the girls were class-mates, except one — a newcomer, who stood at a little distance from the others. Suddenly the door opened: there was the sweep of a black gown, and a very young professor faced both the maidens and the sun.

His black college-cap threw into relief a face somewhat fair and now aureate;[31] grave eyes, half-cold, half-bashful avoided the glances that met them; and the mouth had that look of adolescent repulse to soft emotion that one imagines on the mouth of Hippolytus.[32]

He passed through the maidens as quickly as a gust of bright wind — chill, independent of their sex, yet self-conscious.

How Venus must have laughed at this disguise of Cupid's!

All the girl-students were heart-sick. To the newcomer a God had filled the college … it was the Temple of her first love.

---

[28] Written by Cooper *c.* 1895. Treby speculates that the story may be inspired by J. F. Main, one of Cooper's tutors at University College Bristol (*Michael Field Catalogue*, p. 85).

[29] A large marine reptile of the Jurassic Period.

[30] Euclid (third to fourth centuries BC) was a Greek mathematician whose *Elements* was a key mathematical textbook in the nineteenth century.

[31] A brilliant golden colour.

[32] The son of Theseus and Hippolyta in Greek myth. Hippolytus is repulsed by marriage and refuses to worship Aphrodite, the goddess of love.

Published Prose Works

An Old Couple[1]

Un paradis perdu est toujours, quand on veut, un paradis reconquis
— RENAN[2]

Se nuova legge non ti toglie Memoria
— *Purg.* II[3]

They lived in a simple cottage, very much like ordinary folk. Their children had left them — married, and settled at a distance, as children will; so, once more, they were all in all to each other. They had obtained permission to return to the garden in which they had spent their happy and innocent days. They found the gate swinging on its hinges, and the fiery cherub was not there.[4] It consoled them to return to the old spot, though their conditions were so changed. The air around the rose bushes was as sweet as ever, and they soon grew accustomed to the prickles.

During their exile they had become acquainted with those arts that provide men with shelter against the heat and cold. Accordingly, Adam built a small hut of stones, and Eve plaited wool and fibres into coverings for herself and her husband. As the ages went on, and the population of the world increased, they no longer lived in solitude. The fact that the spring came full three weeks earlier to the valley where they had built their cottage than to any of the even more sheltered nooks among the hills, led men who were beginning to look on the earth with practical, business eyes to settle near them. The old gate, swinging on its hinges, presented no obstacle to the enterprising young colonist, and the

[1] First published in the *Contemporary Review*, 51, February 1887, pp. 220–25. Published under the name Michael Field but written by Katharine Bradley.
[2] Taken from Ernest Renan's Preface to *Souvenirs d'enfance et de jeunesse* (1883). We have corrected an error of transcription in the original. It translates as 'A lost paradise is always, if that's what you wish, a paradise reconquered'.
[3] Taken from Dante's *The Divine Comedy*, *Purgatorio*, Canto II, ll. 106–07. 'If no new law has robbed you of your memory'; Dante Alighieri, *The Divine Comedy*, trans. by Robin Kirkpatrick (London: Penguin, 2012), p. 167.
[4] A reference to Eden; see Genesis 3. 24.

inhabitants of the moss-grown tenement smiled, and held sacred the secret that the newcomers had intruded on the precincts of Paradise. From the settlers they learnt many facts concerning the advance of the world, the arts of navigation, commerce, government and war. But they remained a recluse old couple. It was only rarely that a neighbour looked in, and chatted with them, as one does chat with the aged, of those matters that will interest and delight them. Women pitied Eve, believing she was childless, and noticed with compassion her maternal manner to their little ones. To lovers she was somewhat austere; it was impossible to her to imagine courtship otherwhere than in the bowers of Paradise. She listened attentively when any spake to her of death; without violence or bloodshed she thought it must be tranquil as the deep sleep from which she woke when life was given to her. Tidings of war greatly affected her, but beyond all other things she was distressed at the sight of children quarrelling. She would part the little disputants, and taking them on her knee, would tell them a story of two brothers who quarrelled till one of them grew so angry he slew the other in a field, and then went away from his parents very sorry, and could not come to live with them again for shame.[5] But she did not speak, even to the little children, of God. Now and then she dropt a quiet tear on them, and their mothers would draw them away, saying they were sure now she must once have held in her arms a baby of her own.

In appearance Eve was exceedingly gracious and beautiful, full of reticence and dignity; people always spoke of her as a lady, and whispered to one another that she had come of good stock. To her husband she was full of wistful courtesy; it seemed as if he had made some sacrifice in marrying her, and her devotion was mingled with gratitude. In Adam there was less that was peculiar than in his wife. He would stand often on his threshold in the evening and look out. He had forgotten that centuries had passed by, and was still yearning for the return of his firstborn — the wanderer. It was Eve who in the spring-tide turned to the meadows where the lambs were playing, and she always went alone. When she came back she would put her arms around her husband's neck and kiss him. He did not understand that she had come from a grave; but he was grateful for the kiss, and drew her away to look at the young sprouting blades of corn. He had become a husbandman, and was skilled in the tilling of the ground. Eve never looked happier than when he came home hot and hungry from working in the fields. She loved to set his meal, lay her head on his knee, and listen to his talk of the wonderful new ways of raising crops and planting vineyards. He was busy and contented, and there was no regret in his face. But their conversation did not always turn on commonplace matters. On winter evenings they often discussed

[5] Cain and Abel, the sons of Adam and Eve. Cain, the firstborn, killed his younger brother out of jealousy when God preferred Abel's offering to his own. As punishment, God condemned him to be a 'restless wanderer' on the earth. See Genesis 4. 1–18.

ancient history, and showed a familiar acquaintance with the stories we now read in the early chapters of Genesis. Sometimes they would quarrel and grow sullen, or violently disagree. Then Adam's voice would be heard in reproach, or Eve's in contention, and Adam would walk out, and lean against the old swing-gate that seemed to be the natural boundary of his little domain. When Eve saw him leaning against the gate, and apparently forgetful of her, she would steal up to him softly, and they would walk home together, a new light in their eyes. All age had passed from their faces, and there was majesty in their least caressing touch, for they had no suspicion of intruders, and thought only of each other. After these hours of reconciliation, they would speak of quite another time in their lives, when evidently there had been deep accord between them; then, and then only, was Eve heard to laugh, — a silvery, ringing laugh, full of unimaginable mirth, and Adam, drunk with the witchery, would grow eloquent and tender.

As the ages passed on, though somewhat old-fashioned, they learned to read and write, for they were of strong, vigorous faculty; and, as they attracted and retained the love of all who visited them, they had intercourse with friends in various parts of the world. One traveller — he was an American — kept them regularly supplied with newspapers; these Adam read diligently to his wife; and his keen brown eyes looked up at her from their pages, without spectacles, as lustrous and fervid as when he repeated to her his conversation with the archangel Raphael.[6] He learnt all about the slave-trade, and the excitements of Livingstone's discoveries;[7] stories of travel and exploration were particularly interesting to him, for he was haunted by the superstition that one day one of these wonderful discoverers would come across his lost boy. Cain, he felt sure, was still a wanderer, and an exile: he looked for tidings of him, when he heard of the discovery of a new world; and later on, in the nineteenth century, when no murderer — but he checked himself, and resumed, in his thoughts, — when no *lost person* could remain hidden, even though he were lying at the bottom of some deep Alpine cleft, there seemed really a fair expectation that some clue to the missing one would be found. He even began once a description of his boy, as he looked when he last saw him, with the intention of forwarding it to the *Times*, but his wife bade him reflect that, if their son were still living, his costume, his skin, and the manner of wearing his hair would be changed.

A little before the time at which I am writing a serious grief befell this worthy old couple, and I fear it will be long before they recover from the effects of it. Though, as I have hinted, they to some extent kept pace with the world, and had

---

[6] In Book v of *Paradise Lost* the archangel Raphael visits Paradise to admonish Adam and Eve. Milton's poem is a key background text to this story.

[7] David Livingstone (1813–1873) was a Scottish missionary and explorer whose *Missionary Travels and Researches in South Africa* (1857) was a popular and influential book in the nineteenth century.

probably heard of the French Revolution, the works and influence of the great thinkers were unknown to them. They could scarcely, indeed, be expected to feel interest in philosophy, holding as they did the simple clue to the mysteries of the universe. The literature of the Middle Ages they had always found excessively tedious, but they were well versed in modern poets and authors, and would sometimes remark of a favourite volume that it might have been written in their own garden. One day 'The Earthly Paradise' was brought to them by an English traveller.[8] They were sitting together under an almond tree — one that they had planted in Eden, because it was the first fair creature that had greeted them in the wilderness, when they were driven from their home by the flaming sword. The tree stretched a bough of pink blossom, clear against the blue sky, above their heads, and they sat — the young Englishman noted as he turned back to look at them, after bidding farewell — serene and without curiosity, the book unclosed upon their knee. This was before they had received the intelligence that so troubled them as quite to overcloud their lives. I cannot enter into the details of their religion, enough that they had always believed it a happy thing to be born, and had never regretted that they had peopled the world, even though they had brought sin and death into it by their one rash act of disobedience. For, though God has forced them and their offspring to labour and to suffer, He had never withdrawn from them the comfort and solace of love. It is doubtful indeed whether they would ever have learnt to care much for each other in Paradise, where there was neither peril nor discomfort. Adam once confessed to his wife that it was not until he saw tears in her bright eyes that he felt the longing to cherish her replace the old covetous desire of her beauty. In like manner it was when Adam returned from his first day of distress and fatigue with the spade that Eve felt a wifely tenderness spring up towards him in her bosom, and from that hour it was her chief happiness to mend his clothes, prepare his food carefully, and make his seasons of rest from labour full of refreshment and delight. 'In Eden,' she said, 'there was nothing we could do for each other, and now we are quite dependent.'

It must not be imagined that these two old people never thought regretfully of the days when everything happened just as they had planned; they often grew gloomy and impatient, and when they found bad desires and selfish hopes creeping into their minds, their terror and astonishment were indescribable. But, as I have said, they never doubted that life was a blessing, that Providence was kind, and happiness within reach of each human creature. I now come to the cause of the great misery that is at present disheartening and disturbing them. It had reached their ears that over wide tracts of Europe there are people, not

[8] A collection of poems by William Morris, published 1868–1870. Drawing on Greek and Icelandic myth and set in the medieval past, it narrates the story of people looking for the land of everlasting life.

suffering from war, famine, poverty, or pestilence, who yet bitterly bewail their lot, are inclined to think that the most satisfactory moments of their lives are those spent in sleep or in forgetfulness, and desire only to divert themselves, at whatever cost, till they die. When Adam heard of the strange lunacy that had thus befallen his offspring, he exclaimed, 'Let these young people fall in love and marry.' 'That they cannot do,' replied the young European they were questioning; 'they love no one but themselves. If they see a beautiful object or creature they no longer desire to foster it, but to destroy or to consume it.' 'They are afraid of God; it is as when we hid ourselves in the garden,' Eve whispered to Adam. 'On the contrary,' rejoined their guest, 'they do not believe in any God, and they have no fear of punishment.' 'Yet surely sometimes they feel grateful; that, it seems to me, is one of the things that make up for having done wrong. In my youth I lived a quite blameless life; afterwards, when I had fallen into grievous sin, those whom I had injured were kind to me. It is the blessings one does not deserve that are so precious,' added Eve, timidly, and hid her face, that was blushing like a girl's, behind her husband's shoulder. 'But these people, who believe everything is getting worse, consider life gives them much less than their desert; even their poets, one of them especially, who was once full of marvellous hope, seem to think that, unless men can retain in their grasp for ever the delights and affections that they prize, it would have been far better never to have possessed them.' 'And do the poets say this?' cried Adam, in astonishment. 'Why, we two were scarcely in Paradise a twelvemonth, and yet ——' Eve softly laid her hands on her husband's lips, and turning to the stranger, continued: 'There is a little bit of Paradise still in every human life, and its duration is probably as long as that enjoyed by the first two dwellers upon earth. We are old people, and our children are dead; I do not think I shall ever see my little ones again; by-and-by one of us will be left alone; but we shall remember till we die: perchance the unhappy people of whom you are speaking have never made any memories?' 'Either they have been happy once, and lost the secret of living over again their happy days, or they care nothing at all about the past, and hold that every moment should contain its special little portion of felicity, as a dewdrop its spark of light.' 'If they have lost the secret of hoarding the hours,' rejoined Eve, very gravely, 'they may well wish they had never been born.'

After this, nothing was said: over ill-news old people brood; they do not get excited, or change colour, but they wake in the night and turn over all they have heard, and repeat it to one another for many days, like a piece they would get by heart. I felt that this would happen, when I left them, as I did, abruptly; for I had divined their secret, and, though I am but a careless young fellow, I had no mind to witness the affliction of the worthy old couple, whom in some sort I regarded as my grand-parents. I have never visited them again, and I shall tell no man the way to their cottage. They will live in my memory as I left them — simple, majestic figures, their faces full of astonishment and pain. I think of them frequently after a hard business day, or an evening spent in fashionable society. And my one hope with regard to them is that I may live old enough to see men desire the simplicity they have never lost. Can it be that, in obscurity as great as that which hides them from the eye of the busy world, the young and ardent are planning the conditions of a life that shall be blessed in desire and fruition as that of two young lovers, who, after the shedding of a few 'natural tears' at the loss of their early illusion, accepted their lot, endured its hardships, and, redeemed by patience and hope from degradation, find the ample years of age all too few to recount the consolations of memory?[9]

[9] Bradley invokes here the final lines of *Paradise Lost* XII, 645–49:

> Som natural tears they drop'd, but wip'd them soon;
> The World was all before them, where to choose
> Thir place of rest, and Providence thir guide:
> They hand in hand with wandring steps and slow,
> Through *Eden* took thir solitarie way.

~

Mid-Age[10]

'The Bird of Time has but a little way
To flutter — and the Bird is on the wing.'[11]

Our first cause of distress springs from a deterioration perceptible in all we are or effect. To one with a poignant sense of beauty the change in a flower, a few hours after it has been gathered, is more painful than its withering decay. The body has outlived its ideal moment; coarser materials are being substituted for the delicately woven textures of youth. We walk denuded and impaired. Self-love, it is decreed, henceforth can have no part in our love of beauty. We lose our sense of being welcome in the world. A quality has fallen from our actions, our gestures, our speech — that splendour from the gods that made Laertes lustrous and divine in the eyes of Odysseus:[12] we are no longer young.

Oh deep allure of youth!

From what depths of commonplace does the tradition spring that a middle-aged apple-tree furnished the occasion of man's first offence. We must pierce into Eden, and picture to ourselves our first parents, not under a ripening autumn sun — in a little orchard in Paradise in spring. We must think of a girl set down to rove among our own enchanting, northern blossom-woods, free to smell and pluck and wonder, and then can we for a moment doubt that her ardour, her zest,

---

[10] First published in the *Contemporary Review*, 56, September 1889, pp. 431–32. Published under the name Michael Field but written by Bradley on 23 May 1889 (Michael Field [KB], 'Works and Days', BL Add. MS 46777, fols 68r–71r).

[11] Taken from Edward Fitzgerald's translation of the *Rubáiyát of Omar Khayyám* (1859). Poem VII in its entirety reads:

Come, fill the Cup, and in the fire of Spring
Your Winter-garment of Repentance fling:
The Bird of Time has but a little way
To flutter — and the Bird is on the Wing.

Michael Field would draw on the *Rubáiyát* again for inspiration in *Underneath the Bough* (1893/8).

[12] Laertes was the father of Odysseus in Homer's *Odyssey*. After Odysseus returns home from Ithaca and reveals himself to his aged father, Athena makes Laertes taller and stronger.

her curiosity would hover over the closed buds and yielded, broken blossoms of the apple-flower? Her choice, we must believe, was made in May; it was remembrance of pressed, flushing leaves, of exalting odour that hurried her restless fingers to the fatal twitch.

The immortals, spending an idle hour on earth, share the simple food of the peasant, and pause not infrequently with the poor; seldom do they tarry with the old, unless it be, as in the instance of Baucis and Philemon, to convert their ineffectual mutterings into the perennial murmur of forest-trees.[13]

Whosoever will gain his life, even the life of his youth, must lose it; some freedom from the bondage of personality must be claimed. Barring the splendour of the Divine Presence, one cannot doubt that to St Paul, whose mind as a flashing mirror reflected Christianity, its precious elements were more penetratingly realized than by St Peter.[14] There must be 'a little while' between. We cannot possess what we experience. Why, indeed, should looking forward be synonymous with anticipation, and looking backward with regret? Prehistoric vision, one would fancy, cannot fail to be more nebulous than memory, life's gendered dream. And one would fain say a word about the care of one's memory, the conservation of those moments that may be significant or influential. Selection may be made even of our remembrances; unworthy ones obliterated by repentance, frivolous ones made void by neglect; those that glorify, exalt, or even soften dissociated from vulgar contact or approach. We should even be careful of the moods in which we draw near the 'ruines of time.'[15] An old love-scene, visited by cynicism, may be irreparably defaced. We must not traverse with hurrying, worldly feet places where we have walked with God. We may, notwithstanding, not without prejudice, when ill-treated, or tarnished by the world, resort to seasons in our lives when what is ideal in us has met with recognition, when poets have claimed us of their race, when love has wrought miracle on our faces, or when we have been enabled to confess by deed the scope or intensity of our effort. 'Il mezzo cammina della vita'[16] offers no compensation for the lost pleasures of youth. Life is not a system of indemnification; our losses are not made good; we do not recover our fortune. New powers develop, some the result of conflict or failure, others of contemplative quality. We see better and

---

[13] Baucis and Philemon, a devoted elderly couple from Greek myth, asked Zeus if they could die together, and so he turned them into a pair of intertwined trees.

[14] St Peter and St Paul are both seen as fathers of the Church. St Paul was a Roman Jew who saw the resurrected Christ on the road to Damascus, and from that point on was an apostle and prophet of nascent Christianity. St Peter was one of Jesus's disciples and thought by many to be the first Bishop of Rome, and therefore the first Pope. Michael Field suggest here that St Paul was able to better shed himself of his personality.

[15] Edmund Spenser's poem, *The Ruines of Time* (1591).

[16] This is a misquotation from the incipit of Dante's *Inferno*, which ought to read 'Nel mezzo del cammin di nostra vita', and translates as 'Midway upon the journey of our life'.

deeper, our boundary-lines cut the sky. We are no longer 'im Werden';[17] we accomplish and possess. Virgil, the sage guide, the incomparable master, exhorts Dante at the threshold of the earthly paradise to free exercise of his disciplined judgements and to trust in his chastened senses: —

'Non aspettar mio dir più né mio cenno;
libero, dritto e sano è tuo arbitrio,
e fallo fora non fare a suo senno:
per ch'io te sovra te corono e mitrio.'[18]

Thus crowned and mitred we enjoy a period when the earthly paradise presents enchantments without peril, when we may be left for a while safely to ourselves, to follow our imperious instincts and most immediate desires; in mood to receive as crowning favour of our soul's mistress, 'a corollary.'

Before the poignant vision of Beatrice,[19] before the stormy humiliations of a nature in process of salvation, there is provided for every nobly ordered life a season of revel, relaxation, and satisfied curiosity, when the pageant of the world may be witnessed without intoxication, and art adumbrates truth.

---

[17] German for 'in the making'.

[18] Taken from Dante's *Divine Comedy, Purgatorio*, Canto XXVII, ll. 139–42:

No longer look to me for signs or word.
Your will is healthy, upright, free and whole.
And not to heed that sense would be a fault
Lord of yourself, I crown and mitre you.

Dante Alighieri, *The Divine Comedy*, p. 288. In *The Divine Comedy* Virgil, the Roman poet, is Dante's guide through Hell and Purgatory. These are Virgil's final lines, in which he tells Dante that he no longer needs a guide and is now able to follow his own reason and sense. Bradley suggests that mid-age is such a period, when we are 'crowned and mitred' with self-knowledge.

[19] Beatrice, the embodiment of ideal womanhood, is Dante's guide to *Paradiso*.

A Lumber-Room[20]

It discovers an altar to an unknown god, — humanity in ignorant worship of time. It offends us at the same time that it fascinates; we approach it in impatience; we descend from it in lingering, in dust and tears. As in a vault we look round; we dare not transpose or remove. Our memorial chapel is an attic where grandpapa's crutches touch the long sloping roof, and the moralities are inscribed on a sampler, traversed by mystic signs. Our religion is betrayed in our attachment to the obsolete; the four-post bed in its mouldering uselessness awaits the final trump.[21] Not without hope of ultimate restoration have these rusting fire-irons, this dilapidated furniture, been confined to the custody of the mildew and the moth. Neither are trophies of our mortality wanting. We preserve, as in a crude catalogue, records of our ancient sickness or necessity. We cannot destroy the leading-strings of our childhood: and what of the knobbed stick, the pad, the crutch? Gratitude still leans on these; the horn spectacles, that have ceased to lighten the eyes of our ancestors, dim our own. The nearer an object has lain to life, the keenlier it penetrates our sympathy. A pipe, a ragged purse, a stained palette, a carving half blocked-in, any broken instrument, engage us more than objects stamped with the estranging impress of remoteness or achievement. The globe once habited by gold-fish, the empty bird cage, even the tenantless mousetrap, depress us. Instinctively we moralize. Divines exhort us to an examination of conscience, and we turn a deaf ear: the conscience is too close for impartial survey and censure. Neither must remorse, which is old conscience, be averted to. A past to which we are attached either by prejudice or voluntary affection impedes and constricts us. In a lumber-room we conduct the scrutiny

[20] First published in the *Contemporary Review*, 57, January 1890, pp. 98–102. Likely written by Bradley in 1889. A lumber room was found in large eighteenth- and nineteenth-century houses, often in the attic, and was reserved for unused wood or furniture. Such a room is referenced in Walter Pater's 'A Child in the House' (1878).

[21] The last of seven trumpets sounded on the Day of Judgement: 'We shall all be changed, in a moment, in the twinkling of an eye, at the last trump'. 1 Corinthians 15. 51–52.

of our dead selves without embarrassment: we stand aloof, observe and remember.

Yet why generalize, why speak of lumber-rooms, when it is of one that we are thinking, — the many-nooked attic in an old-fashioned farmhouse, where two rosy-cheeked children played in winter on a floor strewn with store-fruit and ripening damsons? It had been revealed to them that, if a certain curious hair-trunk were opened,[22] with due rites and at propitious hour, the dolls that they had fondled, lost, forgotten, and after many days desired with tears, would suddenly be discovered lying bright and uninjured as on the day of gift. A warming credulity crept through me as I listened to details of the anticipated reunion. We discussed the toilettes of lost favourites that 'suddenly as rare things will, had vanished,'[23] the oddities and infirmity of others taken from us by violence or disaster. We recall the lovable fates of creatures fallen to decay though ill-usage or neglect. We named them by name — Zinga, the Only Son, Antoinette. Everything was ready; faith flowed to the brim of the event. Had the Child Christ been there, immediately must that hair-trunk have yielded up its dead. I remember the chill of heart with which I heard that nothing had been found. There was some quiet weeping on the attic-stairs, then all references to the lost generations ceased. The number of these small children of the resurrection was to have exceeded fifty. Great must have been the depopulating of the imagination!

For the tradition of a millennium, a return of the goodliest creatures that have sojourned with us, is exciting and recurrent, and will never be banished from the hospitable human heart passionate to entertain its heroes. The past must return to us, and something more than the past — the past and our joy in meeting it again. It cannot be that King Arthur and Barbarossa have taken leave of us forever.[24] We want to walk the earth with them again; they kept us in tune; they dispersed the influences that made life spiritless; they set a-ripple the current of our days: let the saints break through to an alien paradise; the children of the earth guard in their hearts everlasting welcome for such as have founded human happiness on worldly triumph, earthliness, pomp, and far-spreading revel. We build monuments to the men who have given order to life: to those who have given colour we render warmer homage; we ask for them back again. We believe

---

[22] A trunk or case covered in hide from which the hair had not been removed.

[23] This paraphrases Robert Browning's 'One Word More': 'Suddenly, as rare things will, it vanished'. This poem, dedicated to Elizabeth Barrett Browning, was the final poem in his volume *Men and Women* (1855).

[24] King Arthur led British forces as they attempted to repel Saxon invaders in the late fourth and early fifth centuries. While little is known of his life, he has been the subject of much mythologization, notably in the nineteenth century in Lord Alfred Tennyson's epic cycle *Idylls of the King* (1859–1885); Hayreddin Barbarossa (1478–1546) was an Ottoman corsair or pirate, and later a Grand Admiral whose leadership was essential in the Ottoman navy becoming dominant in the Mediterranean.

they are stored for us in some cavernous lumber-room of earth, and, returning, will one day cast a processional majesty on life. We have not the courage of the children; we dare not lift the lid of the hair-trunk that contains our hopes; we enshrine them, and let no man approach them with unreverent feet. For we are tempted to call mystic what we shrink from discovering, equally with that we are impotent to penetrate. Awe of contact with intolerable power operates more rarely than the fear of exposing emptiness in retaining us in an attitude of worship.

Belief in a millennium, as we have suggested, may justify the more honourable contents of our lumber-room, some hope that one day they may be reunited to the glory of the ball-room and the banquet; but what shall we say of the objects stowed away in its lowlier corners, the homely, discarded things an elder world esteemed beautiful, buried by us out of sight with revolt and a struggling shame; or, it may be, the creatures of our own caprice, the fad, the extravagance of an hour, the ephemeral display, the relic of a season's finery that instead of rotting with last summer's leaves continues to grin on us from an obtrusive peg? Why did we not give these things to the elements? What prompted us to preserve them? Has the savage, we cry in our irritation, his lumber-room as well as his idol-chamber? Does he revere his rubbish and his gods? We respect the squirrel's instinct to hoard nuts. What animal, even of the more sober Scripture kind, has been known to retain and consecrate its tarnished weapons, its frayed garniture, or forsaken cell. Is then the habit of storing a spiritual habit of which we may be proud, or one for which a future architect will make no provision? As we reflect on the great lumber-rooms of the world, on the difference in quality between the warehouse and the museum, our conclusion visits us as a smile: had man destroyed universally, instead of discarding, had he never learnt to spare that from which his vital interest was withdrawn, antiquity would not now be lying about us as the hills round about Jerusalem, protecting us against those gusts from chaos that sweep across the plain of time.

One of the peculiar and moving attributes of lumber is its persistency. We are for ever confounding it with rubbish, but rubbish is ephemeral lumber and not worth a thought. Lumber incommodes us, the grim fostering it requires is burdensome; rot, that woody rheumatism, may infest its bones; it has need of air, in certain cases of light and warmth. Yet it does not reward our solicitude. The indefinable grace of length of days, a shadow as from the under-feathers of time's wing, rests over it; its corporeal presence is disconcerting. Our respect for it is mingled with admiration of our own long-suffering. Comfort, luxury, convenience, counselled its removal; it owes its conservation to a lenient reliance on the hereafter. Its 'patient continuance' in uselessness impresses us.[25] For how

[25] Romans 2. 7: 'To them who by patient continuance in well doing seek for glory and honour and immortality, [God will give] eternal life'.

strong is the impulse in living things to get done with themselves when their best is accomplished! 'The flower fadeth' — in that is its happiness.[26] The pathos of life lies, not in its transience, rather in its survival of beauty, its monotony, its instinct for the formation of habits.[27] It is natural that the blossom should scatter and the leaf drift. We suffer with the withering flowers that linger, the uncomely creatures that cannot remove, the things that corrupt and do not find a grave, that alter, and yet wane not nor slip away. If a traveller, roving our northern coasts in November, turn from one of the inlet coppices of its cliffs, silver with that curled up meadow-sweet and gold with wide-floundered fronds of blemished bracken, to the bare winter sea, he will learn the harshness of imperishable life. The great water lies as under a spell, stricken by its impotence to suffer change, to abandon itself to the passionate, capricious misery of the wind. It is sick of its own monotony; the currents of summer sunshine withdrawn, it would fain grow old, break up and perish. Its tides heave in lethargic revolt against the oppression of their own routine; eternity clings to it as a fetter.

It were not difficult to ponder till one pondered oneself into the paradox that nothing is useful till it has lost its use. From the moment anything is put aside its leavening potency begins. Our awe of the dead springs in part from the sense we have of their being no more subject to life's daily wear and tear. We think of them in the perfect employment of perfect leisure. Again it is the lumber on old faces that attracts us. The reason we feel so keenly the loss of even a commonplace, old acquaintance is that with him is destroyed so much of old-fashioned experience, philosophy fallen out of repute, and inconsequent religion. Evidence harasses us, tradition consoles. Today is for the craftsman, yesterday for the artist. We cannot reverence what we are ever handling. The sculptor sees his work as it will be when it cools into immortality. He who would attain distinction in the use of speech must have knowledge of the undisturbed, monumental languages. The England we touch and converse with today is not our country. Our country is where the moth and worm corrupt, on the battlefield, and in the crypt.

Precious as we have proved our unprofitable effects, we can by no means unreservedly maintain that all things fallen into discredit should be harboured in hope of future spiritual authority. We must discriminate between dead and lively lumber. Dead lumber is that which, before it became lumber, fatigued and disgusted us; lively lumber is that which in its pre-lumber stage gave us interest and delight. What once genuinely excited us may be spared, so only it pertained not to controversy; for controversy, as St Paul points out, should set before close

---

[26] Isaiah 40. 8: 'The grass withereth, the flower fadeth: but the word of our God shall stand for ever'.

[27] An echo of Walter Pater's 'Conclusion' to *The Renaissance*: 'it might even be said that our failure is to form habits'. Walter Pater, *The Renaissance: Studies in Art and Poetry* [1893], ed. by Donald L. Hill (Berkeley: University of California Press, 1980), 189.

of day. But any work of art, utensil, instrument, or paper that depressed us or wrought us evil, should, when its term is over, be obliterated cleanly as by flame. Though we would deal tenderly with the pious practice of, as it were, providing almshouses for our infirm and unserviceable chattels, it has, like other graceful customs, its abuse; we hoard documents less than intimate, and more than official. 'On ne peut écrire que les choses *dures*; quant aux choses *douces*, elles ne peuvent s'écrire et ce sont les seules choses amusantes.'[28] Truth, Marie Bashkirtseff! the only amusing things, and of them, though you affirm they cannot be written, your own journal affords delicious examples. In correspondence 'les choses dures' should be consigned to the waste-paper basket; 'les choses douces' to the pigeon-hole. We should be able to recur to favourite passages in our letters with the ease and familiarity with which we turn to favourite passages in our books. Instead of this possession of our friends' luminous suggestions and happy eloquence, we crowd our drawers with manuscripts which will never be handled till they are flung by impatient hands in basketfuls on the furnace.

To judge of this habit of accumulation in its fondness and extremity, we must take cognizance of it in the amassments of a lifetime, when the secret places of cabinets and bureaus expose black profiles no personal recollections can tint; miniatures of ladies who open on us the full sweetness of their wide, shining, trustful eyes; locks of hair, alas! not the shade of auburn of the miniatures, a cloudier brown, yet lovable in their strong-fibred curl — baffling and beautiful tokens! We cannot interpret; we should be more at home among the catacombs. From this cynical thought we, guardians or distributors of the worthless treasure of the dead, are recalled by the manifestation, 'mid official files, of a packet curiously corded with flushed ribbon, giving glimpses of a handwriting intricate as fine trellis. Love-letters, modernity! We have reached the heart of our mystery. Our 'dark tower' is upon us.[29] We attain the very essence and underlying reality of rubbish in a packet of yellow love-letters. Whether we read them or not matters little. They are the sacred writings, the civilizing scriptures of mankind. We do not open a Bible when we come upon it in foreign characters in a heathen land. We touch it and give thanks.

---

[28] From *Journal de Marie Bashkirtseff* (1887). Translated by Mathilde Blind as: 'one can only write *hard* things, *soft* things cannot be written, and they are the only things that are amusing to read' (*The Journal of Marie Bashkirtseff*, trans. by Mathilde Blind (London: Cassel & Company, 1890), pp. 78–79). Bashkirtseff (1858–1884) was a Ukrainian artist whose journals were phenomenally popular across Europe and translated into English in 1889.

[29] Most likely a reference to Robert Browning's 'Childe Roland to the Dark Tower Came' (1855), or to Shakespeare's *King Lear*, from which Browning took inspiration for this poem.

Effigies[30]

If men had not lost their sense of the perpetually renewed divineness of existence, they would not, as now, confine their interest to its more impassioned phases. But being no longer in continuous and veritable contact with life, they take stimulus from selected passages of experience; and the choice of propitious hour and season becomes a duty. Westminster Abbey itself,[31] so excellent a place of pilgrimage for all sorts and conditions of Englishmen at all times, has its secrets of initiation and approach. If you would be present when the great reliquary unlocks its most precious influences, you must mingle with the congregation on a Sunday afternoon, in the closing month of the year. From your seat in the choir, lighted only by tapers, look up to the far roofs, where the mists assemble and are blue. While the canticles rise, while the responses, caught in brief, pathetic chant, lose themselves in the hollow vistas of the building, you will feel Night enter like a worshipper. Sable-vested, eldest of things, as Milton saw her when she sat by Chaos,[32] the centuries have changed her nature: she has received into her original darkness and void their whole content; she has gathered their yearly flowers, their

---

[30] First published under the name Michael Field in *Art Review*, 3, March 1890, pp. 89–91. By Edith Cooper. The essay was based on two prose sketches in Cooper's hand documenting two separate visits to Westminster Abbey in December 1889, the first on 9 December to look at the effigies, the second on 31 December for the funeral of Robert Browning, who had died in Venice on 12 December.

[31] Westminster Abbey is one of the most important church buildings in Britain, the place in which the monarch is crowned and royalty and aristocrats buried. Geoffrey Chaucer was interred in a part of the South Transept, now known as 'Poets' Corner', and was followed by many of the great writers of English literature, including Dr Samuel Johnson, Edmund Spencer, Charles Dickens, and John Dryden.

[32] John Milton (1608–1674) was one of the greatest early modern English writers. Cooper here is echoing his masterpiece, *Paradise Lost* (1667/1674), Book II, ll. 959–63:

> when strait behold the Throne
> Of Chaos, and his dark pavilion spread
> Wide on the wasteful deep; with him Enthron'd
> Sat Sable-vested Night, eldest of things,
> The Consort of his Reign.

men and women are her heritage. She is no more outcast and pagan; the holiest relics are in her bosom. She is one of the *Mothers* now, one of the great pregnant powers of the universe — from her tombs and obscurity half the inspiration of mankind is born.

As you sit or kneel the solemn shadows come down through the arches, while the candles sink and soften their shine. This is the vital hour for the dead: a sense wakes in the monuments that reaches the living like a very touch. Sounds from the clouded chapels creep through the music as if ghosts walked among the notes of the organ. Only a few effigies are touched by the flickering light — notably Dryden's pale and dominant head.[33] Here and there a scroll, a flamboyant tablet, a tall human outline erect by the columns, attest the monumental wealth of the Abbey; but the sovereign sculptures lie withdrawn behind that aureate screen, dim in shade; and the Poets' choice corner is almost out of sight. Nevertheless our mind is with the sleepers, with rough Ben Jonson — 'rare Ben Jonson' — his earthy bulk, the firm set of feature,[34] the grand lines of individual fecundity; with gentle Spenser in his woe, in his honoured rest by the Thames side;[35] with Chaucer, quaint, shy, sincere, broad-hearted:[36] nor less do our thoughts turn to the kingly band, who mark our history with the compass of their lives, and themselves slumber on *in saecula saeculorum*.[37] Those whose full effigies remain are stretched on their slabs as if for eternal rest; they are placid and unworldly: some are beautiful. My imagination visited Queen Mary of Scots.[38] I could see the last winter daylight on her brow — that brow which mirrors every change of skies as it endures beneath a window of the Chantry.

And note, in these sculptures — quiet, contained, cold in substance — there is no trace of those qualities which are, as it were, the accidents of the universal End. There is no sinking of the flesh, no depression about the eyes, no frayed outline prophetic of corruption.

---

[33] John Dryden (1631–1700) was a poet, playwright, translator, and literary critic who was an influential literary figure in Restoration London.

[34] Ben Jonson (1572–1637) was an early modern dramatist and poet. His memorial stone in Westminster Abbey bears the inscription 'O rare Ben Jonson'.

[35] Edmund Spencer (1552/1553–1599) was a Tudor and Elizabethan poet most famous for his epic *The Faerie Queene* (1590, 1596).

[36] Geoffrey Chaucer (1340s–1400) was the great poet of mediaeval Britain and is considered to be the father of English literature.

[37] 'Unto the ages of ages'. The phrase appears numerous times in the Bible to express the eternal quality of God.

[38] Mary, Queen of Scots (1542–1587) was Queen of Scotland and a devout Catholic who was beheaded after being found guilty of a plot to assassinate Queen Elizabeth. Michael Field would publish a verse drama — *The Tragic Mary* (1890) — about her later the same year in which 'Effigies' was published.

The company in Edward the Confessor's Chapel,[39] in Henry the Seventh's,[40] and in the many minor chapels to the east, are not portraits but images — essentially conceptions. The sculptors have endowed them with the wholeness and serenity of art; for it is through art alone that a mortal can put on immortality, and yet remain in the world of creatures. The pleasure and confidence we experience by the side of memorial figures — 'the great doom's images,'[41] in a freer and more final sense than Shakspere[42] gave the phrase when he attached it to Duncan's corpse — are due to their ideality, victorious over the details of death as of life.

Now let us turn to another band, dwellers also in the dusk and remoteness of Westminster Abbey: effigies in wax, models of dead kings and queens, each a copy of some corruptible face with its lines of wear and custom.[43] 'O the heavy change,'[44] the creeping shudder, as we turn from the monuments of stone to this show of imitations.

Few sightseers get glimpse of a certain small room over one of the small chapels near Henry the Seventh's. It is a weird, desolate little chamber. We are saddened by the dusty finery of robes and paste-jewels, by fixed features, the closed and opened eyes, the garishness and ruin. Charles the Second fronts us as we mount the steps,[45] with his libertine degeneracy of visage and his pathetic Stuart eyes. At his side couches a Duke of Buckingham in the full array of his

---

[39] Edward the Confessor (*c.* 1003–1066) was one of the last Anglo-Saxon Kings of England. He commissioned the original Westminster Abbey.

[40] Henry VII (1457–1509) was King of England and the first monarch from the House of Tudor.

[41] This quotation comes Macduff's speech in Shakespeare's tragedy *Macbeth* (1606):

> Ring the alarum-bell! Murder and treason!
> Banquo and Donalbain! Malcolm, awake!
> Shake off this downy sleep, death's counterfeit,
> And look on death itself! Up, up, and see
> The great doom's image! Malcolm! Banquo!
> As from your graves rise up, and walk like sprites,
> To countenance this horror!
>
> (*Macbeth*, II. 3. 74–80)

[42] Cooper here uses the spelling that Shakespeare used in his own signature. It was adopted by many in the nineteenth century as being more 'authentic' than the standard modern spelling

[43] The wax effigies to which Cooper refers had been removed from the Church floor to the Upper Islip chapel in the 1840s and are now housed in the new Queen's Diamond Jubilee Galleries in the triforium.

[44] From John Milton's 'Lycidas' (1638).

[45] Charles II (1630–1685) was King of England after the Restoration of the monarchy in 1660. He was renowned for his hedonism and is known as 'the Merry Monarch'. His reputation suffered in the Victorian period from the negative appraisal of Whig historians, most notably Thomas Babbington Macaulay.

rank,[46] and death's sunken aspect spread over him — an imperishable corpse. The Duchess and her little waxen lad are in an opposite case,[47] and next to them a lady, whose rank and name I have forgotten, turning rigidly to an immovable parrot.[48] Queen Anne sits in stricken comfort,[49] no longer drinking tea, indifferent to the obedience of her 'three worlds,'[50] as she faces the bit of grey wall that encompasses her. Further on, without historical sequence, William and Mary stand together[51] — the whole distance of stationary death betwixt them, nevertheless. Old Elizabeth,[52] with wretched wizen form and 'lack-lustre eye'[53] fills a corner, and turns her head away with a dense glare: she is uninterested in her pearls, once strung by insatiable vanity; she is miserable as a lost spirit in polar hell; her pain and disappointment are ice. By her stands Nelson in the clothes worn at Trafalgar.[54] How tender the eyes are! They could even make appeal for a man's kiss;[55] and, though the body is so small, the lips have the heroic, rigid expressiveness of a bronze. The bold seaman, who did his duty, comes out from the trial of representation in a defaming material as easily as out of a sea-fight. But the others, his comrades in portraiture! if we stay with them but a few moments we feel 'chilly and grown old.'[56]

How different is monumental sleep from the perpetuation of life! The statues give us the form and presentment of our close; the waxworks mimic indelibly a transient existence. We have in an effigy the ideal lines of life with the *imprimatur* of death.

The meanest country, the most trivial in incident, assumes after sunset a dignity of aspect; the humble green hills of cultivation, dotted with sheep and scribbled over with hedgerows, lose all pettiness of detail when clothed in deep shadow

---

46 There are a number of Dukes of Buckingham who have monument or effigies in Westminster Abbey. From this description it is most likely to be Edmund Sheffield, Second Duke of Buckingham and Normanby (1716 –1735).

47 Catherine Sheffield, Duchess of Buckingham (1681–1743) and her son Robert Sheffield, Marquess of Normanby (1711–1715).

48 This is an effigy of Frances Teresa Stuart, Duchess of Richmond (1647–1702).

49 Anne (1665–1714), Queen of England, Scotland, and Ireland, and, after the Acts of Union in 1707, Queen of Great Britain and Ireland.

50 Most likely a misquotation from Alexander Pope's 'The Rape of the Lock' (1712), Canto III: 'Here thou, great ANNA! whom three realms obey, | Dost sometimes counsel take — and sometimes tea.' The three realms are England, Scotland, and Ireland.

51 King William III of England, Ireland, and Scotland, where he was William II (1650–1702) and his wife Queen Mary II of England, Ireland, and Scotland (1662–1694) who co-reined from 1689 until her death.

52 Queen Elizabeth I of England and Ireland (1533–1603).

53 The likely source here is Shakespeare's *As You Like It*, II. 2. 21.

54 Vice-Admiral Horatio Nelson (1758–1805), legendary naval commander who died in the Battle of Trafalgar.

55 As he was dying Nelson allegedly asked his flag captain, Thomas Hardy, to kiss him.

56 From Robert Browning's 'A Toccata of Galuppi's', in *Men and Women* (1855).

from the west. The clear, tranquil curve remains against the sky: the rest is obliterated in the majesty of night. In like manner death with its solemn mantle covers all trifling circumstance, caring only to insist on the simple supreme outline of our history, and even calling the golden heaven to its aid to define more sharply our relation with another world. Yet we have often been tempted, when bereaved of those we love, to wish that the accidents of human living should continue and be immortal; we are not ready to render to Time the things that are Time's in the faces and bodies of our friends. In such mood, if we could visit the Abbey, and pass from the tombs up into the museum of casts from mortality, into that little dusty room with its affrighting cases, we should be healed of our longings, our sickness of desire.

It is not pleasant, at service-time, when the candles, the music, the far-off voice of the reader accord in their low tones with the dead, to think of those half-lively demised people upstairs: it is shocking to hear the talk of men beneath that little dusty room, — it is an irritation to the nerves; we feel that the singular inhabitants are tortured and apprehensive; they might each cry, like Keats' Lorenzo —

'Many a chapel bell the hour is telling,
Paining me through: those sounds grow strange to me.'[57]

Repugnant, an insult to the modesty of nature, are such types of death-in-life. At the midnight hour, when the sculptured dead 'walk,' as we must fain believe, what incongruity, if the tall, plain figures meet the parodies of their flesh, and the forgotten chafing, dullness, or anguish of the past nod at them in their *doubles*! Glorianna herself dismounts her pile and goes assured,[58] imperial, through the Tudor Chapel: she is accosted by another, a woman in rich, dingy dress, her own state dress of three hundred years ago; just the colour and stuff, but smutted — 'foul,' her contemporaries would have said. She sees a distracted, bony face, and eyes stiff with age — a virgin, barren age. The likeness speaks to her: she could shake it as she once shook a dying countess in her bed.[59] 'How handsome you are, dear Self!' it says to her: 'you did not mind when I told you that in the year sixteen hundred. Why, you really have none of these wrinkles which the mirror branded across my heart when I saw them; nor have you a thinness about the jaw; and you do not turn your head like a worried animal. You have not the pangs

---

[57] From John Keats's *Isabella, or the Pot of Basil* (1818), ll. 311–12.

[58] Queen Elizabeth I was also known as Gloriana.

[59] Catherine Howard, Countess of Nottingham (1547–1603) was the lady-in-waiting and confidante of Queen Elizabeth I. There is a legend that the Queen had given a ring to her favourite courtier (and, many believe, her lover), Robert Devereux, 2nd Earl of Essex, that he could send to her if he ever found himself in trouble. Just before his execution for Treason in 1601 he attempted to send the ring to the Queen, but it found its way to the Countess, who did not inform Elizabeth, as Howard's husband the Count of Nottingham was a sworn enemy of Essex. She is said to have confessed this two years later on her deathbed and the Queen reacted furiously, shaking her and telling her that 'May God forgive you, Madam, but I never can'.

of starvation in your muscles; you have not known years of profitless love, nor days of dying on the floor. Won't you acknowledge me, Glorianna? I am old Queen Bess, the most beautiful woman of her time — alas, alas!' The royal form addressed is silent; then, with a moan such as we hear among the rocks of a cave, she turns away in soliloquy: 'I must have come too near my cousin Mary's tomb for such disaster to have fallen me.[60] I will lie down.'

We share her feelings; we cry *Avaunt!* from the depths of our souls when we face these unreal mockeries.

'Let the earth hide thee!'[61] Such is the entreaty with which ghosts are met — they who have passed through the experience of death, undergone and been vanquished by the grave, who rise on the vision of men after uttermost transformation. The Abbey waxworks are far more terrible than ghosts. They have known life: it is a thing of the past, yet they have not lost its temporality; its expressions are mummied, egregiously embalmed. For — arrest corruption, stop one of Nature's processes, bid her slacken her pace, and the penalty is the incongruous and the grotesque. The peering framework of the skeleton hurts less in exposure than the stationary hideousness of the mask. The ways of nature are true and righteous altogether, so are the ways of art, though the methods of each are opposed. The one scatters to recombine, the other synthesises to liberate. The falling dust of the corse[62] asserts nature's method in its swiftness and indiscrimination; the fixed effigy affirms the fine selective method of art, and both combine in the fulfilled and perfect monument. A symbol cannot be accepted in place of the veritable mould: a cenotaph[63] gives us the kind of chill we experience from contact with a hollow heart. Men will not yield their lives to preserve it from the spoiler; they will die at the altar for the sake of the bones beneath its pavement. Yet there are Englishmen who would have Westminster Abbey swept of its monuments, who complain that they damage its architectural beauty. True, yet they make its walls half human in appeal and invincible against neglect. Something can be said even for the unfamed monuments, so lovable in their crudity and shapelessness, so resembling the religion to which they are witnesses, so protesting, so individual. We suffer doggerel on the gravestones and weep over it: Gray himself, when he attempted the composition of his own epitaph, fell into

[60] In 1568 Mary Queen of Scots appealed to her cousin Queen Elizabeth for her help to reclaim her throne after she was forced to abdicate following her trial and conviction for her part in the murder of Lord Darnley. Mary was kept in custody by Elizabeth for the next eighteen years before being tried and executed for an alleged plot to execute her cousin. The suggestion here is that Elizabeth feels cursed and wracked with guilt for having betrayed her cousin.

[61] William Shakespeare, *Macbeth*, III. 4. 92. Macbeth's words to Banquo's ghost. The previous sentence's 'unreal mockeries' echoes Macbeth's words to the ghost a few lines later.

[62] The term corse is another (now obsolete) word for a corpse.

[63] A term for a monument which is most often used to commemorate those who died elsewhere, particularly in war.

stilted commonplace, which is scholar's doggerel.[64] Tolerance is an essential element in piety: the idols that have influenced the fate of nations have been squalid often and obese. They died — those second-rate admirals, soldiers, statesmen, and were buried under monstrous heaps of stone; we would not disturb them. Through them, we, by proxy, can lie under the shadow of the arches. They are laid there that we, by patience and comfort of their sepulchres, may have hope. Their painful and unpicturesque lives are not without significance. Westminster Abbey is a record of English life, not a Pantheon;[65] and to be a faithful record, it must devote large space to the fantastic and the commonplace. Presentations of even extravagant and unlovely sorrow may be suffered with a humorous patience. Art is not made a liar when a militant skeleton is withdrawn from his vault to shake his bones and weapon at a fair woman; the spirit of Hamlet is in that mason's work: 'Now get you to my lady's chamber, and tell her, let her paint an inch thick, to this favour she must come: make her laugh at that.'[66]

Let not the zeal of eliminating therefore possess us. The look of crowd about the Abbey suggests the fulness of the ages from which it has gathered its relics: the contest for place is stimulating.

It has been suggested that there should be no more burials within its precincts, on the score of health. If it be unhealthy to draw near to the dead, let the living leave them; let them be visited as we visit Paestum,[67] with a trembling anxiety. The little singing-boys and the white-robed clergy may officiate elsewhere — not elsewhere can we touch sacramentally our accumulated past. Shall we be kept by terror of a pestilence from communicating with eternal things? Let the organ cease, if it must, and the 'choir invisible' remain![68]

As for those who ventured to intrude the question of health when the body of a great poet was on its way to sepulchre at Westminster — the reek of them goes up to heaven; one fears that they should infect, not a neighbourhood, but a whole nation, with, not their physical remains, but the unforgivable thoughts of their hearts.[69] The Church Catholic is founded on relics, on the worship of the dead: one marvels not that she endures; she has recognised the gulf fixed between the

---

64 This appears to refer to the final three stanzas of Thomas Gray's 'Elegy Written in a Country Churchyard' (1751), entitled 'The Epitaph' and added to the second, revised version of the poem.

65 The Pantheon, an Ancient Roman temple, was a place of important burials from the sixteenth century onwards. It was a model for the Panthéon in Paris which, after the French Revolution, was used as a mausoleum for the most important citizens of the Republic.

66 William Shakespeare, *Hamlet*, v. 1. 188–90. The final lines of Hamlet's 'Alas, poor Yorick' speech.

67 An Ancient Greek city located in what is now the Campania region of Italy. It is the home of three Doric temples and was an important destination for many travellers.

68 George Eliot, 'Oh May I Join the Choir Invisible' (*The Legend of Jubal and Other Poems*, 1878).

69 There was some debate in the press about the unsanitary decision to inter Browning's mortal

church and the sanitorium; she apportions the worshipper cold stone and damp, ghastly light, and creeping odours from the tombs — her incense, her illuminations are for the shrine. To disturb bones, to forbid the increase and store of mortal relics, is to put away from us what is concrete in religion.

. . . . .

We[70] are fresh from a grave in the rich acre of Poets' Corner. Who that was present at the burial of Robert Browning could deny the elevation given to ceremony by the presence of the sculptured dead? Recall the crises of that last service. The tolling bell made blind plunges down through space; there was a hush — human breath waiting, withdrawing itself from the air, becoming a reserve power, tragic, perceptible. The great expectation was motionless, while the mist kept steady and dense above the arches. At last we recognised the labouring movement of those who bore, under screen of the luminous purple covering, the small, octagonal coffin, crossed with violets — dark some, and some dim — wreathed with premature, frail lilac, to its station before the golden altar. During that solemn rest under the lantern, it was well to feel there was another throng than that of the curious or eager spectators — a throng represented in the persons of long-past statesmen and poets. It was well indeed to turn from the row of vivid pressmen under the altar-rail, note-books in hand, typifying by their very position the sacrilege of the age, to the unemployed and timeless company overhead. So, one meditated, would the famous spirits of Elysium have received a newcomer,[71] without eagerness and without curiosity.

Again, when the grave was closed round its treasure, and the words, 'Earth to earth, ashes to ashes, dust to dust,' fell on the ear — themselves smiting like shards, in their outrage on our mortal nature — the sight of Ben Jonson's sturdy front was a beacon of triumph. He is said to have been buried upright, with the ruddy head erect, for the Last Trump.[72] Square-set against every kind of annihilation after near three centuries, his bust was a dramatic comment on hopelessness.

---

remains in Westminster three weeks after he had died. Sir Robert Rawlinson, a sanitary engineer, argued that the advanced decomposition of the corpse posed a public health risk. See Samantha Matthews, *Poetical Remains: Poets' Graves, Bodies, and Books in the Nineteenth Century* (Oxford: Oxford University Press, 2004), pp. 238–40.

[70] This final section of 'Effigies' is adapted from the entry Cooper penned in 'Works and Days' after they had attended Browning's funeral. Michael Field [EC], 'Works and Days', BL Add. MS 46778, fols 1r–3v (1 Jan 1890).

[71] Elysium was, in Greek Mythology, a paradise to whom the gods sent those whom they had made immortal.

[72] Ben Jonson was buried upright in the Abbey. This is thought to be because he was too poor to afford the space for a horizontal burial. On 'Last Trump', see above, n. 21.

After all rites came the elemental music, the elegiac yet confident words, of Watts's hymn —

'O God, our help in ages past,
Our hope for years to come.'[73]

We, the living, on the rim of a new year — a black crowd, minute under the great walls and roof of the Abbey — sang as we looked before us into the future; above us, just over the clustered, singing heads, stood larger figures, fewer, white with unsunned whiteness — the assembly of the sculptured dead, attesting in eloquent silence the unison of the Past with the prophetic Present, as they both turn to Him, 'the ineffable Name.'[74] Last of all came the 'Dead March'[75] — the muffled thunder of it like a far-off avalanche among the stony heights of the tower and transepts, with something in it of apotheosis, of divine reception to a soul in worlds away.

I paused, after passing the new tomb, near Shakspere's monument. The finger of the royal dramatist points to the writing in his hand: —

'The cloud-capped towers, the gorgeous palaces,
The solemn temples, the great globe itself,
Yea, all that it inherits, shall dissolve,
And, like an insubstantial pageant faded,
Leave not a rack behind.'[76]

On the opposite wall is another writing, held forth by corpulent Handel: 'I know that my Redeemer liveth.'[77] The great poet, whose open grave was hard by, had learnt the Scripture displayed by each hand of stone. Yet it was not so much the transience as the inadequacy, the initial character of mortal life, that affected him; and the work of redemption was to him

'God's task to make the heavenly period
Perfect the earthen.'[78]

---

[73] Isaac Watts, 'Our God, Our Help in Ages Past' (1708).

[74] In the Bible the name of the God of Israel is spelt יהוה (in English YHVH) and there is no consensus as to pronunciation, hence it is the 'ineffable' name of God.

[75] 'The Dead March' from George Frideric Handel's oratorio *Saul* (1739), which is played at state funerals in Westminster Abbey.

[76] William Shakespeare, *The Tempest*, IV. 1. 152–56.

[77] The composer Georg Frideric Handel (1685–1759) is buried in the south transept of Westminster Abbey. 'I know that my Redeemer liveth' (a quotation from Job 19. 25 which also appears in the Church of England's An Order for the Burial of the Dead) is an aria for soprano from the third part of Handel's oratorio *Messiah* (1741).

[78] From Robert Browning's poem 'A Grammarian's Funeral' (1855).

The Fate of the Crossways[79]

The roads met and crossed in front of an angle of wayside grass, across which ran the wall of an olive-farm. Along the top of this wall a dozen or more pollard cypresses grew together,[80] the elastic forwardness of their growth restrained by informal wattles. Two cypresses, unstinted in height, stood erect at either end of the dark hedge, with beautiful formality like towers, a little in advance of the others, since the wall made a shallow curve just where they rose. Against the wall, half-way up its grey surface, a stone seat had been built, a seat transformed by weather and use almost to a natural object.

It seemed as if the builders expected that many people would sit down on the long bench at that place; yet as I approached I only saw one figure in the centre — a woman's. Her dress was dark and her thin fingers lay on it at the knee, quite white and without movement of any kind. Her feet had such hold of the ground they seemed to chain it. But the veil round her head was fluttering and milky, her pale eyeballs drew in the light till they were full of its beatitude, and the whole face conveyed to the beholder such activity of an indwelling mind, in spite of the unusual features, that the impression weighed down one's breath. She seemed to be a goddess, to belong to the universe just by the way she sat in that common afternoon glow, beside that bit of wall.

I could not speak to her, and she did not move to look at me, although I felt she drew me into her eyes, as she drew the light. I stood before her, because I had to choose my road, for I was at crossways in my journey. Should I turn to right or left? As I hesitated and cast about, a most singular sense came over me that the seat was crowded. I could see nothing; but as one feels there is teeming life in the grass, or in the stream, when one's perception is sensitive with its own life, so I felt that seat occupied by presences, from the woman's figure in the centre to the cypress towers at each end. And I knew that as I was drawn into the goddess's

---

[79] Written by Cooper on 25 April 1895 (Michael Field [EC], 'Works and Days', BL Add. MS 46783, fol. 58r). Submitted to *The Pageant*. First published under the name Michael Field in *The Dial*, 5, 1897, p. 11.

[80] A tree which has had its branches removed to encourage new growth is a pollard.

eyes like the light, so these unseen companions of hers hung on my choice as earthly things hang on the changes of the weather. With a fear that was nearly blind, and intensity that was actual anguish, I made my choice I will not say whether to right or left.

But I had not gone far along the road, before all the fierce dogs in the neighbouring farms began to howl in chorus, as if it had been midnight instead of afternoon. I looked back — the woman was gone and the seat was empty with the extreme voidness of a church at mid-day.

Then the truth came to me clear.

I had been in the presence of Hecate[81] — the dogs howled again — of Hecate and the Souls of the Dead who wander with her.

I sank down on my new road — if with adoration or mere collapse I cannot tell.

Ye Fates of the Wheel of Necessity, Clotho, Lachesis and Atropa,[82] ye are nothing as compared with the Fate of the Crossways, Hecate, who wanders with the Dead.

The dogs no longer howled, but whimpered, and I went on direct.

[81] Hecate is an Ancient Greek goddess associated with magic, necromancy, and crossways.

[82] In Greek myth Clotho, Lachesis, and Atropa are the three Fates who spin the web of life.

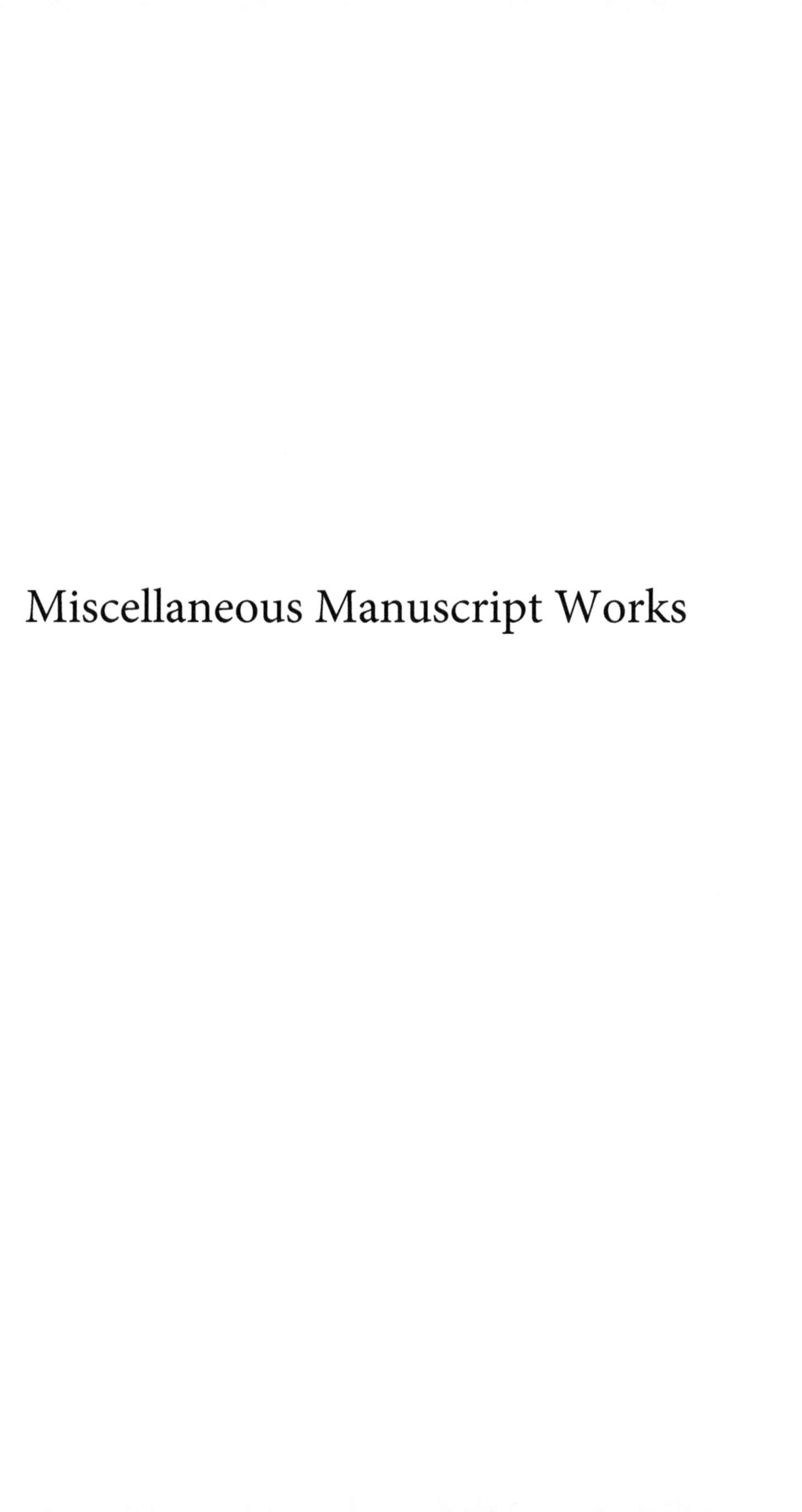

Miscellaneous Manuscript Works

~

Rhythm[1]

'We did not come together, and we cannot go together.'

An old woman said this to me two days after the burial of her husband.

She had lost many children. I tried to recall these to her. She remembered them as one remembers the violets gathered for one in youth — with a flush of pleasure, no distinctness. She was very old. Before her lay a few more years at the washing tub, and then the grave.

No one wanted her to live. She lodged under the roof of a sickly married son, with many little ones of his own to feed.

In her cold room at nights she did not read her Bible — she thought of her husband's body slowly rotting in the churchyard. When she went down to the warm house-place it was to rock the baby to sleep by the fire.

'We did not come together and we cannot go together.'

Life had taught her one of its own rhythmic laws.

[1] Written by Bradley on 25 September 1893 (date given in KB's hand, Oxford, Bodleian Libraries, MS Eng. misc. c. 303). Appears in both manuscript and as a typescript. This prose poem was seemingly accepted by Henry Harland for the second volume of the *Yellow Book*, but subsequently withdrawn by Bradley. See Introduction (pp. 28–29) for an account of this episode.

A Death Bed[2]

One wondered how she would die. Her life had been full of uncriminal vice. She had a bitter tongue and moments of fantastic rage. She was a monthly nurse,[3] an old, peaked, thin woman, with occasionally an exquisite, outbreaking smile. She had herself been gay in youth; of her daughters only one had been married before becoming a mother. It was my custom to visit her about six times a year: during one of these visits made on a sharp, frosty morning, she told me that whatever she gave her husband for dinner, she always served it to him hot. Then I understood why he seemed lonesome when a cruel, cancerous disease, involving operation, kept her away from him three months in hospital. After her return from the hospital she rallied: for a year or two she was wheeled to communion on fine Sundays. Suddenly she fell sick of her last sickness. The house became loathsome. Her children complained they were too tired after their day's work to sit up with her. It was impossible to feed her, except through an artificial opening in the side. But she was not left to starve. One of her neighbours, a tender, homely woman, accustomed to laying out the dead, came daily and fed her through the open wound. She was not thanked. For four days she continued, feeding, washing, waiting for the end. On the fifth morning her patient awoke, from a sleep of thirteen hours, inquisitive — restless.

'Are you better?'

'No.'

'Are you happy?'

'No.'

---

[2] Oxford, Bodleian Libraries, MS Eng. misc. c. 303 Written by Bradley *c.* 1893. A manuscript and typescript version exist. At the bottom of the typescript, in a hand that resembles that of Mary Costelloe, there is a critique of the sketch. Seeing as we know that Bradley and Cooper solicited feedback on their *croquis* from Berenson it is likely that he dictated these thoughts to Costelloe: 'It seems to me that the [illegible] wants unity of impression — you begin in her mind, then introduce yourself, and then at the end the other woman hears her talk. I didn't like "outbreaking" smile, it is too strong — so also "uncriminal vice," and "cuddled". The realism of the wound is (to me) too much — the effect is too strong.'

[3] A now-obsolete term for a nurse employed for the postpartum period.

'Then pray, before it is too late. All night I have been praying for you.'

'Praying for me, *really*?'

'Yes, and do you pray?'

'I will' — but with the knowledge that Love was near her, she cuddled up and went to sleep.

On her face in death there was the strange, outbreaking smile.

Sunset[4]

As a child I loved to sit in the window-seat and watch the sky. I liked the way in which the clouds interpenetrate without pushing each other out of place. One day my mother came up to me and asked:

'What do you see?'

'Nothing.'

'But God lives there.'

'Then,' I answered crossly, 'I have seen God.'

And I continued watching.

But the conversation formed the basis of a very curious dream, dreamed in manhood, years after it had taken place. I arrived in the midst of things, beginning well on in the story, with a strong purpose at my heart. I was on a visit to fairy-land, and I knew definitely what had brought me there. I wanted to see God, and I had been assured by scientific men, it was only the fairies who had any acquaintance with Him. I walked through an unnatural forest that broke into elfin forms. Robin Goodfellow was there and the rest.[5] I felt they would have plenty of smart answers, but I could not put my question to them. It seemed such a foolish question, now the time came for me to put it, I grew hot and fought my way through the thorny brushwood as fast as possible. The wood soon lay in my rear, and I found myself facing an old Etruscan Gate,[6] with grey olive-groves shining through. 'Ah,' I thought, 'this is a better dream,' and passing quickly through the gate, for I recognised the path, I made my way through the olives to a high terrace-walk. There, propped against the stones of an unused, half-decayed church, I rested and looked out. It was evening. The vineyards of the mid-plain were yellow and lustrous, the sprinkled mountain cities scintillated in the sun. Unconsciously I fell into my old habit of watching. It annoyed me when a voice

[4] Oxford, Bodleian Libraries, MS Eng. misc. c. 303. Written by Bradley *c.* 1893. It exists as both a manuscript and a typescript.

[5] Robin Goodfellow, also known as Puck, was a mischievous fairy in English folklore.

[6] The Etruscans were an ancient civilization (ninth to first centuries BC) in the area of the Italian peninsula which, more-or-less, maps on to the region now known as Tuscany.

close to my ear said, as it seemed to me, in a resonant ironical tone — 'Can I do anything for you?' I turned round sharply — a traveller in a grey suit similar to my own was seated on the ledge beside me. 'Can I be of any service to you?' he repeated, 'your secret has been made known to me: you would see God!' With the sunset still making red globules in my eyes, I turned to the quiet figure, and trembled. I saw he was not 'sincerely so'. I saw that the felt hat and ordinary travelling suit were worn as a ghost would wear them. A ghost who wished to engage in easy conversation with his friend. The luminous eyes were deprecating.

'Can I do anything for you?'

'Nothing: leave me alone.'

But there were tears in my eyes as I turned them back towards the universe, to watch, and to wonder as of old.

Dies Irae[7]

I have always been a lover of daybreak, but I cannot get up early; I am too sickly. I remember a June morning in boyhood. My three brothers had left me, whilst a delicate crêpe was still hanging over the toneless atmosphere. They went to see the sun rise over the fells. I felt bitter and afraid, and, curling myself up in bed, I made a picture of the Dies Irae.[8] It was always over the Roman Campagna that I saw the onslaught of that day — the huge tomb of Caecilia Metella stood out immovable.[9] With intense curiosity I waited for the first, little crack in the solid masonry.[10] 'Will it fall on her?' I speculated, 'or will she come out, roused up by the noise, as if it were a simple earthquake?' So very far, it seemed to me, she had to come. That was why there was no quaver in the outline of her tomb. I waited and looked through all that silver space on to the Alban hills. The light was rising steadily without fleck of sunshine, providing no shelter as it travelled, forcing the thinnest blade of grass to assert itself. Volume after volume of undazzling clarity — what would become of it? There was no room on the little plain for the unwrapping of its tides? They pressed and swelled on to me like a wind, like the blast of a trumpet, and in response as from the four quarters of the earth, there was a great cry; — deprecating, ribald, delirious, it hissed up to me like water splashed against hot metal.

And Caecilia Metella?

Her tomb stood impenetrable. It was useless waiting any longer. I came away.

---

[7] Oxford, Bodleian Libraries, MS Eng. misc. c. 303. Written by Bradley *c.* 1893. There are two versions, one in Bradley's hand, the other typed.

[8] 'Day of Wrath' (Latin), or the Day of Judgement, marks, in Christianity, the Second Coming of Christ and the ultimate judgement of God. It is a prayer sequence in the Latin church that has been a staple of choral musical settings, in particular the Requiem Mass.

[9] The tomb of Caecilia Metella — the daughter of the Roman Consul Quintus Caecilius Metellus Creticus and wife of Marcus Licinius Crassus, a senior Roman official — lies on the Via Appia outside of Rome. We have corrected Bradley's misspelling of the first name as 'Cecilia'.

[10] It is traditionally believed that on the Day of Judgement the dead will emerge from broken tombs and graves.

Let Me Help You Along[11]

'Let me help you along; you are looking so weary' — and with rapid decision he drew her arm through his; then, still doubting if he had quite secured it, he caught her wrist imperiously in his right hand, and held her fast by his side.

This bit of boldness was curious from him, for he had about him a great quiet and modesty; he had chosen never to be married, and was honourable as he was courteous. She, on her part, would never have dreamt of giving him love: but they had been much together and their natures were in unison at that time.

He plunged into the darkness for a troop of friends lagged behind, and he wished to be safe from their notice. The night was black, with a pile like velvet that hindered the shining of the lamps as a carriage passed, and that almost seemed to muffle sound.

Through her glove she felt his pulse beat, thrill on thrill — a magnetism shaking the nerves, nourishing pleasure. The vital force of nature struck her wrist; the contact gave her a sense of oneness with her companion and with the whole earth.

His pulse spoke for him — he let himself go now if never again with the sweep of that stream of being from which he had chosen to sever his life. He was out on a holiday, he knew it was ending, that he and she would say goodbye tomorrow — these were facts and he was still young.

When they got home, she drew her arm away the moment his grasp loosened from her wrist — drew it away quickly as the light sloped through the pane above the door, and then said in her friendly voice:

'Thank you for having helped me along.'

[11] Untitled in MS. Oxford, Bodleian Libraries, MS Eng. misc. c. 303. Written by Cooper *c.* 1893.

Quai d'Anjou[12]

Her fellow-watcher was called away, and she was asked would she remain with the corpse. She nodded to show she would not be afraid, and fixed her eyes on it steadily.

All she saw was a dark head laid deep in the hollow of the large French pillow, the line of the sheets and ordinary coverlet below the beard, and, where the heave of the chest showed, a large crucifix. The very thick lashes lay in settled fringes on the cheek — that was the only sign of death. The girl sat quite still as she had been left by her fellow-watcher. She would have liked to remain so, by herself without stirring — and she knew that when she became an old woman she would desire the same thing.

[12] Oxford, Bodleian Libraries, MS Eng. misc. c. 303. Quai d'Anjou is a dockside area in Paris, running along the Seine. While the version in misc. c. 303 is in the hand of EC, another copy exists in 'Works and Days' in the hand of KB, where it is prefaced by the following note: 'This November 11th twenty six years ago Alfred Gérente died: I have been looking at the old journals. Goodness. What a sentimental girl I was. It's marvellous God suffers such creatures to continue.

How diffuse, and boring, and ridiculous youth is! And yet the passion of those days, in the midst of all this folly, was perfectly genuine. Why then do I feel that past self break into dust as I read?' (Michael Field [KB], 'Works and Days', BL Add. MS 46782, fol. 133r (11 Nov 1894)).

Alfred Gérente (1821–1868) was an artist in stained glass who designed windows for Notre-Dame. During her stay in Paris in 1868 (while studying at the Collège de France), Bradley became infatuated with this man, who was twenty-five years her senior, and a widower. He died unexpectedly on 11 November 1868. Bradley viewed his body at Quai d'Anjou, recounting the death-bed scene in her diary, expressing resentment towards family members being present and admiring Gérente's corpse: 'I should have loved to be all alone, learning these glorious lineaments by heart' (Michael Field [KB], 'Works and Days', BL. Add. MS 46776, 1868–69, fol. 23r). Bradley's journal from this period later became Volume One of the full-scale diary project of 'Works and Days'.

Between Rome and Ancona[13]

They were in a railway-carriage, and were travelling from Rome to the Adriatic Marches: two were women, the third a quite young man. Clearly there was a confidential relation between the fair-haired woman and the young man, who were sitting side by side at one end of the carriage, while their fellow-traveller sat at the other end, with a window all to herself.

She looked out: a deep plain like an arena curved among stunted peaks of a very bad, grey colour; the plain was filled with a coming harvest of maize, and

---

[13] Untitled in MS. Oxford, Bodleian Libraries, MS Eng. misc. c. 303. Written by Cooper in August 1893. The couple here are clearly modelled on Berenson and Costelloe, while Cooper is the unhappy woman sitting alone. For more on this dynamic see the Introduction (pp. 6–8). The landscape they are travelling through around Celano is a drained lake, not a crater, as Cooper suggests. It is uncertain whether she was mistaken or whether she altered the landscape to fit the bitter and scarring nature of the experience.

This appears to be one of those instances in which Cooper wrote prose and Bradley wrote poetry inspired by shared fraught emotions. On 19 August 1893, Bradley writes: 'For P. [Pussie, i.e., Cooper] croquis, for me, moments and cries and beyond these some new verse forms for wh I wait God to give the body' (Michael Field [KB], 'Works and Days', BL Add. MS 46781, fol. 53v). She follows this with the poem 'Meeting at Bergamo', which begins with the line 'We had parted at Ancona' (54r). The poem was later published in Michael Field, *Wild Honey from Various Thyme* (London: T. Fisher Unwin, 1908), pp. 117–18. We reproduce the published version:

We had parted at Ancona, for there was so much to see —
The Love Temple built about Isotta's tomb at Rimini,
With Correggio's dome of angels he had scarcely time to show:
It was simpler to be candid … When we met at Bergamo,

He was sure we had been happy? — 'Oh, most happy!' How it shined
On the solid chestnut-ramparts — [all was just as he divined]
On the grass an emerald instant, on the wide plain at our feet
That we gave our voices' jar to! Suddenly I said, 'Be sweet,

Be yourself.' — 'I will.' The willing cleared the temples of their spite,
And his eyes were given to me rich in their caressing light;
Dropt the devil, dropt the malice, and I drank his beauty in.
Oh, what seals there are to open — not to open them is sin!

above the crops aspen-poplars grew, ill-balanced in shape, but exquisitely sensitive in every motion. The sky was not so much blue as a whitened purple — an impure, burning sky: and the air could hardly carry the heat; sometimes indeed it seemed to throw down its burthen flat on the Earth in desperation. The plain was an old crater, the peaks once formed the rim of the enormous volcano — and the time of year was June.

The history of the spot was all of fire — and the present was a glow of unmitigated sun. But this was not all: the present was making history as torrid as that which the country confessed in its every line and tint. The girl at the window looked out for long whiles, but in the end always turned toward the man and woman at the other window; and as her eyes rested on them she looked as if she hated one or the other, or both. Her face, indifferent on the surface, glowed deep like metal at white heat — and her expression of indifference did not deceive her companions; not the man, who very genuinely was her friend, and drawn to her by many affinities of temperament; nor the fair-haired woman who possessed his love. This love of his was a passion that had been kept platonic and had become with time an habitual clinging to a strong serviceable nature and to a beautiful face. It was unconventional, for the fair-haired woman was a wife, who lived no longer with her husband.

Men agree best with women who are their complete opposites; who give them the full advantage of a different sex; in whom their ideas charm them as instincts — and this absolute unlikeness was the ground of harmony between the two travelling-companions seated together: on the other hand the girl who watched them was far too like the man she loved for him to love her — even too much like him for them to be friends. They had mutual understanding of what each other thought and felt, but they chafed each other almost as much as they animated. The chosen woman was old-fashioned in her womanhood, but very independent in her actions; the girl was of a newer type of womanhood, but old-fashioned in her conduct — leaving circumstance to settle her life. The young man's interest was aggravated by this defect of character, and perhaps it was in a measure magnetically dominated by the strength of her passion for him.

The train went curving round the old crater, and at last stopped for a few moments at Celano, birthplace of that Thomas who wrote *Dies Irae*.[14] A sterner place it would be impossible to imagine: it stood out harsh on the purple sky, while its lava-rocks sloped toward the crater with an incline that suggested they went down to hell.

---

[14] In the original Cooper writes Peter, which we have corrected to Thomas. Thomas of Celano was a Franciscan friar and poet who wrote the medieval Latin hymn 'Dies Irae'. See also note 8 above.

Of course the great poem rolled through each of the travellers' memories, naturally they talked of it, and connected the intensity of its images of conflagration with the volcanic home of its writer.

Dies irae, dies illa![15] The words were no longer of the future — no longer of *that* day but of *this*! So at least the girl felt, for judgement that burns through all covering of secrets had come on her: she realised her mortal passion for the man who could not be hers, her hatred for her fair-haired friend — above all she realised that the beloved man and the hated woman saw as openly as she herself the privacies of her own nature.

She had hidden nothing that was not made manifest: fire was at its work of desecration, do all she could to restrain it, for the fire within her blazed up in response to the fire of this Italian day, among fire-blighted hills as naked as her own soul. She knew that in every glance she revealed what she experienced absolutely, with final truth. The ages might dissolve in smoke when their time came! What was that to her! She herself, her personality, had dissolved in self-confession before the awful flames of a single love and hate. O Sibyl, witness of the Last Day, has your woman's heart ever suffered imaginatively as this girl's actually did![16]

She endured the splendid shame of loving, the implacable shame of hating; and she who was closely reticent by habit underwent the torments of her doom before the very eyes that made her shrivel up, like a parched scroll, with the sense of exposure to uttermost publicity — so personal and at the same time so universal was the judgement that for her loomed in the sunshine, loomed over the ashen slopes as the train moved on through the valleys — while the air in the travelling-compartment become brutally stupid with the smouldering of afternoon.

No-one spoke: a sigh that was the ghost of a groan broke now and again the incandescent lull of the hours; no other sound was audible, except the rattling pant of the train. The lovers still sat together, and the girl watched them from time to time. At last the woman laid her head — with a glance of triumph towards her miserable friend — on the young man's shoulder: she slept, and as she slept she looked lovely and rose-coloured as a field of sainfoin.[17] The young man gazed fixedly out of his window and bore her head without pleasure, as if some masculine disgust at a false step chilled him. Only once his eyes met the girl's in a flash as brief as lightning and who knows how like it in essence. She had reached

[15] The opening line of the hymn, which translates as 'Day of Judgement! day of mourning!'.

[16] There were numerous Sibyls who were prophetesses in ancient Greece. The figure of Sibyl was appropriated in medieval Christian iconography as prophesising the Second Coming. In the third line of 'Dies Irae' it is stated that David and Sibyl will be witnesses on the Day of Judgement: '*Teste David cum Sibylla*'.

[17] A perennial herb (Old French 'healthy hay'), grown as stockfeed for cattle.

that pitch of phrenzy when an emotion becomes its opposite, when love is hate and hate itself finds its object precious. She was not very far from that still higher pitch of madness when emotion bursts into some act that has nothing to do with choice. She was in hell — not the hell of what is over and done with, but the living hell of what can and may be done under temptation.

The fair-haired woman woke up roseate from sleep and looked straight before her with satisfied eyes. It relieved the tension when she smiled at her lover and tried to persuade him, sportively and without mercy, to settle himself for a little sleep, as she had done. He looked forlorn, limp with fatigue, yet quite unlike sleeping, but to please her he closed his eyes. With something in the action emphasising that *she* did it and that no other woman could, she drew her long white forefinger across his eyebrows caressingly. If she had been the arch-fiend she could not have thought of anything more cruel to do as a sign of her possession; and there was a gay malice in the movement that made it intolerable. The girl clenched her hands; the very throb of murder quickened in her heart: then, with an effort she did not think she had power to make she turned her back on the couple and endured in herself all the agonies of a murderer while standing as if impassive, her eyes as hard as a corpse's, fixed on the broiling mountain-sides.

Suddenly, the horizon grew spacious, its light free, imponderable; the mountains seemed to retire up country and their curve to be driven back by what was not yet a breeze but the possibility of coolness.

Something very wonderful happened in the girl — a rush of every sense and feeling toward liberation, like that of the people in Limbo when Christ threw down the door and dazzled them.[18] *Castel a Mare*![19] — The Sea!

It glittered on into the very sky, it came with the divine sympathy of breezes toward the hot land, opaline as a spirit, yet stronger than the hills, it stretched across the girl's eyes, it filled her throat with refreshment, it gave her the hopefulness that motion can always inspire. Little sails waved to and fro with red suns on their blackness or yellow stars and moons on their cow-hide brown — there were even pictures in their folds that had been repeated for cycles by the Adriatic fishers.

These little sails mingled with the little rippling half-discs of light all over the top of the sea, played together a fantasia of merriment. The girl lent bare-headed out of the window, drinking in the brine through every pore, letting her passion go outside her and rock on the wind and sweeten itself from closeness; bathing

---

[18] In the period between Crucifixion and Resurrection Christ is believed to have descended into Hell (or in some accounts/translations Limbo) and granted salvation.

[19] Castle on the Sea. There is no place with this name around Pescara where their railway journey would have given them the first glimpse of the sea before they travelled north along the coast to Ancona.

her eyes in the tides, in the light of the divine presence that had burst on them in the midst of horror. Life swelled her breath, reached her heart — in her imagination added a cubit to her stature; made her lips fresh and kissed her to the roots of her hair.

How restful the sand of the shore, how the tamarisks were blown though like her hair;[20] how open the coast lay for her to watch! The stifling mountains were on the other side; they could not catch her any more between their infernal hollows, burn her, desecrate, judge, punish. She was saved by the lustre that had broken in on all this — to which she had rushed instinctively: the Adriatic!

When she sat down again, she looked at the two who were also looking toward the sea, and they were to her, for that moment, a man and woman who belonged to each other. She could meet the lover's eyes almost as the waves met hers — impartially, offering no evil.

Between Rome and Ancona she had passed through Condemnation and Redemption, among the physical surroundings of our Earth, but with the absoluteness of the spiritual world that is beyond Time and Space.

[20] A large, deciduous shrub, also known as salt cedar, that grows along the Mediterranean.

~

Wanting is — What?[21]

Three long steps had been cut in the steep, wooded rock and the year before…

But *this* year, as I sat on the low ground amid a matting of the close, rounded leaves of the golden saxifrage,[22] and looked up, I only saw a dribble as of a stalactite cavern from the topmost step; then the high stems of the willow-herb, its feathery seeds caught apparently in its own long fingers: in the middle of the second ledge an arum in a pot; and, on either side of the third steep, rocky step, osmunda,[23] lady-fern, a solitary root of alkanet,[24] water-avens.[25]

---

[21] Oxford, Bodleian Libraries, MS Eng. misc. c. 303. Written by Cooper *c.* 1893. The manuscript page has 'For That Moment Only' struck through above the title. The title comes from Browning's poem of the same name which serves as the prologue to his collection *Jocoseria* (1883):

Wanting is — what?
Summer redundant,
Blueness abundant,
— Where is the blot?
Beamy the world, yet a blank all the same,
— Framework which waits for a picture to frame:
What of the leafage, what of the flower?
Roses embowering with naught they embower!
Come then, complete incompletion, O comer,
Pant through the blueness, perfect the summer!
Breathe but one breath
Rose-beauty above,
And all that was death
Grows life, grows love,
Grows love!

Robert Browning, *Jocoseria* (London: Smith, Elder, & Co., 1883), p. 3. Cooper reviewed the collection favourably, which was the beginning of their friendship with Browning. Edith E. Cooper, '"Jocoseria," By Robert Browning', *Modern Thought*, 1 July 1883, pp. 297–300.

[22] Small herbaceous plant. The name translates from Latin as 'stone-breaker'.

[23] A deciduous fern.

[24] A green perennial with blue flowers when in bloom.

[25] Small wild flowers common to the British Isles from May to September.

Absolute stillness, save for the stalactite — dripping at the top! The place was not melancholy: the banks around that black stairway were covered to their very edges with abounding green. Sunshine lay in patches on the verdant leaves of the saxifrage, and the blossoms of the blue alkanet looked almost dewy —

Wanting was — what?

A Superstition[26]

'There is a Wishing-tree on that little hill,' I said. 'You can just see it.'

The young man who was walking with me struck his hands together and looked at me with an alert, unnatural smile. 'Oh, let us go there; it would be such fun.'

So he and I climbed on spongy mountain-grass in the direction I had pointed out. We were guests together in the same house, and had known each other but a few days. He was the grandson of two duchesses, the only son of an ill-used and beautiful woman. His eyes were blue; something in them rambled like wind through the sky on a summer day. Lank, bright hair edged the straining forehead, the mouth hung loose, but occasionally twitched the left cheek and eye from under a broad-ended strong moustache of the same colour as the hair. He was dressed in grey — a forlorn elegance, a gentleness of breed and of temper being apparent in the very way his clothes sat on him. A pathetic creature! For he had youth with none of the passions of youth; he was a poet with no poetic power, full of ambition in a world that could never be his, scrupulous so that his conscience befooled him, thoughtful to such a degree that his powers of observation were those of a baby. At college he broke down under the discipline of a tutor who was a casuist in moral philosophy. Nervous exhaustion, meeting exhaustion of blood, had blurred the effectiveness of his face completely so that expression haunted it rather than dwelt in the features, and his smile had the ghastliness of music to an old dance.

---

[26] Oxford, Bodleian Libraries, MS Eng. misc. c. 303. Written by Bradley *c.* 1893. Large parts of this sketch appear in an account of a holiday Bradley and Cooper took to the Lake District. 'Herbert' is based on Sidney de Vere Beauclerk (1866–1903), who privately published a slim volume, *Poems*, in 1897. In the account of the holiday, he recites his poetry to the other guests at the house in which they are staying and is met with hoots of laughter. 'Poor Sydney shrinks, deplores, and suffers like a dog of exquisite breed that men make a fool of'. He is not to be confused with Charles Sidney de Vere Beauclerk (1855–1934), a Jesuit priest who was, for a time, an associate of Frederick Rolfe. See Michael Field [EC/KB], 'Works and Days', BL Add. MS 46781, fols 58r–63r (Sept 1893).

We soon climbed the hill, for all his movements had rush in them; but as we came alongside the tree we were almost thrown backward by the congregated snort of a flock of wild fowl as they fled from our intrusion. At the same moment the flame of the setting sun, hidden as we ascended, struck toward our faces. Turning in pain from such violent light, we fronted the old holly. It was the sole tree to be seen on the fell: its trunk looked as if built of mountain-stone, its scant and obstinate leaves made a prickly sound to the wind — a chilling sound. It stood among rocks, sodden grass, weather-stained clumps of heath and mown bracken, lying in soft frizzles like those that strew a barber's floor. We were breathless when we reached it. Then Herbert panted in his deprecating voice 'I must have a short time to prepare,' and struck away to the left, while I from my seat on a boulder looked across the valleys and mountains and distant lake. From time to time I glanced round: the grey figure was pacing rapidly at ten yards off, with twitching fingers and responsible face, backward and forward; now and then there was a nod, now and then I saw the escape of a fervent smile. The moments went by, the pacing went on. The sun sank behind a mountain, then the whole rippling mountain-line became sympathetic, as if it had been drawn by a hand that shook with passion at the beauty it expressed. The sounds from the valley came up close to the ear, yet with a refinement that solemnised the humblest among them. From the height where I sat the wild ducks on the little tarn below looked like crumbs broken on the water. Herbert's figure seemed shut out from this wonderful evening loveliness; one could tell from his stoop that his perceptions were blank while his thoughts were weighing the good wishes that rose up in him for his beloved mother, and for every friend and relative. There was something ironic in the impassive old tree as it stood ready for the confidences of its devotee.

The air was tranquil, the sun had set in resigned peace: Herbert alone was distracted and bursting with petitions. At last he came near and placed himself by the trunk of the holly with his hand against it and his feet balanced on a sharp stone. In this attitude he broke into an uncertain laugh and looked at me with suspicious smiles in his eyes, turned aslant. 'I feel such a goose standing here' — 'Oh no, not more of one than I was when I spent a quarter of an hour here at noon. You must remember to wish something for me.'

In one moment a religious intentness had taken the place of the giggle; his lips moved spasmodically and at the end of each silent spasm he patted the tree, swung forward over the point of the stone on which he stood and then fell back on his heels. His grey suit made him look almost like another stem to the grey holly, the sharp green leaves were about his head; his colourless face was as stern as the cold pallor that came from the trunk in response to twilight. His wishes were long, his pats many, the rhythm of his incantation was unbroken to the end. Then with the unconscious egoism of devoutness he turned to me at last and said gratefully 'I am a spoiled child! For I believe in prayer and yet have this thrown in'. I smiled to myself: what were his prayers but his wishes. Yet this wise old tree was to him a superstition though a good and powerful one. We ran down hill, leaving our holly-stock to its loneliness, and at the foot of the hill Herbert told me his wish for me, repeating it like a proposition: 'that I might have the key of joy and the key of tears and use them well'.

The Broken Pediment[27]

Humanity in relation to the object of its worship is like the broken pediment of the Parthenon.[28] Nike and Isis are not wanting;[29] fronting the face of the central mystery stand the figures of the messenger and the herald; we learn from the lips of these what they have beholden, and, turning our eyes toward their vision, find, in place of the throned majesty they announce, a rent — the irrelevance of a blank unsculptured void. In the world's happier days there was unity; the agitation of those nearest the divine was an agitation of diffusive energy and desire: we see the same exultant figures, sublime on the borders of a chasm, and pity, in our forlorn misery, their passion of deluded hope. Despair prevents us from re-piecing the fragments of our broken gods. We lose heart the moment our antiquarian curiosity is checked; and forget that amid the ruins of a revelation imagination should take the place of industry.

[27] This short essay, in the hand of Bradley, is to be found in Oxford, Bodleian Libraries, MS Eng. misc. 653, fols 137–39. The title is on a small envelope, below a little sketch of a pediment rent in two. It is signed K.B., but the K could be an R, raising the possibility that this is Robert Browning, with whom both Bradley and Cooper were close prior to his death in 1889. Yet there is no record of this essay or of the phrase 'broken pediment' in Browning's work.

[28] A pediment is a triangular gable found in Ancient Greek architecture. The pediment of the Parthenon in Athens is rent and there are very few marble statues remaining within it, many having been appropriated by the Earl of Elgin in the early nineteenth century. Bradley and Cooper were not in favour of the Parthenon marbles being returned to Greece and wrote a poem to that effect. Michael Field, 'On a Proposal to Restore the Elgin Marbles to Athens', *The Academy*, 3 January 1891, p. 13. The 'broken pediment' is not to be confused with the Baroque architectural feature of the same name.

[29] Nike is a Greek goddess, the personification of victory; Isis is an Ancient Egyptian goddess who was worshiped by both Egyptians and Greeks in the Hellenistic Period.

The Past[30]

Never fear disloyalty to the past. A man went to a fish-monger's one Friday, bought fish, and had a good dinner. The next Friday he went to the same shop, repeated his action, and became very ill. The fish-monger in response to his complaints said — 'But you took away a slice from the same fish.'

Becoming something different from what one has been is just like turning over a leaf in a book.

30 This little fragment is found in a notebook of Katharine Bradley's that documents their trip to France and Italy in 1893. Oxford, Bodleian Libraries, MS Eng. misc. e. 341, fols 3r–3v.

Selected Prose Sketches from 'Works and Days'

Botticelli's *The Birth of Venus*[1]

She rises from a shell that floats on scallop-shaped wavelets, her back hair is bound in a sheaf, her locks about her face are bright and possessed by the wind. This Venus born out of her time is shy at her own naked loveliness, and will greet the rosy garment of daisied broidery Spring carries to wrap her. This attendant woman-form is clad in white sprinkled with blue cornflowers, her necklet of flowerless rose-leaves, her girdle of the rose in bloom. Zephyrus and Flora mingle their dusky, gilded wings,[2] their grey and olive raiment, their dark and golden heads — incorporated to breathe on the goddess, to wonder and desire. The foot of Zephyrus moves the water shoreward. Roses fly like birds in the crisp air, which likewise makes the ends of Venus' hair flamboyant. To the right are lemon-trees — in the left hand foreground some rushes that tell of the coming to land of the Queen. Her eyes have the loveliness of the waters in them — the waters growing sweet with dawn. The sky is of early blue, and no habitant of the world is awake. On the grass which her coming makes golden is a root of violet with round leaves and desultory little flowers.

But what is this cool, cool sea, sprinkled with blown rose-leaves — and the shy recoiling girl-form that seeks to veil itself in its coiled wrappings of lucent hair? Not the Greek Venus, joyous and unabashed: she will slide gratefully into the

---

[1] Michael Field [EC], 'Works and Days', BL Add. MS 46778, fols 64r–65r (June 1890). Both of these responses to Botticelli's painting are in Cooper's hand. The second response — on a separate page — is headed 'Sim [Bradley] on the Venus'. They would write a poem drawing on these notes for *Sight and Song*. Sandro Botticelli (1445–1510) was one of the most prominent artists of the Early Renaissance. *The Birth of Venus* was most likely painted in the 1480s and is housed in the Uffizi Gallery in Florence. Algernon Charles Swinburne and Walter Pater were key figures in establishing the importance of Botticelli's artworks in the nineteenth century. Michael Field's response to *The Birth of Venus* is in dialogue with Pater's imaginative description of it in his essay on Botticelli (1870), subsequently revised and included in his *Studies in the History of the Renaissance* (1873).

[2] Zephyrus is the god of the west wind in Greek mythology; Flora is the Roman goddess of flowers and spring.

great outspread rosy cloak the figure on the right is wanting to lay over her — not the Greek Venus; she does not even by amorous bend of the head indicate her knowledge of that lusty, sweeping male-force on the left. Flora is contemplative, as woman, of woman's beauty — the lips apart in wonder; but Zephyrus is covetous and blustersome.

This then, if we must have nudity, is how a Christian artist draws it: the soft guardian eyes of almost tearful shadow, the whole body timid, full of the instinct of flight.

The little green waves are indicated by their faint foam-tips treated decoratively — How happy this girl would be in the forest if she could become a Dryad and be deep in the bank![3]

That the things of Love are unspeakable, that the sorrow of it cannot be told — that shadow face expresses to us. There is strong covert in the great orange-trees,[4] and underneath them sombrest earthly shade, exquisitely contrasting with the lovely lucent frilly pucker of the ripples under the shell.

---

[3] A nymph or nature spirit who is to be found in trees in Greek mythology.

[4] A covert is a place of refuge; a thicket.

Botticelli's *Primavera*[5]

An hour or more before Botticelli's *Spring* — the most imaginative and therefore suggestive picture in the world. As in all Botticelli's best compositions there is a tranquil central figure (or group) and all the marvel of the picture consists in the variety and disposal of the side-groups in movement round this quiet subsisting at the heart of the design.

Venus is this fixed point in *Prima Vera* — on one side of her is all the distraction of March and April — even the orange-vista is beaten into turmoil by the brazen feathers of the wind — on the other side the harmony of May under the classic aisle of orange trunks.

On one side Development and its dangers —

On the other Perfection and its doom.

The lining of Venus' cloak, folded in her arm, is grey as Arno under the Tra Montana.[6] Hermes' helmet is a precious bit of colour[7] — of the depth of uncut sapphires.

Venus has an expression that is intimate, pensive, overwhelming, as if she were in love with Love as we all are in spring and she were the mother of that private but ideal pain.

I have never noticed before that there is a shock of sappy red, the inward purples of fruit blossom, in the white of Flora's dress.

Eos has the most perfectly naked form in Art[8] — under her veil we realise the very shiver and loveliness of flesh exposed to wind, and the azure head on her side gives an impression of curious shame.

---

5 Written by Cooper: Michael Field [EC], 'Works and Days', BL Add. MS 46783, fols 44r–44v, 48v (13 April 1895). *Primavera* is believed to have been painted in the late 1470s or early 1480s. It is housed in the Uffizi Gallery, Florence.

6 The Arno is a river that runs through Tuscany, including Florence. 'Tramontana' is an Italian word for a northern wind.

7 Hermes was the herald or messengers of the gods in Greek mythology.

8 Goddess of the dawn in Greek mythology.

In harmony with the rhythm of fulfilment on Venus' right hand a beautiful arc is suggested from the figure of Love (the beginning), the ripe orange touched by the Herald of Death (the end).

What a tragic figure Hermes is! The lover Juliano,[9] with the death of love and life in his stricken blue eyes!

The flowers are real, just because they are a divine cypher, with the meaning of a whole Italian hillside in their symbols.

How elastic that grape-hyacinth springing up under the second nymph's raised sole!

---

[9] Giuliano de' Medici (1453–1478), patron of Botticelli. In the nineteenth century some suggested that Giuliano's mistress Simonetta Vespucci was the model for Venus in *The Birth of Venus* and the *Primavera*, though this was disputed by later critics. Giuliano was sometimes said to be the model for Hermes or Mercury.

Botticelli's *Venus and Mars*[10]

In the National Gallery we sat long within sight of Botticelli's *Venus and Mars*. It is a masterpiece — the tone is perfect, the design has fearless simplicity — it is ideal, it is ironic, it is true. Venus lies alert, her body lifted like a shoot after thunder-rain, triumphant — for she has but received the storm: in him it is spent — a fury and power that he has lost. He sleeps as if dead — the conch that is blown into his ear through the rust-red locks is silent to his senses — his lids are closely-moulded over his eyes, his lower lip falls with a sharp ridge, his nostrils have the arrested delicacy seen in those of the dying who are unconscious, this fulfilment of love is so like the fulfilment of life! How tragic are the two great figures — male and female — he sleeping in illusion, she already above it, and watchful lest it cheat her even again — while the lusty little powers of nature are frolicsome over the sleeper and roll their tongues with comic knavery as they sport with his forsaken armour. She is beyond the aim of their jest — she is modern, cold, she is sad, she is awake.

Ah, nature, nature! It laughs in its satyrs at 'la vieille ironie, L'Amour';[11] it enjoys its own laughter, but above the rust-red locks of the sleeping lover it has set the wasps to swarm, with a dim fierceness of movement, round the bole of a tree.

Where are there greens or divine rose-colours such as Botticelli's — where else is there such harmony of line and tint — where is there more firm, more exquisite pessimism?

---

[10] Michael Field [EC], 'Works and Days', BL Add. MS 46779, fols 56v–57r (27 July 1891). *Venus and Mars* (1485) is housed in the National Gallery, London.

[11] Paul Verlaine, 'L'Angoisse' (Anguish): 'as for that old irony, | Love' (from *Poèmes saturniens*, 1866).

Greiffenhagen's *An Idyll*[12]

A young shepherd takes to his lips and his breast a yielding girl. She is huddled up to him — the blessedness of receiving, of being passive under love softly moulds the look of her face. Her arms fall straight to the left, her bosom is pressed toward her throat by the lover's arms, her head nestles against his insatiable mouth. There is summer in her eyes and on her mouth while her cheek is kissed. The dark shepherd-boy, in hat and violet-shadowed goatskin, takes a simple possession of her that is ardour at its purest heat. Her dress is gay blue, her hair burns a sorrel-brown; poppies flap knee-deep round her — breezy flakes of scarlet against her skirt, dangling patches in the lighter, grey-green herbage. The slope rises by apple-trunks to the sky, where a red sun sets submissively, while it turns the last poppy that climbs toward it into a tiny blaze of vermillion. There is an astonishing truthfulness in the picture — its subject is old as the meadows, its treatment modern, modern — life in every sweep of the brush. It is instantaneously passionate. The figures are seen as if by someone standing upright as they.

It is one of those works of art that 'reveal what woman in herself must feel'.[13] The diverse sexual frankness of enjoyment in giving (or rather taking) and receiving is clear as in Michael's *Tiresias* — also woman's more cloudless delight in her part than even man's in his. Rossetti's conventional poppies[14] are lustreless and of the past beside this Impressionist dance of poppies.

---

[12] A description of the painting *An Idyll* (1891) by Maurice William Greiffenhagen (1862–1931). Michael Field [EC], 'Works and Days', BL Add. MS 46780, fols 78v–79r (25 April 1892). Bradley and Cooper viewed the painting at the Guildhall Art Gallery, London.

[13] Cooper quotes from Poem LII of *Long Ago*, written by Bradley, which tells the story of Tiresias, who experiences life as both a man and a woman. He is punished by Hera for revealing that women experience greater sexual pleasure: 'As sacrilegious lips reveal | What woman in herself must feel'. Michael Field, *Long Ago* (London: G. Bell, 1889), p. 77.

[14] Perhaps the painting they have in mind is Dante Gabriel Rossetti's *Sibylla Palmifera* (1866–1870), or the poppies, white and symbolic of death, that appear in his *Beata Beatrix* (1870), Tate Britain.

Manet's *Olympia*[15]

She is a little thing (her proportions are too small — almost stunted) yet in her is the queenship of sterile passion, an attractive majesty, complete in itself. Her couch is red; her bed and cushions inky-shadowed white; she lies on a lovely dust-coloured silk, trailed over with red oriental flowers. Her body has the colour of very old marble; the outlines and shadow are dark, for the room is hung with dark-green curtains. In her hair is an old-rose bow, narrow black-velvet round the throat, a bracelet on the arm. The union of nudity and ornament marks the self-consciousness of the body — that it exists to fascinate. The head is thrown against a brown screen. She has a little chin, a mouth expressing strange complaisant pride, dark eyes assured of receiving homage and ennui from everything on which they look, accepting coolly the marvellousness of this continual reception of what is not pleasure. A negress in faint pink, chocolate and grey turban (her head of the intensest brown) brings a bouquet, ostentatious, flattering. A black cat stands at Olympia's feet.

I can only stare at the firm, alert features, the simple directness of the face: no stain of scruple is on the brow or mouth; the deep eyes have made terms, they have not smiled meretriciously, they have not wept hypocritically. There is in her none of the simulation of a mistress. The brown eyes have a deaf look: they have

[15] Michael Field, 'Works and Days', BL Add. MS 46780 fols 118r–119r (24 June 1892). The first response is Cooper's. The second is an inserted page, in Cooper's hand, with 'Sim [Bradley] on Olympia' at the top. They had been taken to see the painting by Berenson, who made the following pronouncements before leaving them to ponder the painting: 'It is Cleopatra, who has just unrolled herself from mummy clothes, and the cat knows it'; 'C'est la prostitution eternelle'. He also christened the painting 'Manet's *Venus*' (fol. 118r). Édouard Manet (1832–1883) was a key figure in the development of modernist painting. *Olympia* was painted in 1863 and was first exhibited at the 1865 Paris Salon, where it was widely condemned as immoral. Much of the anger was a response to the respectability with which the central figure, a prostitute, was depicted. It was acquired by the French government in 1890 and has been on display in the Musée d'Orsay ever since.

never listened to love. The clear cheeks are unpainted. Art is brought to allure her in the coloured bouquet; she herself simply dominates in her nude verity. This is all she wills to do. There are strange reserves about her face — no abandon; it has never given itself; the eyes are undisturbed, the pretty soft-lipped mouth quite resolute.

A Renaissance Dream[16]

I cannot really write of this month — I have felt like a ghost walking over a desert. It has been cold, so cold that the snow has scarcely been able to push through the hard sky — the black evergreens are topped with parsimonious whiteness and the ground is scantily covered. Even by the fire one has one's own peculiar little breezes about one's back.

We have worked well — but after work nothing remains to be done, but to rest one's tired head and look into bitter hollows that one has dug or that have been dug round one.

On the night of January 29th I had this dream. Michael [Bradley] and I were in an Italian Duomo visiting a Tomb on which was the Effigy of a beautiful youth, painted to look like life. The board-floor was shaky around the tomb, but treading lightly we came close: then the Effigy turned over from supine to prone, and we saw the inch-long lashes of oaten-gold lift and pale mocking eyes opened on us, while a fine, smiling tremor quickened the mouth, and I cried out *I have seen the Renaissance*! The effigy then came down and Michael would kiss its hands and cheeks while I shivered lest she should catch the plague. Then the figure returned to its tomb, and sitting with drawn-up legs watched us go toward the door — I heard a strange noise like a pebble being rolled about: 'it's his tongue moving' I thought with indescribable fright — and sure enough these slow, stony words came from the beautiful mouth 'I — can — lend — you — a — pair — of — scissors.' We fled at the highest pitch of terror.

---

[16] Michael Field [EC], 'Works and Days', BL Add. MS 46783, 13r–14v (Jan 1895). Untitled in original. At the time this entry was written, Bradley and Cooper were increasingly disillusioned with Berenson. On the morning of 29 January, Bradley reports receiving a letter from Costelloe stating that 'the Doctrine is too busy to write, and will never write again, at least until he has finished decorating his walls'. Bradley immediately drafted her reply: 'And now I want you and Mary to sail out of our lives as if you were dead. Bon voyage. Illusion perdue. Michael' (Michael Field [KB], 'Works and Days', BL Add. MS 46783, fol. 12r). Cooper was clearly devastated at this severing of ties, and her dream reflects this, drawing connections between the 'Renaissance youth' and Berenson, the proffered 'scissors' and the 'severing letter'.

And in the morning came the cruel letter from Florence, and the severing letter was written to Bernhard. Oh, if it would sever — we might grow strong but .... we feel that all the while fate is watching us with a subtle Renaissance smile.

Hallucinations[17]

It is twilight; milk is brought and I drink it; then we are left and the lamp put out. I see my Love by the window — she opens the striped blinds that I may watch the August full moon, making a poetic daylight throughout the sky, and defining with stern blackness the roof of the near station, and touching the green of the embowered plane-trees till they are magical as an enchantress's robe in colour. I feel the outside beauty has an ominous calm about it — I am fervidly hot; the white beams lie on my brain, and provoke it — they enter it clear, quiet, precise; they make it vague, distracted, visionary. They evoke their contraries. I create phantasies, that come so fast that they form an element round me in which I sink, sink — then float along under them, then sink again. It is a stream the particles of which are impressions, and memories, fortuitously held together, and active as they have never been and they were never intended to be. My Love, finding how it is with me, lies on her bed and in a grave low voice recalls the lovely things we enjoyed in Italy — the Adige[18] 'rolling coolness along'[19] under the red arches of Ponte Vecchio,[20] which we saw through the gay green of the acacias; the great bluish mountainland we watched from Fiesole,[21] the Duomo of Florence small

[17] Michael Field [EC], 'Works and Days', BL Add. MS 46779, fols 94r–95v (22 Aug 1891). During a trip to Dresden in August 1891, Cooper became ill with scarlet fever. She was hospitalised on 19 August; Bradley insisted on staying with her. Due to her illness, Cooper's hair was cut short and she was re-christened 'Heinrich' by her nurse ('Schwester'), who became rather infatuated with her during her stay. The nickname stuck, and later became modified to 'Henry'. Cooper was discharged from the hospital on 26 September 1891.
[18] A river in north-eastern Italy that flows through Verona.
[19] Most likely from Lucretius' *De Rerum Natura*: 'the earth has in her first bodies out of which springs rolling coolness along replenish without fail the boundless sea, she has bodies out of which fires rise up; for in many spots the earth's crust is on fire and burns, though headstrong Aetna rages with fires of surpassing force.' Lucretius, *On The Nature of Things*, trans. by H. A. J. Munro (London: G. Routledge and Sons, 1880), pp. 54–55.
[20] The bridge they are referring to is most likely the Ponte di Castel Vecchio which crosses the Adige in Verona.
[21] A town overlooking Florence. Bernard Berenson was resident there, while Vernon Lee lived a short distance away. The two women would stay there with Berenson and Costelloe in 1895, a visit that would precipitate the final break between the two couples.

and impressive,[22] in the midst; the plain of Lombardy golden with maize over which the stripped mulberry trees grew like an untimely winter. As she speaks her words change into fair, hurrying visions. The moonlight through the blind becomes more and more powerful — delirium is glorious, like being inspired continuously. Forms of art and poetry swim round and into me. Every moment is plastic.....

A great dromedary comes along,[23] with red trappings and trophies, in the midst are set the words *Two weeks at Dresden*!! The ironic beast passes.

Vast Bacchanals rush by, Rubenesque, violent — (Here 'Tannhäuser' feeds the phantasy.[24]) I fall into an attitude of sleep, like an Antinous on the ground.[25] I am Greek, Roman, Barbarian, Catholic; and this multiform life sweeps me toward unconsciousness — only the shine through the blinds tortures me so that I cannot lose myself. I beg my Love to keep a candle lighted to put out the moon, with all its terrible spectral frilliness — to obliterate the white cavern-arch of the door — Death's Door that I keep approaching, that I cannot pass, for as soon as I am near it the brilliant swirl of images is round me and I am caught back to life. Again and again I am magnetically drawn to the grey portal and as often rescued.

Then I see our two straight beds — they are coffins — we lie near one another in noble peace........

At last I am carried away into Unconsciousness...... I become aware of a figure in a short nightdress — a girl, almost at the other end of the Ward, who has leapt to embrace a hero, a dark, magical man in the corner (a cloak-stand) who does not respond. In horror at his coldness she struggles back and falls across the bed half-faint. That is how my escapade appears to me — I see that wan creature on the bed. (an ocean of gold pouring down)[26]

I could not tell to moonshine

What I would tell to *light* or to *dark* — that is the dilemma. (I spring into bed away from it), and am saved to consciousness. (Then a message arrives from the Doctor I am to have wine). Schwester drenches me — the gold-red wine runs down my night-dress and the sheets... Oblivion... I fling myself down toward the foot of the bed, half-uncovered..... I am covered by nurse, turned back on

---

[22] The Duomo di Firenze is an iconic church in the centre of Florence, famous for its massive dome, which can be clearly seen from Fiesole.

[23] A one-humped Arabian camel.

[24] Bradley and Cooper went to the opera to see Richard Wagner's *Tannhäuser* on 16 August 1891 in Dresden, despite Cooper's worsening condition.

[25] A Greek youth who was the beloved of the emperor Hadrian. After Antinous's death Hadrian had him deified and he was worshipped across the Roman Empire. He was revered by homosexual men and women at the *fin de siècle* and Wilde referred to him in a number of his works.

[26] The oddities of presentation here reflect the diary manuscript, which captures Cooper's frenzied state of mind.

the pillows and again drenched with Mavrodaphne[27]...... oblivion...... I have my Love close to me and I am telling her about the tones of the light, that is coming in by the window — she says I was wonderful on it, but I do not recall a word I said, nor can she.

The sun shines broad and yellow over the ward. I lie half-slumbering with deep, blissful breaths and with the sense that cornfields, harvest-meadows, the great, enlightened, fruitful Earth is all round me and the joy of life — *here* — in the world, enters my soul and body, stays with me and re-consecrates me a mortal being. It is beautiful to feel the ideally familiar claiming me with delicious insistence; the sun as much sending life down to me in his August ray as the Angel sends it with his voice down the trumpet to the skeleton in Blake's drawing on the first page of Blair's *Grave*.[28]

I stretch my limbs on the hospital-bed with a luxuriousness of enjoyment and an out-of-doors weight in their pressure, feeling under every part that the earth supports my life. It is like being born again to Light, — a religious recognition of its divineness, geniality, its tremulous qualities of colour and movement. I am so unutterably happy. The Doctor comes — I sleep on, and yet I cognise this sleep, though I hear no sound. It is a peace of which I am conscious, as I lie on the bosom of sunshine ... I remember nothing more.

[27] A sweet fortified wine made from black wine grapes, produced in Greece.

[28] In 1805 William Blake was commissioned to produce engravings for Robert Blair's *The Grave* (1745).

Study For a Krankenhaus 'Conte'[29]

Two trees grow in a mournful, shady thicket under the great back of a hospital, with windows hundred-eyed. One is an apple tree, one is a quince.

Men and women walk the garden sick and severed. It is autumn, late September: the fruit on the Tree of Life is hanging plenteous, but where is its sturdy colour, its fervid stain, the basking indefiniteness of its form in the sunlight? The apples rest wan — a wan yellow — on the boughs. If we turn from the tree and look over the garden, all the human creatures have the same sad pallor; they are dedicated to Life, but the beauty of its health has not come to them. They grow strong as they sit in the sun; but the ambers and roses of the orchard may not visit the cheeks of fruit nor mortals within this garden.

And the other tree — the Tree of Love — whose fruit united bride and bridegroom in the Golden Ages! Among its round leaves here and there is a shape of sunken leather, a thing of skin, very white for a quince, as mournful as the dry relics in a tomb. Where is the sweetness, where is the breath — where is the nuptial joy in these unlovely circles grown beneath shade?

But the garden is spectral and full of strange things. There are green paths where men and women walk: the men are by themselves, the women are in companies, restricted from breaking up and crossing over to the sunny side where the men must stay — neither sex has happiness from the other. Hearts are pale, eyes indifferent ... and the quince tree in the shadow is unseen.

(I had stood long before these two trees, on nurse's arm, the previous afternoon. There stood near a doleful figure of stone pouring out water under a weeping willow)

---

[29] Michael Field [EC], 'Works and Days', BL Add. MS 46779, fols 110v–111r (26 Sept 1891). 'Krankenhaus' is German for hospital, while 'conte' is French for tale. The 1880s saw the popularity of 'contes cruels', a cruel or sardonic short story mastered by Auguste Villiers de l'Isle-Adam and Octave Mirbeau. This was the first work Cooper wrote after she had left hospital, having recovered from scarlet fever in Dresden.

My green hat sought below and I walk out with Schwester to feed the fishes.[30] I call her the old *Katze*[31] who must keep about Station 44 lest the little mice should play. She murmurs I am her mouse whom she loves, but whom she can love best *im Bett*.[32] I hasten to meet my Love in the woody paths and we visit hand in hand the quince and apple.

In the afternoon, while walking with Schwester in the men's garden, we see a violet-dove, glowing green and rose under a hydrangea, with many leaves and a single blue-empurpled blossom. Timing glances askance at passing litters on which glower mighty blankets, and once or twice the pale, devoted heads of the sick.

---

[30] See note 17 for the amorous Schwester.

[31] Cat.

[32] Translation: 'in bed'.

Gentle Death[33]

And with regard to the fourth part of our life, by which I mean that which a noble spirit attains in its last state of old age. Two things may be said — one that the soul should return to God as to that part whence she set out when she began to enter on the sea of this life; the other that she should bless the road by which she has come, in so far as it has been direct and good, and without the bitterness of tempest. And at this point it should be understood that, as Cicero says in his treatise on *Old Age*, natural death is, as it were, a port and reposeful haven to us, after long voyaging.[34] And, as the good mariner when he is drawing near to port, lowers his sails and softly with gentle conduct enters therein, so we ought to lower the sails of our worldly operations and turn to God with all our understanding and heart, so that the entrance to that haven may be effected with all suavity and peace. And of the benignity of nature we have witness in this that in such death there is neither grief nor bitterness, but as a ripe apple lightly and without violence detaches itself from its branch, so our spirit without struggle severs itself from the body where it has been dwelling. And — as in the case of one who comes home from a long journey — before he enters the port of his city, its citizens come out to give him welcome, so the citizens of the eternal life make haste to meet the noble soul, comporting themselves in such wise that they constrain it to see those whom it believes to be with God. I have heard that Tully in the person of old Cato said 'I appeared to see, and I raised myself up in my great desire to see your parents whom I loved, and not only these people whom I had known myself, but others of whom I had heard tell.'[35] Let then the noble soul resign itself to await the end of this life with much desire, for this in good truth is to exchange the inn for the homestead, to cease from journeying and turn into the city, to abandon the sea for the haven.

---

33 Michael Field [KB], 'Works and Days', BL Add. MS 46804, fols 14r–15v (27 May 1889). This appears to have been written at the same time as 'Mid-Age' and designed as a companion piece.
34 Marcus Tullius Cicero, *Cato Maior de Senectute* (*Cato the Elder on Old Age*), written in 44 BC.
35 From Cicero's *On Old Age*. We have not been able to locate which, if any, translation Bradley was using here.

~

It Was an Old House[36]

It was an old house; the inhabitants were very old. It stood in a garden full of great trees — the leaves were never swept up in autumn; they rotted gradually away. In spring there was crude flowering of self-sown plants, gilly flowers and foxgloves, the seeds of which had been blown on to the high banks by chance. It was pleasant to feel that in this house nothing was disturbed, nothing was altered. One was not conscious of any unnatural arrest of events, as, when the furniture and trifles of one dead, are left in the disposition in which they were when he quitted them; the processes of accumulation and decomposition seemed to be those of nature; one did not remark there was anything old-fashioned in the ornaments and hangings — one would never feel there was anything old-fashioned in a landscape where little had been disarranged by war or by the elements. There was about the inmates of this house the same air of continuity: they did not seem near their end; they were assuredly far from their beginning. And there was no mark of catastrophe about them. I was accustomed to spend with them three months of every year; and these months were usually the months of late autumn. My own life was full of desolation and misery, and when I became their guest the chill of alienation was added to solitariness. There was some reference to their head-aches at meal times — the rest of the day they spend, I imagine, in their bedrooms (for I heard slow footsteps overhead) readjusting old finery, praying possibly. I was a child and myself never prayed, except with hands folded against the patch-diamonded quilt. Or they were nursing themselves, or else, but this was in the early morning occasionally, sorting their preserves. No one visited them. In their youth they had been betrothed — one to a fine old naval captain, the other to a clergyman with slender income. Fear of exposure to climate in the one case, dread of penury in the other, prevented marriage. The elder female, I noticed, never complained of headaches on stormy nights: the younger occasionally asked me to read the prayers for the sick. Once when I was in the

[36] Michael Field [EC], 'Works and Days', BL Add. MS 46778, fols 143v–144r (1890). This prose piece is found at the back of the 1890 diary, and thus it is difficult to specify an exact date of composition.

midst of these I glanced across towards the gaunter sufferer, and I asked if I should continue the form of prayer for those at sea. She came to me, closed the book, and sharply slapped my ears. Yet the proposal was prompted by kindliness: I wanted to quiet the dread excitement in her eyes, and I knew of no other remedy against the grating effect of the wind on her nerves. As I grew older I was never asked to read. In the morning I wandered a little amid the dropping leaves; the afternoon I lay listlessly on the sofa of the faded pink drawing-room, and watched all that happened to the minute-and-finger hands of an old timepiece. The cuckoo-call call of this old clock was the one lively sound in the house. It woke me at times from a sleep in which it seemed to be I had been vainly seeking to entertain myself by dreams. I wondered at first how it was that the clock was kept going. On enquiry I was told that an old man came once a week to look at all the timepieces in the house. It was therefore no matter of surprise to me when one afternoon I saw before me — he must have come in while I slept — an old man with remarkably keen eyes, the keenest and dearest I have ever seen. 'You are the timekeeper' I said to him, and he answered 'I am Time' — 'Are you here to do repairs?' 'Have you heard of the millennium?' was his sharp reply. I was shaping my lips for the orthodox rejoinder when he continued 'it will be a grand bit of work, a first-rate bit of craftmanship! — I am a lazy fellow — hitherto I have but tinkered at Chaos; the effort is so tremendous to really re-adjust the centuries — but I mean to do it' and his face glared........

The Morgue[37]

To the morgue this morning quite early in the glowing sunshine. It has been our worship; that temple of death loves the temple of the living God. Liberté, égalité, fraternité[38] — true there — realised in the grey, marred faces within laid brotherlike — freed from the mesh of life, and equal at last in their destiny — bound all these voyagers for God. I saw first an old man lying very calm — the whites of his eyes giving the appearance of spectacles, so that he looked like time lying dead in glasses — then a deeply bronzed face, full one would say of sin and experience, finally a rather kindly, commonplace fellow, gentle enough in his fixity. It is Michael's church that little morgue and he found it quite impossible to remain afterwards in Notre-Dame, amid the mumbling and the lights.[39] God has provided for worship in the facts of life — if we will but look deep into birth and death — unflinchingly — accepting all the physical repulsion, and read on through the letter to the indwelling mystery, we shall learn how to conduct ourselves between — under the tricolour,[40] and with the runic gospel written on our hearts.

---

37 Michael Field [KB], 'Works and Days', BL Add. MS 46778, fol. 44v (8 June 1890). It was a popular pastime for residents and travellers alike to visit the morgue just behind Notre-Dame on the Île de la Cité. Here the bodies of vagrants and those fished from the Seine would be exhibited with the aim of their being identified and claimed by relatives and friends. In reality most visitors — including Robert Browning, Charles Dickens, and Frances Trollope — were going to experience the morbid spectacle. For many of these British visitors the morgue was symptomatic of lax French morals. See Paul Vita, 'Returning the Look: Victorian Writers and the Paris Morgue', *Nineteenth-Century Contexts*, 25 (2003), 241–55.

38 The national motto was emblazoned over the entrance to the morgue. It was a popular slogan during the French Revolution, first used by one of the most prominent revolutionary figures, Maximilien Robespierre.

39 Michael here pertains to either Bradley writing of herself (she was Michael while Cooper was Field) or to the shared Michael Field identity. A few months later Cooper writes of the visit: 'As of all the objects I saw on my journey I retain with most singular sharpness the faces at the Morgue — so of all the days I have lived I remember these days last year with the most indelible and sensitive exactitude.' In the comments that follow it is clear that she links the experience with her broader reflections on mortality following the death of her mother on 20 August 1889. Michael Field [EC], 'Works and Days', BL Add. MS 46778, fol. 106v (21 Aug 1890).

40 The tricolour is a name given to the French national flag.

The Morgue Revisited[41]

Two years roll back — I feel I am again in Paris for the first time as my Love leaves me at the back of Notre-Dame under the chestnuts, and crosses the road. While she is away I look up at the apse — I have a wish to see the people of the Morgue, but I no longer feel that strain at my heart that nearly killed me in this place two years ago, when I first prepared to look on death — death I had never seen, though my beloved mother had passed through the change. It was something like the desolate terror I felt when I first looked at the sea into which I was to be dipped — I had to come point blank into contact with a new element.

Now I am simply anxious to increase experience.

My love comes and with her I go to the moral den in which death is confined. One's whole nature seeks to escape in what, if one were alone, would be a cry of surprise. Then all goes quiet in one, and the dead figures become as objective as waxwork.

There are three men — one a dusky, tragic old man, with bent head, folded-in lips, and clenched hand; the second a most open-faced corpse, with a smooth, French pleasantness on the unwrinkled alabaster features; the third a boy with fierce pitiful brows and a mouth that has become triangular. Their clothes lie over them — such utter 'lendings'. What strikes me more than anything else is the smallness of death, the way in which it makes limits that cannot be passed. I have before me the shapes of men some few feet long — but where is the magnetism that passing from these shapes could fill a room, fill other hearts, fill those flat clothes — where is the expansiveness that only used these features as the centre of its flight over the world? Yes, death is the smallest thing in the universe — with no beyond, no emanation! Thank goodness it breaks up! And in so far as we live shut up in bonds without self-expression, mobility, freedom — we are but corpses and are becoming every day more like these little models on their backs beyond the bars of the Morgue.

[41] Untitled in original. Michael Field [EC], 'Works and Days', BL Add. MS 46780, fols 123v–123r (26 June 1892).

Yes, this is my Sunday lesson — that life, life is what the living must seek with heart and soul and strength and might.

The only poor escape from the fixedness of a corpse is through the psychology that traces a past in the forms — a past is always piteous — it is sorrow or happiness that is over: present and future have alone to do with life — heigh-ho, we must live, till this machine is cast from us.

The Waxworks[42]

The waxworks; to see Cardinal Newman in the round;[43] Tennyson too is there in an alcove. Can it be done like sister Helen's waxen man?[44] Can one be given a place in these ranks of the eternal dead? For this is death's very kingdom — corruption is the break up of death, and running away again of the precious atoms to work at life; but this is first how death would like to keep everything, always smooth, and round, and full of fleshly cold.

[42] Michael Field [KB], 'Works and Days' BL Add. MS 46779, fol. 141r (8 Dec 1891). This note was written following a visit to Madame Tussaud's waxworks. The waxworks was first opened in 1835 and moved in 1884 to a purpose-built museum on Marylebone Road.
[43] Cardinal John Henry Newman (1801–1890), an Anglican priest and influential figure in the Oxford Movement, who later converted to Catholicism, becoming a cardinal in 1879.
[44] An allusion to Dante Gabriel Rossetti's poem 'Sister Helen' (1853).

~

Omissions[45]

Michael Angelo omitted to kiss the lips of Vittoria.[46] It is the sins of omission that have the tragic note — 'I was sick and in prison, and ye visited me not.'[47] Forgetfulness is the unpardonable sin to love: the 'first faint neglect' stirred Lear's rage;[48] offences can be forgiven; omissions are spectres. One may strive to lay them by incantation or by curse — but they will return. In as much as we did it not we are damned. You may crucify and be forgiven; but you may not neglect.

---

[45] Michael Field [EC], 'Works and Days', BL Add. MS 46778, 142v (1890). This short prose piece is found at the back of the 1890 diary, and thus it difficult to specify a date of composition.
[46] Vittoria Colonna was the muse of the poet and painter Michelangelo.
[47] Matthew 25. 43: 'I was a stranger, and ye took me not in: naked, and ye clothed me not: sick, and in prison, and ye visited me not.'
[48] William Shakespeare, *King Lear*, I. 4. 64–68.

> Thou but rememberest me of mine own conception: I
> have perceived a most faint neglect of late; which I
> have rather blamed as mine own jealous curiosity
> than as a very pretence and purpose of unkindness:
> I will look further into't.

Hyacinthus[49]

The slope with level horizon-line at the further end of my valley is a rare tawny-purple, for the brown withered bracken is illuminated by the Tyrian hue of mingled hyacinthus,[50] and their brilliant colour is mitigated and diffused by the wintry tints. On the left slope the flowers are close together and uncompromisingly violet, making the cloud-shadows as they pass imperial for a moment. Above are oaks — young oaks in sunlight, and over all is a blue sky frank with the West Wind.

49 Untitled in Original. Michael Field [EC], 'Works and Days', BL Add. MS 46777, fol. 6v (31 May 1888). On 26 May, Bradley wrote of the hyacinths: 'In Edith's valley the other evening we found a bank of hyacinths. Above them, overlooking the oaks, was a full pale moon, not shining, not yet an influence — a steady, dominating presence; before and beneath which swifts were fretfully crossing' (fol. 7r). Bradley's entry is followed by drafts of 'Poem LX' ('She loved the perfumed inlet') from *Long Ago*, which describes Leda discovering an 'egg hid in the hyacinth-bed' (l. 109). That Cooper uses the classicized spelling suggests that the hyacinths conjure up Hyacinthus, lover of the god Apollo in Greek myth. This is confirmed in the allusion to the west wind: Zephyrus was the god of the west wind and was an admirer of a Hyacinthus; Zephyrus killed him in a fit of jealousy that Hyacinthus preferred Apollo.

50 Tyrian, or imperial purple, refers to a highly coveted dye used for clothes in Ancient Rome, usually reserved for kings and emperors. Produced from the glands of snails, it was so difficult to make and expensive to acquire that it had connotations of wealth and power.

~

An Oat-field in June[51]

We strolled along the path, a ditch on one side and on the other a world of oat-stalks, shooting out their signpost blades, juicy lightsome green below where the sun hid, and on the top of the field an unconcerned blue. In the midst of the movement of the stalks — their soft and yet crackling movement — swaying with it noiselessly, the poppies, just up to the shoulders of the grain, flickered and uncreased their flowers. Their blots of pure red, that close to the eyes become one consternation of wings, with their broadness emphasised the strokes of the harvest, and their green buds hung with a barley-like droop among the husks of the oats. Food and sleep, the two restorers of life, breathed together as grain and poppies in the wind of a summer day.

The large, inert, blight-varnished leaves of June.

---

[51] Written by Cooper in the summer of 1894. Michael Field [EC], 'Works and Days', BL Add. MS 46782, fol. 70r (June/July 1894). Exact date of composition unknown, but the sketch appears between the 22 June and 5 July 1894 diary entries.

An Oat-field in September[52]

Then my Love takes me to her oat-field, where the sheaves rest, sunk in fondling beams. Nature, in spite of Oscar,[53] has made a seat that is perfect — a group of oat-sheaves — it has spring and curve fit for any royal race. The moors, inflexible against the suave oat-crops, shine no less delicately in spite of their strength, for like the oat-fields they have a special disposition to do honour to light, to all aerial effects. Nearly at the top of Gallow hill[54] we rest against a ladder-stile, in the eye of the setting sun.

Round us wave the upland outlines, a reverent blue, very passionate along their edges; in front of us is a standing oat-field, shot with pink ripeness here and there in the masses of its primrose — almost opaline. The middle-distance is a grove of spruce-firs, so velvet-dense one wants to stroke them; while bits of heather intensify in spots the pink stipples among the rocks. At the top of Gallow Hill we feel the shudder of the place. It is getting grey evening; round the boughs of the trees a dismal secrecy grows up — the plateau where the gibbet must have stood is strewn with trunkless fir-roots, very much lopped, lying deadly in the long grass; the country on which the condemned once looked, before all of a sudden it disappeared, lies wide and still gentle although darkening. As we glide down the hill between firs and bracken we hear plunges, and shattering of leaves on the ground — shockingly restless movements like those of the 'deaders' — and we see half-hidden birds.[55]

---

[52] Untitled in original. This sketch is from a holiday in the Scottish Borders. Michael Field [EC], 'Works and Days' BL Add. MS 46782, fols 120v–121r (9 Sept 1894). On the same day, Bradley wrote a brief companion poem entitled 'An Oat-field in September': 'How blue! | I am looking through | the sunshine, and green, and grey combined | Of the feathery oat-fields in the wind | to the sky behind'. Michael Field [KB], 'Works and Days', BL Add. MS 46782, fol. 119r (9 Sept 1894).

[53] A riposte to Wilde. In 'The Decay of Lying' Vivian states: 'But Nature is so uncomfortable. Grass is hard and lumpy and damp, and full of dreadful black insects. Why, even Morris's poorest workman could make you a more comfortable seat than the whole of Nature can.' Oscar Wilde, 'The Decay of Lying', in *Intentions* (London: Osgood, McIlvaine, 1891), pp. 1–58 (p. 4).

[54] Gallow Hill lies just outside the town of Moffat. Whether it was a site of a gallows at some point is uncertain, but Cooper clearly finds the atmosphere a little morbid.

[55] 'Deaders' is a slang term for a corpse or dead person.

~

Daffodils[56]

Through firs and gorse, down the brow of a hill — and under a hedge we saw our first daffodils (two open flowers and a bud). They were growing in awful peace — I have never seen anything look so still, except the eyelids of the little work woman in the Morgue. Their unfaltering lemon-gold sloped towards the grass, severe and — ah, so devotional, they made me say in a whisper 'and having prayed together we Will go with you along.'[57]

Then we climbed into a cleared copse where hundreds of daffodils must have flowered before they were gathered, even to the buds; but in a circle of wands from the hazels we found a company, showing lustrously against the wands … and then under a burthen of wands further on a single flower. The sun was setting — it had reached the tranquil, not the coloured stage; the air held more of its effect than the sky yet showed. We did not pluck a daffodil — they grew inviolable.

Later we came though the firs and saw a round glow behind them — it was the pascal moon rising.[58] A chafer passed,[59] like the twang of one string of an Aeolian harp;[60] the firs throw back the atmosphere, as only their strong spiny boughs can! The insistent darkness compels aerial perspective.

Later still, after supper, we went out in the moonlight. Pines are the trees for moonlight — they are night itself in visible shape. We went over the brow of the

---

[56] Untitled in original. These passages were written during a holiday Bradley and Cooper took to Hermitage, Berkshire, over Easter in March 1894. Michael Field [EC], 'Works and Days', BL Add. MS 46782, fols 17v–18r, 20v–21r (21 March 1894, 23 March 1894). In this passage they are developing a dialogue with William Wordsworth — in particular his poems 'I wandered lonely as a cloud' and 'Ode on Intimations of Immortality from Recollections of Early Childhood'. See Alex Murray, 'Michael Field's Wordsworth', *Victorian Poetry*, 58 (2020), 427–50.

[57] From Robert Herrick, 'To Daffodils' (1665).

[58] Cooper here has misspelt Paschal Moon, or the Ecclesiastical full moon that is used to determine the date of Easter in the Northern Hemisphere. The word Paschal comes from the Aramaic 'Pascha', meaning Passover.

[59] A large flying beetle found in grasslands.

[60] A stringed musical instrument that is played by the wind. The Aeolian harp was used as a symbol by Percy Bysshe Shelley and Samuel Taylor Coleridge.

hill again, and directly under the moon we saw our first-seen daffodils once more, blanched, solemn and dewy — almost ghostlike beneath their hedge.

The sound of the wind in fir-trees is cosmic — the gathering of many waters etherealized; and with the pertinacity of effort that can throw continuance itself into the background.

This afternoon we go on, 'wandering still'. First away to the thicket, to break through thorns and boughs into the presence of sunlit daffodils. The little cloistral society we spied out last night is still undissolved. What could be lovelier than daffodils with plenty of space round each flower, the gold of the sun on the deep and pale gold of each; shadow moving on the perianth,[61] shadow lurking under the fringes of the corona.[62] Daffodils seem to be solitary by election; they respond to the breeze as if they savoured it (comme ils le savaient[63]). And they too light up from the earth, as if they felt its stimulus immediately — they are so fine, so chastened, and withal so quiet that they are votaries of the most exquisite pleasure, when the sun shines and the wind stirs. Coming on them is like coming on Dian's companions.[64]

We slip away from the holy sight, through thorns and boughs.

---

[61] The non-reproductive part of a flower surrounding the sexual organs.

[62] The corona is the name given to the inner appendage that sits in the centre of a daffodil, inside the perianth of outer petals.

[63] 'as if they knew it'.

[64] The Roman goddess Diana, associated with the countryside, the moon, and virginity, was often depicted alongside female companions, such as wood-nymphs (dryads).

Bramber[65]

We wake at Bramber to a lovely morning. I open the parlour window: — the castle-wall stands white above the glinty mist of the village-street. Then I gaze at a meadow opposite, with dew-shine over it — poetic as grass can be. There is a squared yew-tree just in front of the inn; beyond the yew-tree apple-boughs, green with lichen, attractive through the gleaming air. We stroll down the part of Bramber away from the castle:

The roofs and the downs are in delicious tone — grey and red and lilas[66] — the richest tint being emphasised by the crimson elm-blossoms. Chalk-country is made to be ploughed, grazed, — to have austere farmhouses on its slopes and black barns. It is not meant to be built over, inhabited, gardened. No, no — the cabbages become a gangrene across it, and all houses that are not agricultural suburban. Best sight of all is that of horses ploughing on the beautiful rims of the land; — and a few sheep lying together in the bleached hollow are valuable — they look to be made out of small humps of chalk, so like are their lines to those of the countryside.

The precise elder is in leaf — old, dark-natured, punctual, no Bacchic delirium in its spring!

Also the arum-leaves are lush.[67]

We see a few speedwells[68] and think of our darling Mother One.[69]

I plucked for my Love some wayside violets — minute but sweet to smell.

We are happy to the brim.

---

65 Michael Field [EC], 'Works and Days', BL Add. MS 46781, fols 26v–26r, 27v–28r (7–8 March 1893). Bramber is a village in West Sussex. The River Adur runs through it, and it has a ruined Norman castle.

66 'Lilas' is French for lilac.

67 A flowering plant found in Europe and sometimes called an arum lily, even though they are unrelated to actual lilies.

68 Blue perennial wildflowers commonly found in Britain.

69 The 'Mother One' was Cooper's mother and Bradley's sister. She died in August 1889 and is regularly recalled in 'Works and Days' throughout the 1890s.

Then we pay homage to the castle — There I startled two wood-doves from the keep, and see a rook whizz off with a green stick in his possession.

We toil up a hill — on the top is a duck-pond, the ducks reduced to tails upright in the water and beating feet: a bound of farm-buildings beyond the pond and then a long down.

We find a little further that we can rest in a farm-close on some logs of wood. There we sun ourselves like cats; the logs are marvellously-toned greys and weeds are vivid between them. Oh, we are so inexpressibly happy!

~

Pevensey[70]

The day is blue from the beginning — We cross the Marsh, preceded by Tramps — On the rail-lines we see Millet's effect — figures in the typical actions of toil against the sky.[71] We reach the shore — the tide is far away — in the shallows shrimpers push along; above the stone are the definite little forts. Sim[72] suggests they are there because Englishmen have never got over the nervousness from William the Conqueror's landing. We walk in front of the tiny successive shadows that are waves on the blue water, watching the freedom of the wave-lines in the sand. No pencil is ever so delicate, so effortless in its design as the waves. We love this shore — here the Earth is not trafficking with the sea — they are not bargainers but lovers, and full of the delicious vagueness of dreams.

We lie on the pebbles, bury our hands like children, wind a trumpet with our lips and make the hands rise again — games come naturally to us, and we are so blissfully happy.

---

[70] Michael Field [EC], 'Works and Days', BL Add. MS 46781, 27v–28r (7–8 March 1893). Pevensey is a village in East Sussex near where William the Conqueror landed in 1066. Nearby are the remains of a Norman castle built over a Roman fort.

[71] Jean-François Millet (1814–1875) was a French realist painter famous for his rural landscapes.

[72] 'Sim' was one of Cooper's many nicknames for Bradley. It is short for Simorg or Simurgh, a mythical bird from Persian literature.

Herstmonceux Castle[73]

A west wind is blowing over the marshes; there are no primroses on the inland banks. *The Castle* — low set, very domestic, ivy-hung, complete. Each tower worth a visit to see its roof of ivy, shadow and piercing-green combined deliciously in those tiles of leaves.

To the north a bridge over the dry moat where hazels grow, blanched with lichen, full of disorder, straining for height.

The bridge is the way into an old garden. The espaliers are thick with lichen as if it were grey hair; the lichen covers their thousands of little boughs. Most of their props are gone and they stay as rigid as old people. The very rose-trees have lichen up to the brown leaf sprouts; the pinks are powerfully tangled. Mistletoe hangs, leather-like, from one apple-bough, gold and silver in fatal clasp. Bees house near the wall — peach trees — one of the peach-blossoms is a deep and precious cup. The bees hunt among the great violets in a weedy corner. Their winged shadows fly across the wall. The creatures themselves wrangle with the petals for their sweetness. I see one eager bee accost a violet-bud; then, realising that it is shut and secret, hiss out some tetchy music and go. A lyric moment — that coming of the bee too soon, when the honey is kept virgin from mere youth.

73 A fifteenth-century brick castle in East Sussex. Michael Field [EC], 'Works and Days', BL Add. MS 46781, fols 31v–32r (10 March 1893). This description is presumably the basis for EC's poem 'Great Violets in a weedy tangle' in *Underneath the Bough*, Book IV. Berenson and Costelloe were satirical about the apparently innocent use of the words 'Each heart receives | The prick that takes its bliss' in this poem; Ricketts loved the word 'tetchy'.

Haslemere[74]

Next morning I was introduced to the garden Logan is making out of the wood. It lies south-west, and the flowers are never quite windless; it is a smooth terrace, with grassy forest-ground below and the close copse above, restricted by wooden lattices, on which creepers are beginning to hang. Suddenly the terrace curves up beyond the lattices into a semi-circle of green foliage, and at the end of the garden a common little gate opens into a nutty glade, where the blue dampness of Surrey lingers all day. Over this copse one can see hills, loaded with trees and here and there high-topt pines on knolls and ridges above the trees.

The gravel-path of the terrace runs beside a long bed of flowering plants, some wild, some old-fashioned, some beautiful new kinds — but the colour always chequers the green as it should in a delightful garden — never puts it out of court. Here a lily with yellow ruts down its petals and speckles as of pure mud on its toneless petals is seen bowing down among tufts of goldenrod, and tawny sal piglossis waves in front of it.[75] Clematis makes a sudden diamond-pattern of violet behind the reserved droop of the *Hyacinthus Candidus* in flower over pansies.[76] Then opposite the semi-circle of lawn, at the further edge of the terrace, pinks and picottees[77] tremble rigidly in the south-breeze against their sticks, and Shirley poppies[78] fade with a lavish yielding of their bright selves to ruin, and in a bed, close against the wild hedgerow, tiger-lilies square their buds over maiden-blush roses, that grow low down on their bushes in August.

---

[74] This description of the garden provides the setting for 'By the Sundial' (p. 84). The garden, in Surrey, belonged to Logan Pearsall Smith (1865–1946), brother of Mary Costelloe, and in the early twentieth century a well-known essayist. Michael Field [EC], 'Works and Days', BL Add. MS 46782, fols 104r–105r (Aug 1894).

[75] *Salpiglossis sinuata*, or 'Painted Tongue' plants as they are known.

[76] Cooper is likely referring to *Galtonia candicans*, otherwise known as summer hyacinth. *Candidus* is Latin for white, the colour of the flowers of summer hyacinth.

[77] Cooper's misspelling of 'picotees', most likely meaning carnations. 'Picotee' designates a flower whose petals have an outer margin of another colour.

[78] A type of ornamental field poppy that was created through hybridization by Reverend William Wicks of Shirley in what was then Surrey (now part of London).

This garden among the leaves and hills, fresh and so quiet except for the click of insects and piping calls — no longer notes — of the birds, only wanted one object to complete it, to bring out its significance — a sundial — for in a sundial we see what a garden is to man, a place where time passes in light, and destiny slips a lovely thing through forms and colours that pass away with the hand-shadow on the hours.[79]

Mrs Burroughs,[80] a little American sculptor, has had the honour to design the dial for this sylvan garden, this chequer-work of blossoms on the dense woodlands: of course the design should have been perfect — it is only timidly harmonious. A pensive woman, almost ill with dreams, crouches on the top of the pillar, leans her shoulders heavily over the disc, and lays her left index finger on the fateful hand.

The next morning she was put in her place, and it was curious how the quietude became positive as soon as she rose in its midst, the green more green, the sun a mere sequestered radiance, and the flowers more sacred in the brevity of their vividness.

---

[79] The phrase 'hand-shadow' is seemingly Cooper's own. The central piece on a sundial, the shadow of which tells the time, is a gnomon.

[80] Most likely the American sculptor Edith Woodman Burroughs (1871–1916). She visited England in 1893, marrying the American artist Bryson Burroughs (later curator of paintings at the Metropolitan Museum of Art, New York). The couple spent time in Paris and Florence during 1894 and 1895. Woodman Burroughs designed two fountains for the 1915 Panama-Pacific International Exposition in San Francisco, winning a silver medal for her 'Fountain of Youth'.

The Magic Corner[81]

First came a granular mist — lilac and windy — the mist of the grasses; then sprays of wild-rose with great white stars caught in their briars forming a heavenly tangle; then behind the rose-branches the austere grey wheat fields, and last of all the hills, grey, ripening into blue vapour.

Here and there as one drew close to the wild-roses one saw a branch of buds, orange-red, flecked by the warm diffused violet of the blossoms' glow against the blanched corn, sweet and steady in loveliness.

Above this world of vagueness, tint and fragrance, the few little trees on the bare chalk down seemed toiling uphill — on the curve of land against the sky; and as we looked at the downs-side we saw it palpitate with movements like those of passing clouds — but really the wind was lifting the grasses as it breathed. On the summit we could see the regiment of grass-stems infinitely delicate in their line, almost imperceptible.

[81] An account of the garden at 'the Magic Corner' to which Bradley and Cooper took their friend 'Lion' FitzPatrick. Michael Field [EC], 'Works and Days', BL Add. MS 46782, fols 67r–67v (22 June 1894).

Selected Prose Poems and Sketches of the *Fin de Siècle*

This small selection of prose poems and prose sketches is designed to offer readers some sense of the variety of short experimental prose forms that were circulating at the *fin de siècle*. We have chosen here pieces that either have a direct connection to Michael Field (we know they read Schreiner and Meynell), connect Bradley and Cooper to wider developments (the Decadence of Wilde, the writing of contemporaries such as Egerton and Macleod), or offer some sense of the movement of the prose poem into modernism (Mansfield). This is only a small selection, and details of the broad range of prose poems produced at the *fin de siècle* appears in the section of this volume titled 'Further Reading'.

~

Olive Schreiner, 'The Gardens of Pleasure'[1]

She walked upon the beds, and the sweet rich scent arose; and she gathered her hands full of flowers. Then Duty, with his white clear features, came and looked at her. Then she ceased from gathering, but she walked away among the flowers, smiling, and with her hands full.

Then Duty, with his still white face, came again, and looked at her; but she, she turned her head away from him. At last she saw his face, and she dropped the fairest of the flowers she had held, and walked silently away.

Then again he came to her. And she moaned, and bent her head low, and turned to the gate. But as she went out she looked back at the sunlight on the faces of the flowers, and wept in anguish. Then she went out, and it shut behind her for ever; but still in her hand she held of the buds she had gathered, and the scent was very sweet in the lonely desert.

But he followed her. Once more he stood before her with his still, white, death-like face. And she knew what he had come for: she unbent the fingers, and let the flowers drop out, the flowers she had loved so, and walked on without them, with dry, aching eyes. Then for the last time he came. And she showed him her empty hands, the hands that held nothing now. But still he looked. Then at length she opened her bosom and took out of it one small flower she had hidden there, and laid it on the sand. She had nothing more to give now, and she wandered away, and the grey sand whirled about her.

[1] Olive Schreiner, *Dreams* [1891] (London: T. Fisher Unwin, 1900), pp. 51–55.

Alice Meynell, 'A Pilgrim'[2]

Now and then a firefly strays from the vineyard into the streets of an Italian city, and goes quenched in the light of the shops. The stray and waif from 'the very country' that comes to London is a silver-white seed with silken spokes or sails. There is no depth of the deep town that this visitant does not penetrate in August — going in, going far, going through, by virtue of its indescribable gentleness. The firefly has only a wall to cross, but the shining seed comes a long way, a careless alien but a mighty traveller. Indestructibly fragile, the most delicate of all the visible signs of the breeze, it goes to town, makes light of the capital, sets at nought the thoroughfares and the omnibuses, especially flouts the Park, one may suppose, where it does not grow. It hovers and leaps at about the height of first-floor windows, by many a mile of dull drawing-rooms, a country creature quite unconverted to London and undismayed.

This *flâneur* makes as little of our London as his ancestor made of Chaucer's.

Sometimes it takes a flight on a stronger wind, and its whiteness shows dark with slight shadow against bright clouds, as the whiter snow-flake also looks dark from its shadow side. Then it comes down in a tumult of flight upon the city. It is a very strong little seed-pod, set with arms, legs, or sails — so ingeniously set that though all grow from the top of the pod their points together make a globe; on these it turns a 'cart-wheel' like a human boy — like many boys, in fact, it must overtake on its way through the less respectable of the suburbs — only better. Every limb, itself so fine, is feathered with little plumes that are as thin as autumn spider-webs. Nothing steps so delicately as that seed, or upon such extreme tiptoe. But it does not walk far; the air bears the charges of the wild journey.

Thistle-seeds — if thistle-seeds they be — make few and brief halts, then roll their wheel on the stones for a while, and then the wheel is a-wing again. You encounter them in the country, setting out for town on a south wind, and in London there is not a street they do not recklessly stray along. For they use our arbitrary streets; it does not seem that they make a bee-line over the top of the

[2] Alice Meynell, *London Impressions* (London: Archibald Constable: 1898), pp. 4–5.

houses, and cross London thus. They use the streets which they treat so lightly. They conform, for the time, to human courses, and stroll down Bond Street and turn up Piccadilly, and go to the Bank on a long west wind — their strolling being done at a certain height, in moderate mid-air.

They generally travel wildly alone, but now and then you shall see two of them, as you see butterflies go in couples, flitting at leisure at Charing Cross. The extreme ends of their tender plumes have touched and have lightly caught each other. But singly they go by all day, with long rises and long descents as the breeze may sigh, or more quickly on a high level way of theirs. Nothing wilder comes to town — not even the scent of hay on morning winds at market-time in June; for the hay is for cab-horses, and it is at home in the clattering mews, and has a London habit of its own.

White meteor, lost star, bright as a cloud, the seed has many images of its radiant flight. But there is only one thing really like it — the point of light caught by a diamond, with the regular surrounding rays.

Fiona Macleod (William Sharp), 'Mist'[3]

A dense white mist lay upon the hills, clothing them from summit to base in a dripping shroud. The damp spongy peat everywhere sweated forth its over-welling ooze. Not a living thing seemed to haunt the desolation, though once or twice a faint cry from a bewildered curlew came stumblingly through the sodden atmosphere.

There was neither day nor night, but only the lifeless gloom of the endless weary rain: thin, soaking, full of the chill and silence of the grave.

Hour lapsed into hour, till at last the gradual deepening of the mists betokened the dreary end of the dreary day. Soaked, boggy, treacherous, as were the drenched and pool-haunted moors, no living thing, not even the restless hill-sheep, fared across them. But towards the late afternoon a stooping figure passed from gloom to gloom — wan, silent, making the awfulness of the hour and the place take on a new desolation.

As the shadow stole slowly across the moor, it stopped ever and anon. It was a man. The heavy moisture on his brow, from the rain passing through his matted hair, mixed with the great drops of sweat that gathered there continually. For as often as he stopped he heard footsteps anigh, footsteps in that lonely, deserted place — sometimes following, sometimes beyond him, sometimes almost at his side. Yet it was not for the sound of those following feet that he stopped, but because on the rain-matted cranberry bushes, or upon the glistening thyme, or on the sodden grass, he saw now bloody foot-marks, now marks of bloody fingers. When he looked there was nothing below or beyond him but the dull sheen of the rain-soaked herbage; when he looked again a bloody footstep, a bloody finger-mark.

But at last the following feet were heard no more — the bloody imprints were no more seen. The man stood beside a deep tarn, and was looking into it, as the damned in hell look into their souls.

---

3 Fiona Macleod, *The Sin-Eater and Other Tales* (Edinburgh: Patrick Geddes, 1895), pp. 137–40.

At times a faint, almost inaudible sigh breathed behind the mist in one direction. It was the hill-wind stirring among the scaurs and corries at a great height on a mountain to the north.[4] Here and there a slight drifting of the vapour disclosed a shadowy boulder; then the veils would lapse and intervolve, and the old impermeable obscurity prevail.

It was in one of these fugitive intervals that a stag, standing upon an overhanging rock, beheld another, a rival with whom it had fought almost to the death the day before. This second stag stood among the wet bracken, his ears now laid back, now extended quiveringly, his nostrils vibrating as he strove to smell the something that moved through the dense mist by the tarn.

The upper stag tautened his haunches. His lips and nostrils curled, and left his yellow teeth agleam. The next moment he had launched himself upon his enemy. There was a crash, a sound as of a wind-lashed sea, sharp cries and panting breaths, groans. Then a long silence. Later, a single faint perishing bleat came through the mist from the fern far up upon the hill.

The restless wind that was amid the summits died. Night crept up from glen and strath — the veils of mist grew more and more obscure, more dark. At last, from the extreme peaks to where the torrent crawled into hollows in the sterile valley, there was a uniform pall of blackness.

In the chill, soaking silence not a thing stirred, not a sound was audible.

---

[4] Scaurs: a sheer rock; corries: a hollow in a hillside (Scots).

Oscar Wilde, 'The Disciple'[5]

When Narcissus died the Trees and the Flowers desired to weep for him.[6]

And the Flowers said to the Trees 'Let us go to the River and pray it to lend us of its waters, that we may make tears and weep and have our fill of sorrow.'

So the Trees and the Flowers went to the River, and the Trees called to the River and said, 'We pray thee to lend us of thy waters that we may make tears and weep and have our fill of sorrow.'

And the River answered, 'Surely ye may have of my waters as ye desire. But wherefore would ye turn my waters, which are waters of laughter, into waters that are waters of pain? And why do ye seek after sorrow?'

And the Flowers answered, 'We seek after sorrow because Narcissus is dead.'

And when the River heard that Narcissus was dead, it changed from a river of water into a river of tears.

And it cried out to the Trees and the Flowers and said, 'Though every drop of my waters is a tear, and I have changed from a river of water into a river of tears, and my waters that were waters of laughter are now waters of pain, yet can I not lend ye a tear, so loved I Narcissus.'

And the Trees and the Flowers were silent, and after a time, the Trees answered and said, 'We do not marvel that thou should'st mourn for Narcissus in this manner, so beautiful was he.'

And the River said, 'But was Narcissus beautiful?'

And the Trees and the Flowers answered, 'Who should know that better than thou? Us did he ever pass by, but thee he sought for, and would lie on thy banks and look down at thee, and in the mirror of thy waters he would mirror his own beauty.'

---

5 Oscar Wilde, 'The Disciple', *Spirit Lamp*, 6 June 1893, pp. 49–50. This differs significantly from, and is much longer than, the version that was published as part of *Poems in Prose* in the *Fortnightly Review* (July 1894).

6 A famously beautiful hunter from Greek myth. The most well-known version of the myth is found in Book III of Ovid's *Metamorphoses*, in which Narcissus spurns the attentions of Echo, a mountain nymph, and as a punishment Nemesis leads him to a pool where he falls in love with his own image and is destroyed by his unfulfilled desires.

And the River answered, 'But I loved Narcissus because, as he lay on my banks and looked down at me, in the mirror of his eyes I saw ever my own beauty mirrored. Therefore loved I Narcissus, and therefore must I weep and have my fill of sorrow, nor can I lend thee a tear.'

Ola Hansson, from *Young Ofeg's Ditties*[7]

I do not dwell behind locked doors and closed blinds; every passer-by can look through my windows — ye who have suspicion that I sit up to my neck in filth and that blowflies buzz in swarms around my head — come and see!

I shall stand on my threshold and receive ye, shall accompany ye through all my rooms, shall open all cupboards, and let ye peer into all drawers. But first ye must change your shoes and scour your hands, for no scouring has any much effect upon your kind of dirt, and I am not going to have the marks of your fingers upon my things.

Ye will find here well-polished vessels, furniture without a grain of dust, the perfume of many flowers, and rooms filled with sunshine; but ye will hear no blowflies buzz save those that always swarm in your own brains. Mayhap ye will point to a few flies that lie dead in the window frame, but we all sail with corpses in our freight, and flies are not the worst of corpses.

'Come to me! I fear ye not. It is ye who are the cowards, I know ye so well. I shall follow ye out into the desert, and ye shall carry naked knives in your girdles, and I alone shall only have my bare hands. I know ye; ye are like the snapping curs that dare to bite my heels but slink away like cowards with their tails between their legs if one fix one's eyes upon them. So much ye will dare do — stick a knife in me if I inadvertently turn my back on ye; but if I look into your eyes ye slink away with hanging head. I know ye, — ye are cowards.'

[7] Ola Hansson, *Young Ofeg's Ditties*, trans. by George Egerton (London: John Lane, 1895), pp. 77–78.

~

Katherine Mansfield, 'Leves Amores'[8]

I can never forget the Thistle hotel. I can never forget that strange winter night.

I had asked her to dine with me, and then go to the Opera. My room was opposite hers. She said she would come but — could I lace up her evening bodice, it was hooks at the back. Very well.

It was still daylight when I knocked at the door and entered. In her petticoat bodice and a full silk petticoat she was washing, sponging her face and neck. She said she was finished, and I might sit on the bed and wait for her. So I looked round at the dreary room. The one filthy window faced the street. She could see the choked, dust-grimed window of a wash-house opposite. For furniture the room contained a low bed, draped with revolting, yellow, vine-patterned curtains, a chair, a wardrobe with a piece of cracked mirror attached, a washstand. But the wallpaper hurt me physically. It hung in tattered strips from the wall. In its less discoloured and faded patches I could trace the pattern of roses — buds and flowers — and the frieze was a conventional design of birds, of what genus God alone knows.

---

[8] This prose poem was written by Mansfield in 1907. It was sent with a number of other works to Vere Bartrick-Baker where it was kept, later to be published as an appendix to Clare Tomalin, *Katherine Mansfield: A Secret Life* (London: Penguin, 1988), pp. 259–60. 'Leves amores' translates from the Latin as 'casual or light loves'. As Gerri Kimber notes, Mansfield's prose poem was titled after an Arthur Symons poem ('"Always Trembling on the Brink of Poetry": Katherine Mansfield, Poet', *Humanities*, 8 (2019), 1–18). Mansfield explores a similarly fleeting erotic encounter to Symons's poem and utilizes some of his language and imagery; for instance, the opening of Symons's lyric is echoed in the end of Mansfield's prose poem:

> Your kisses, and the way you curl,
> Delicious and distracting girl,
> Into one's arms, and round about,
> Luxuriously in and out
> Twining inextricably, as twine
> The clasping tangles of the vine.

Arthur Symons, 'Leves Amores', in *Selected Early Poems*, ed. by Chris Baldick and Jane Desmarais (Cambridge: MHRA, 2017), pp. 112–13.

And this was where she lived. I watched her curiously. She was pulling on long, thin stockings and saying 'damn' when she could not find her suspenders. And I felt within me a certainty that nothing beautiful could ever happen in that room, and for her I felt contempt, a little tolerance, a very little pity.

A dull grey light hovered over everything; it seemed to accentuate the thin tawdriness of her clothes, the squalor of her life, she, too, looked dull and grey and tired. And I sat on the bed, and thought: 'Come, this Old Age. I have forgotten passion, I have been left behind in the beautiful golden procession of youth. Now I am seeing life in the dressing-room of the theatre.'

So we dined somewhere and went to the Opera. It was late, when we came out into the crowded night street, late and cold. She gathered up her long skirts. Silently we walked back to the Thistle Hotel, down the white pathway fringed with beautiful golden lilies, up the amethyst-shadowed staircase.

Was Youth dead? … *Was* Youth dead?

She told me as we walked along the corridor to her room that she was glad the night had come. I did not ask why. I was glad, too. It seemed a secret between us. So I went with her into her room to undo those troublesome hooks. She lit a candle on an enamel bracket. The light filled the room with darkness. Like a sleepy child she slipped out of her frock and then, suddenly, turned to me and flung her arms round my neck. Every bird upon the bulging frieze broke into song. Every rose upon the tattered paper budded and formed into blossom. Yes, even the green vine upon the bed curtains wreathed itself into strange chaplets and garlands, twined round us in a leafy embrace, held us with a thousand clinging tendrils.

And Youth was not dead.

MHRA Critical Texts

Jewelled Tortoise

The 'Jewelled Tortoise', named after J. K. Huysmans's iconic image of Decadent taste in *A Rebours* (1884), is a series dedicated to Aesthetic and Decadent literature. Its scholarly editions, complete with critical introductions and accompanying materials, aim to make available to students and scholars alike works of literature and criticism which embody the intellectual daring, formal innovation, and cultural diversity of the British and European *fin de siècle*. The 'Jewelled Tortoise' is under the joint general editorship of Stefano Evangelista and Catherine Maxwell.

For a full listing of titles available in the series and details of how to order please visit our website at www.tortoise.mhra.org.uk

www.ingramcontent.com/pod-product-compliance
Lightning Source LLC
Chambersburg PA
CBHW070545310726
48982CB00004B/844

* 9 7 8 1 7 8 1 8 8 9 7 3 2 *